Kate Ellis was born and brought up in Liverpool and studied drama in Manchester. She has worked in teaching, marketing and accountancy and first enjoyed literary success as a winner of the North West Playwrights competition. Keenly interested in medieval history and "armchair" archaeology, Kate lives in north Cheshire with her husband and two sons. *An Unhallowed Grave* is her third Wesley Peterson novel.

D0768390

An Unhallowed Grave

Kate Ellis

PIATKUS

For more information on other
books published by Piatkus visit our
website at www.piatkus.co.uk

First published in Great Britain in 1999 by
Judy Piatkus (Publishers) Ltd of
5 Windmill Street, London W1T 2JA
email: info@piatkus.co.uk

This edition published 2000
Reprinted 2000

A catalogue record for this book is available from the British Library

ISBN 0 7499 3173 6

Set in Times by
Phoenix Photosetting, Chatham, Kent

Printed and bound in Great Britain by
Mackays of Chatham plc, Chatham, Kent

For David and Mona Ellis

Prologue

June 1969

The girl looked out of the window. They had come for her.

She watched the cars glide up the gravel drive towards the house, soundless, like the ghostly coaches of legend that fetched the souls of the damned.

The policewoman put a firm hand on her shoulder. It was time to go. Leaving the room, the girl caught sight of herself in the gilded mirror. A waif looked back; a pale copy of the carefree seventeen-year-old who had arrived at the house only six months before.

She walked down the fine oak staircase slowly, carefully, the policewoman hovering behind like a nurse watching her patient take her first convalescent steps. The girl swayed slightly and the policewoman put out an arm to steady her.

The silence hung like glass between the girl and the group of people waiting in the hall. They stood watching her descend the staircase. A man, a woman and a small child, a handsome, fair-haired boy of six or seven.

The girl could hear her own breathing; her own heart beating. But the people at the foot of the stairs made no sound. They stood like waxworks – even the boy – avoiding eye contact.

The girl allowed herself to be led past them to where the police cars waited. She sat in the back of the first car, staring ahead as they swept down the gravel drive.

A gaggle of locals had gathered by the ornate gates. As she passed they thrust their bitter, distorted faces at the car windows. The girl tried to cover her ears but she couldn't block out the word they spat at her.

'Murderer . . . murderer . . . murderer.'

Chapter One

1 March 1475
The jury state that John Fleccer, the blacksmith's son and divers others did riotously and unlawfully assemble near the church and did assault William de Monte. Fined 12d.

The same John Fleccer did then strike Ralph de Neston and drew blood on him. Fined 3d.

From the Court Rolls of Stokeworthy Manor

June 1999

The two teenage girls stood at the churchyard gate, trying to hide the nervousness they felt. In spite of the warmth of the summer night a thin mist was blowing in from the creek, slinking and swirling around the moonlit gravestones.

'We've got to do it. It's part of the ritual. It won't work if we don't.'

'I can't see it working anyway.' Joanne – Jo to her friends – Talbot offered her friend Leanne a cigarette which was accepted with studied boredom.

'Go on, Jo. It'll be a laugh.'

'You reckon it'll work, do you? You think we'll see our true loves?' she said with heavy sarcasm. 'It's a bloody waste of good grass if you ask me.'

'Oh, go on. Me gran said it worked for her. Go on. It'll be a laugh,' Leanne pleaded.

Jo looked down at the tiny plastic bag in her hand. It contained a dried leafy substance. 'Will this do?'

'It says hemp *seed* in the rhyme but . . .'

'Let's get on with it, then. I'm not hanging round in this bloody

3

churchyard much longer. It's giving me the creeps.' She shuddered.

'Scared, are you?'

Jo gave Leanne a withering look. 'Piss off. 'Course I'm not scared.'

'We've got to do it on the path near the church door . . . and we can't do it till midnight.' Leanne was relishing the experience of being slightly, tantalisingly frightened. Anything to relieve the tedium of village life; of the dull routine of catching the bus to Tradmouth Comprehensive each morning and hanging round the village bus shelter and phone box each night.

'We'd better get a move on.' Jo squinted to see her watch in the bright moonlight. 'It's nearly midnight now. Can you remember that verse your gran told you?'

''Course I bloody can.'

The two girls giggled nervously up the church path, not daring to look left or right. The mist prowled like lean white cats around the lichened tombstones.

Jo's hand was shaking as she handed the plastic bag to Leanne. 'This had better bleeding work.'

Leanne opened the bag. 'We walk towards the church door scattering it. Then we look round. That's when we see . . .'

'Get on with it. Hurry up.'

Leanne emptied the contents of the bag into her outstretched palm, then she began to walk slowly, ceremoniously, towards the ancient church, scattering the leaves onto the path.

'Hemp seed I sow. Hemp seed I sow. He that will my true love be, come rake this hemp seed after me,' she pronounced solemnly. 'Now we look round,' she added apprehensively, dreading an encounter with her future lover less than her friend's sarcastic disdain when the ritual didn't work.

As the girls turned slowly, they saw a movement. Something white swayed from the branch of a large yew tree to their left. They stared for a few seconds before they realised that this was no vision of the man of their dreams.

The body hung there, twisting in the breeze that was blowing the mist in from the creek.

It was Jo who let out the first, night-shattering scream.

At ten past midnight Julian D'estry – he had added the apostrophe to impress clients – poured himself another glass of Chardonnay

4

and waved the bottle at the lithe blonde who lay, supine, on the adjacent sunlounger.

Monica Belman shook her head. 'I'm going for another swim.' She sat up and reached across to touch Julian's bare stomach.

Her hand slid lower but he grabbed it before it reached its target. 'Not now.'

Monica pouted in exaggerated disappointment. 'What's the matter?'

'I'm a bit stressed out. Busy week.'

'That's why we come down here. To relax . . . to get away from all that. Come on. What's wrong?' She knelt up on her sunlounger and began fumbling with the back of her bikini top. 'I know the perfect cure for stress.'

'What?'

'Wait and see.' She discarded her top and slipped elegantly out of her bikini bottom – something most women are incapable of doing with any panache. Then she approached the edge of the pool and, after looking over her shoulder to make sure Julian was taking in the view, plunged her slender, naked body into the chlorinated blue waters of Worthy Court's communal indoor swimming pool.

Julian propped himself up on his elbow and watched Monica appreciatively while he sipped his Chardonnay.

'Put some music on,' shouted Monica from the pool, floating neatly on her sunbed-bronzed back.

Julian obliged, placing a CD expounding the merits of 'sexual healing' on the portable player by his side.

'Turn it up. Right up. It'll get us in the mood.' Her voice held a cockney twang and more than a hint of erotic suggestion.

Julian obeyed and, after a few minutes of watching Monica frolicking mermaid-like in the water, pulled off his swimming trunks and joined her in the pool. He swam up to her and she flipped onto her back, a come-hither look in her bright blue eyes.

'Listen to the sound quality of those little speakers – it pays to buy the best,' he called over the suggestive rhythm.

'What? Can't hear you over the music,' Monica replied. She had no need of conversation. She reached for Julian's arm and pulled him towards her, her hand wandering downward to discover that the mad Friday evening drive from London to Devon had taken its toll on his libido. Monica, not one to give in without

5

a fight, attached her mouth to his as the music that echoed off the swimming-pool walls approached its inevitable conclusion.

The silence came like an explosion. Sudden. Unexpected. Shocking. Julian and Monica looked up out of the pool like a pair of startled seals. Standing at the edge of the pool watching them was an elderly couple, well dressed and furious-faced. A tall, grey-haired man and a younger woman with tumbling auburn tresses stood nervously behind them; the man's hand protectively on his companion's shoulder as if anticipating trouble. The elderly woman defiantly held the unplugged CD player above her head.

Monica tried to cover her embarrassment with her hands while Julian, naked and helpless, could only open and shut his mouth in impotent rage as the CD player joined them in the water with a satisfying splash.

'Perhaps now you'll learn to have more consideration for others,' shouted the woman righteously. 'And don't think you can treat us like the local peasants and frighten us with your pathetic death threats. We know you're all mouth.' She approached the edge of the pool and peered at the pink shapes in the water. The corners of her mouth twitched upward. 'And no trousers,' she added before marching away, her supporters following in her wake.

Police Constable Ian Merryweather answered the call in his new patrol car. Suspected suicide in Stokeworthy churchyard. He hoped it wasn't messy. Only last week he'd been called to a farm where a man had put a shotgun in his mouth and pulled the trigger: blood and brains everywhere. As he put his foot down and negotiated the narrow country lanes at considerable speed, he hoped this corpse had been considerate enough to swallow a few sleeping pills before lying down in an orderly fashion.

It was twenty past midnight when he drew up at the rickety lychgate that separated the churchyard from the road. A small group of people milled around the gate: late Friday night drinkers on their way home from the Ring o' Bells, Merryweather thought. It was hard for the constabulary to enforce licensing hours in these scattered villages. He stepped out of his patrol car, donned his cap and drew himself up to his full height as the good, or not so good, citizens of Stokeworthy eyed him expectantly. The group parted to reveal a pair of teenage girls sitting on the lychgate bench,

6

sobbing into disintegrating tissues. They were being comforted by a couple of overweight older women, presumably their mothers. Merryweather took charge of the situation.

'Right, then. Can someone tell me what's been going on?' From the distraught state of the girls, Merryweather feared that the message had been wrong: perhaps they had been indecently assaulted. He contemplated radioing for a WPC right away.

'Go and have a look for yourself,' said the plumper of the mothers defiantly. 'Over there.' She gestured impatiently with her thumb.

Merryweather took a deep breath and set off down the church path.

It wasn't long before he saw it. A couple of the male pub-goers had followed him tentatively up the path. He turned to address them. 'Hasn't anyone thought to cut her down? She could still be alive.' The men looked blank. The idea hadn't occurred to them. 'Move back, now. Don't just stand there gawking,' he said with what he hoped sounded like authority.

He looked up at the figure hanging from the tree. It was a woman in a belted white mac. Her arms hung limply by her side, puppet-like, and her discoloured face, tongue protruding, told that hers had not been a peaceful death. A metal ladder was propped up against the tree: she must have jumped from it to her untimely death. Constable Merryweather climbed up a few rungs and touched her wrist, feeling for a pulse. There was none. The body hadn't yet begun to stiffen but it felt cool to the touch. He descended the ladder and radioed for assistance, wondering whether to cut the body down for decency's sake.

But something stopped him taking action. It was obviously suicide but, if by any chance it turned out to be less straightforward than it looked, he had no wish to be hauled up before CID for destroying evidence. He'd leave that to someone else: Merryweather was always a man to play safe. Besides, his back had been playing him up recently and hauling dead bodies around might be the last straw.

Crowd control: that was the best use of his talents until help arrived. He noticed that the people by the lychgate had begun to edge into the churchyard. 'Come on, now. Move back. There's nothing to see,' he announced in time-honoured fashion. There was nothing he could do for the poor cow who was dangling from

7

the tree, but he could at least keep public order: that was what he was paid for.

'Who found her?' he asked the assembled company, trying not to look at the hanging body which stood out white against the darkness of the great yew tree.

'I ... er ... we did,' said one of the sobbing girls. 'It was 'orrible.'

'I'm sure it was, miss. We might need a statement from you. What's your name, my luvver?' he asked in true Devon fashion.

'Jo ... Joanne Talbot. And Leanne ... she was with me and all.'

'Leanne Matherley,' said the other girl, barely audible.

Merryweather addressed the assembled group, growing by the minute as more villagers, some sporting dressing gowns, left their houses to join in the excitement. 'Does anyone know who the dead woman was?'

'Aye,' said one of the drinkers. 'It's her that works at the doctor's. She lives in Worthy Lane ... opposite them new holiday cottages.'

It was with some relief that PC Merryweather's sharp ears picked up the approaching sound of a police car siren drifting through the night air. Reinforcements had arrived, with the police surgeon following close behind in his Range Rover.

He let them into the churchyard and resumed his crowd control duties, using his time and natural curiosity to find out what he could about the dead woman and whether anyone had noticed if she'd been depressed recently. Apart from the fact that her name was Pauline Brent, a nice enough woman who worked as receptionist for the local GP and kept herself to herself, he discovered very little. She had lived in the village for about fifteen years and was still regarded as a newcomer.

After a few minutes Merryweather felt a hand on his shoulder: the large hand of Sergeant Dowling from Neston police station who had arrived in the patrol car. 'A word, Ian.' Dowling drew the constable to one side away from curious village ears. 'The doc's not happy. He thinks there's something not quite right so he's going to get the pathologist up here to have a look. Get the area taped off, will you. And take names and addresses ... just in case.'

PC Ian Merryweather, glad that he'd not trampled all over the evidence, went about his duties with renewed enthusiasm.

*

Charles Stoke-Brown put the white carrier bag on the floor and fumbled for his key.

He picked the bag up, pushed at the studio door and flicked on the light, a bare bulb in the centre of the ceiling. Something was wrong. He was an artist, not a tidy man, but he knew that the mess in the long, low studio was not all of his making. Drawers had been opened; the mattress on the unmade double bed in the corner had been tipped over; paintings that had been piled against the walls now carpeted the bare wooden floor. A small window pane had been broken to enable the intruder to open the larger window and climb in. He had been burgled.

Charles ran to an open drawer and made a swift search. The photographs had gone. He could feel his face flush red: there was no need to mention them to the police. He began to pick up the canvases from the floor and pile them against the walls, thinking he'd better report the break-in, if only for the insurance. But as far as he could see, very little had been taken. He reached inside the carrier bag he was still holding and drew out a small, framed sketch . . . at least they hadn't got that; it had been with him, safe.

He would tidy the studio and get the window mended in the morning, but at that moment he felt like walking. Walking to forget: to erase the evening's events from his mind. He would call the police later.

He grabbed the door key and went out again into the misty night air. There were police car sirens – quite close. Or was it an ambulance?

He walked on, away from his home in the converted water mill at the far end of the village. Normally when he walked after midnight he had the place to himself, with only owls, screeching foxes and the occasional gaggle of drunk or drugged-up local teenagers to spoil the peace of the sleeping village. Or, more recently, those new people at Worthy Court, with their loud music and weekend parties. But tonight was different.

As he neared the church he spotted the small crowd of people, some seemingly in their nightclothes, standing by the lychgate, deep in speculative conversation. Then he saw the police cars.

He turned, his heart pounding, and began to hurry back towards the mill, moths fluttering at his face, their ghostly wings illuminated by the full moon. A bat swooped from a tree, bringing him to a sudden halt.

Then, out of the bushes beside the narrow road, two shapes staggered towards him. They were young, about seventeen; one dark, one fair. Their faces bore the marks of acne and youthful bravado ... and something else. Wherever these boys' minds were, they weren't in a small village in South Devon on a warm June night. Their eyes were distant, hardly registering Charles. Drunk, thought Charles: the victims of a Friday night session on cans of strong lager behind the village hall, or ...

His worst suspicions were confirmed when the smaller of the pair collapsed on the road. The other looked at him, puzzled, with none of the unfocused bonhomie of the overindulgent drinker. He bent down to address his supine friend. 'Hey, Lee ... there's a man ... he ain't got no face ...' The boy's speech was decidedly local and horribly slurred. The lad on the floor giggled but made no attempt to get up.

Charles moved forward, intending to sidle past.

'Don't go. Come and see the angel ... in the trees ...' The taller lad, his faded T-shirt covered in something unpleasant, approached Charles with outstretched arms. Charles took the opportunity to escape.

He walked swiftly off down the road, trying to put the encounter from his mind. He had come to Stokeworthy to avoid such things; to paint, to return to the simplicity and peace of country life. As a police patrol car flashed past, Charles flattened himself against the hedgerow. The last person Charles wanted to meet at that moment was a representative of the local police force.

Detective Inspector Gerry Heffernan was fast asleep when the telephone by his bed shattered the peace of the room. He always slept well on summer nights, when he could leave his window wide open to let in the sound of the water lapping against the quayside outside his front door. But the telephone meant that his sweet, nautical dreams were to be short-lived. He picked up the receiver and grunted a sleepy greeting, only to be informed by the offensively awake constable on the other end of the line that he was needed at Stokeworthy. Dr Bowman, the pathologist, had been called, he was told in awed tones, and it might be a case of murder.

'Might be? Doesn't he know?' he asked, indignant.

'That's what he said, sir. Might be. He said to call you, sir,' the constable added, apologetic.

'Murder,' Heffernan muttered to himself as he pulled his trousers on. Then he picked up the phone and dialled. When Wesley Peterson answered, he could hear a crying baby in the background. 'Sorry about this, Wes. We're wanted. Suspected murder . . . Stokeworthy.'

As he waited for the sergeant to arrive, Heffernan gazed out of the window, watching the fishing boats, laden with lobster pots, chug down the River Trad towards the sea, and wondering what kind of murder had been committed in a nice quiet village like Stokeworthy.

Chapter Two

1 March 1475
John Fleccer is amerced because he forcibly deprived Robert
the minstrel of his lute and beat his son. Fined 6d.
Thomas de Monte, the stone carver, doth misorder himself
with knocking at the doors and windows of Ralph de Neston in
the night and frightening them in their beds. The said Thomas
did claim to the jury that he would speak with Ralph de
Neston's daughter, Alice, to her father's displeasure. Fined 2d.
From the Court Rolls of Stokeworthy Manor

'Sorry about this, Wes,' Heffernan said with some sincerity as he
climbed into the passenger seat.

The young man at the wheel smiled. He was a good-looking
man; his skin dark brown, his eyes warm and intelligent. 'That's
okay,' he said. 'Michael decided it was time for his feed anyway.
He started to bawl just before the phone rang.'

'That child must be psychic.' Heffernan paused. 'Murder.
That's all we flaming well need with the tourist season upon us.
You've not had the pleasure of a tourist season yet, have you,
Wes? It'll be a whole now experience for you.'

Wesley stared ahead, concentrating on negotiating the narrow
lanes. He had been transferred to Tradmouth from the Met the
previous September, and the changes to the district brought about
by the influx of summer visitors were, as yet, a mystery to him.

'What kind of place is Stokeworthy, sir? Don't think I've come
across it yet.'

'Just a village – church, pub, council houses, cottages. A lot of
weekend places and holiday lets, you know the sort of thing. And

there's a manor house ... medieval, I'm told. It's near Knot Creek, a little inlet off the Trad. I've put in there a few times at high tide.'

'You seem to know it well.'

'Not really. Kathy used to like walking. We'd go all over the place in the old days. We walked from Stokeworthy church down through the woods to the creek once.' The inspector's voice softened as it always did when he talked about his late wife, whom he had met by a happy quirk of fate when, as first officer of a cargo vessel, he'd been winched off his ship by helicopter suffering from appendicitis and taken to Tradmouth Hospital where he had fallen for Kathy, his nurse. After that he abandoned his native Liverpool and joined the force in Tradmouth. Kathy had died three years ago and Wesley, a perceptive man, knew that he missed her very much, although he never put his grief into words: that wasn't Heffernan's way.

'Is the manor house still lived in?' The mention of a medieval manor had caught Wesley's interest.

'Some rich businessman bought it, I believe. No doubt well in with the Chief Constable, so don't you go digging up the foundations.'

Wesley smiled. He was used to his boss making quips at the expense of his archaeology degree.

'Anyway,' Heffernan continued, 'this murder's probably a domestic. They usually are. Some man's come in from the pub and found his missus in the arms of the milkman ... or vice versa in these days of equality.'

'Looks like we're here.' Wesley, having followed the rural signposts carefully and avoided any unpleasant encounters with agricultural vehicles on the narrow, unlit lanes, felt rather pleased with himself as he swept past a sign that informed him that Stokeworthy welcomed careful drivers. He slowed down, looking for signs of life ... or death.

They reached the ancient church at the heart of the village, where a few feeble streetlights glimmered, making little difference to the inky darkness. Wesley slowed down almost to a halt when he spotted the flashing lights of two police patrol cars parked near a large group of curious villagers who were milling around the moonlit lychgate that led to the churchyard.

'Quite a crowd ... no doubt here for the free entertainment,' said Wesley philosophically as he parked the car.

'Like a ruddy public hanging. They can't all be witnesses. Tell the local lads to take names and addresses and pack 'em off to bed, will you ... preferably their own.'

Wesley got out of the car and showed his warrant card to PC Merryweather, who had been eyeing him with considerable suspicion. Heffernan remained in the passenger seat, weighing up the situation.

'I've taken names and addresses,' said Merryweather with some indignation when Wesley passed on the inspector's orders. 'And I was just going to get this lot off home. I suppose you'll want to talk to the girls who found her. They're over there with their mams.'

'Fine. Thanks.' Wesley attempted a smile, fearing that he'd already put at least one local back up.

Merryweather turned away. He had heard they'd got some black graduate whizz kid from the Met down at Tradmouth CID. He wondered how this paragon of modern policing got on with Gerry Heffernan: perhaps the blunt Scouser would be enough to send the whizz kid scurrying back to London where he belonged ... which might not be a bad thing.

When the crowd began to drift off to their beds, Heffernan emerged, bear-like, from the car. To Merryweather's disappointment he gave Wesley a friendly slap on the back. 'Right, Wes, where's this here body? Let's go and take a look, shall we?'

Wesley nodded. 'It's near the church. Two girls found the body of a middle-aged woman hanging from a yew tree. She's been cut down now, so I'm told. The girls who found her are over there. Do you want to talk to them?'

Heffernan thought for a moment and looked at his watch. 'Nah. Let 'em get home and get some beauty sleep. We'll have a word in the morning.'

As Wesley arranged this, Heffernan passed under the lychgate and walked slowly up the path to the church. It was a long, winding path, flanked on either side by tombs of varying shapes and sizes: flat table tombs for the wealthy or pretentious; small headstones for the more humble in purse or spirit. The graves glowed in the light of the full moon, and wraiths of mist crept round them like the ghosts of the dead rising from their earthy beds. Not, Heffernan thought, a place for the nervous to be at night.

To the right of the path, over by the churchyard wall, was an area bathed in bright, artificial light. And, striding towards Heffernan across the grassy graves, a genial smile on his face, was a tall, balding man. 'Gerry. Delighted to see you.' Colin Bowman always insisted on getting the social niceties out of the way before getting down to his gruesome business. He spotted Wesley approaching up the church path. 'Wesley. Good to see you. How's that baby of yours? Pamela well? Not too many sleepless nights, I hope.'

'They're both fine, thanks. And a few years in CID is a good training for sleepless nights.'

'What have we got in the way of dead bodies, then, Colin?' Heffernan steered the conversation towards death.

'Rather interesting, actually.' Bowman led them over to the illuminated area. On the grass lay the body of a woman. In life she must have been reasonably attractive, although the manner of her death had distorted her face. She wasn't young, but neither was she old, and her hair, fair with no sign of grey, was cut in a smooth page-boy style. Her nails were short and neat and covered in clear lacquer. The lightweight white mac she wore didn't look cheap, nor did the navy sandals on her feet. This woman had looked after herself.

'She was found hanging from a branch of this old yew here. You can see the rope up there. The police surgeon got a constable to cut her down.' The policemen looked up. A length of thick rope dangled from the tree. Colin Bowman continued. 'Suicide was suspected at first, of course. There's a metal ladder propped up against the tree. I was talking to one of the churchwardens just before and he said that some work's just been done on the church porch ... that's where the ladder and rope came from. Very handy. She could easily have climbed the ladder, put the noose around her neck and jumped. Not a nice death. It takes a professional hangman to get a cleanly broken neck. Amateurs tend to choke to death: it can take a long time.'

'And this one?' Heffernan bent over the body, studying the woman's face. Wesley stood behind, trying to put a vision of the woman's struggling, agonising death out of his mind.

'Oh, she choked. You can see the face and neck are dark red. That's caused by ...'

15

'Put it in your report, Colin. My stomach's not up to it this time of night. What makes you think it's suspicious?'

'Dr Palmer, the police surgeon, was called first and he noticed something. Here.' He pointed at the side of the neck.

'What?' Heffernan could see nothing he thought unusual. The neck was a mess of red and bruising where the rope had dug into the flesh.

'Can't you see, Gerry? The shape of the marks. When somebody's strangled in the course of a suicide by hanging the rope marks form a classic V shape because the rope's been forced upwards behind the ears by the weight of the body.' He illustrated with his fingers. 'But when someone is strangled the marks are straight around the neck.'

Wesley bent over to look. 'I can see some other marks . . . just there. Looks like finger marks.'

'Precisely. It's my guess that she was strangled manually until she was unconscious then strung up and the hanging finished the job. That's just a guess, you understand,' he added, covering himself. 'I won't know for certain until I've done the post-mortem, but . . .'

'But you'd put money on it?' asked Gerry Heffernan, impatient with all this professional caution.

Colin Bowman smiled and nodded. 'If I was a gambling man, yes. I would.'

'Time of death?'

'She's been dead a couple of hours. Ten thirty or thereabouts. Do you know who she is yet?'

'Apparently her name's Pauline Brent,' said Wesley, who had picked up this precious nugget of information during his brief discussion with the assembled locals. 'She was the local doctor's receptionist and she lives . . . sorry, lived . . . in Worthy Lane, wherever that is. She lived alone, no family, but apparently she was on good terms with her next-door neighbour . . . a Mrs Green. We could ask her to identify the body and see what she's got to say.'

Heffernan looked at his watch. 'It's one o'clock in the morning. I don't see much point in frightening this poor woman to death by hammering on her door at this hour. Keep this area cordoned off and get it examined at first light. We'll have to tell the vicar the bad news about his churchyard first thing tomorrow and get this

Mrs Green to do the identification. What's the earliest you can do the post-mortem, Colin?'

'Half ten suit you?'

'Perfect.' Heffernan looked down at what was left of Pauline Brent, then spoke softly to his sergeant. 'Wonder what the poor woman did to make someone choke the life out of her like that.'

'Or what drove her to climb up a tree and hang herself. Perhaps we'll find it's suicide after all.'

Heffernan shook his head. 'No, Wes. It's murder. I can feel it in my water . . . and my water's never been wrong yet.'

Wesley Peterson yawned. He had felt wide awake first thing, but now, sitting at his desk on the first floor of Tradmouth police station, he was beginning to feel the effects of his disturbed night.

He stared at the file open in front of him and flicked through the pile of reports. Why were so many local vicars reporting small articles of value – pictures or carvings – missing from their churches then, a week or so later, phoning apologetically to say that the prodigal was back, safe and sound? It had happened five times in all, and Wesley's first thought was that a forgery had been exchanged for the genuine article. But each time the vicar swore that the original had returned – and who was he to argue with a man of the cloth?

Wesley had been assigned to the case because he had once served with the Met's art and antique squad. But now the file lay there before him, challenging, mocking. He was staring out of the window seeking inspiration, watching the masts of the yachts as they swayed on the glinting river, when the phone rang, jolting him awake and back to the realities of police work.

It was the inspector. Mrs Green, Pauline Brent's neighbour, had identified the body. Could Wesley go to Stokeworthy and ask her a few pertinent questions? Then could he and DC Rachel Tracey have a look through the dead woman's things? Wesley closed the file on the truant works of art. Murder took priority.

He took his jacket from the back of his chair and slung it over his shoulder. The day was warm enough for shirtsleeves.

Crossing the station foyer, he heard his name being called. He turned and saw a large desk sergeant grinning at him benignly. 'We're a man short next Sunday, Wesley,' Bob Naseby began. 'You can't get that wife of yours to let you out, can you? You'd be batting fifth. I'd have put you further up the order, but . . .'

'Sorry, Bob. There's been a murder over at Stokeworthy . . . looks like we'll be pretty busy.'

Bob Naseby, his body behind the desk of Tradmouth police station but his mind permanently out on the cricket field, nodded sagely. 'That's a shame. We must get you a game this season. With your family history.' He leaned forward confidentially. 'I looked that great-uncle of yours up in Wisden. Top batsman he was in the days when the West Indies were unbeatable.'

Ever since he had revealed the family cricket connection in the course of polite conversation, Wesley had regretted it. He wondered how long he could keep making excuses: how long it would be before he would reveal his mediocrity out on the wicket. But the death of Pauline Brent bought him some time . . . for now. He looked at his watch ostentatiously to signal he was in a hurry, and Sergeant Naseby released him from custody with a friendly wave of his bowling arm.

Wesley ran down the station steps, climbed into his blue police-issue Ford and drove to Stokeworthy, finding the journey much easier in daylight.

He had arranged to meet Rachel Tracey at Mrs Green's cottage. He found Worthy Lane easily and Rachel – who, half an hour before, had taken Mrs Green's arm gently and had led her out of the room where Pauline Brent had lain, neatly and inoffensively arranged, beneath a crisp white sheet – answered the door.

Rachel was relieved to see him. 'She identified the body. It's Pauline Brent.'

'How is she?'

'Remarkably calm in the circumstances.' She gave Wesley a smile and led the way to the living room. Rachel, cool, blonde and efficient, was a good person to have around in a crisis.

Once Rachel had introduced him, Wesley began to ask the inevitable routine questions. Susan Green, he discovered, had last seen her neighbour at around five o'clock on the night she died. This was quite normal, she said: they didn't live in each other's pockets. She had heard no unusual noise from Pauline's house. She hadn't heard her go out of her front door – but then she had had her television on and had been engrossed in the BBC's excellent adaptation of a Jane Austen novel. There had been nothing unusual about Pauline's recent behaviour, but she had seemed a little preoccupied, as though she had something on her mind.

Rachel caught his eye and nodded. Wesley knew and respected her talent for putting people, especially the not so young, at their ease so that they talked freely. So, well trained by his GP mother and later his wife, he went into the spotless cottage kitchen and made three cups of tea while Rachel did her stuff.

'Tell me about Pauline,' Rachel began gently.

Susan Green's hair was short and jet black and her unmade-up face was covered in freckles and small moles. Rachel guessed she was in her mid-forties, but she could have been a well-preserved fiftysomething; it was hard to tell. She was a tall woman with a taste for long ethnic clothing, and her voice was soft, with a slight American accent.

'She was a good neighbour. Very reliable.' Rachel looked up from her notebook. Reliable was a strange word to use about a friend: it made her sound like an employee ... or a domestic appliance. She let Susan continue. 'When I moved here five years back she was one of the few people in this village who made an effort to make me feel welcome. I'd just been widowed and wanted to start a new life for myself.'

'Where did you live before?'

'Birmingham. My husband was a professor at the university there ... I met him when he came over to the States as visiting lecturer. That was thirty years back.' She smiled at the memory. 'I worked as a social worker,' she continued. 'Then I had to nurse my husband through cancer. When he died I felt I had to get away ... change my life. So I gave up my work and came here. I intended to paint but ...' She shrugged and smiled. 'I guess I never got around to it.'

Rachel looked round the low-beamed room. Susan Green's late husband had left her well provided for: a social worker's salary alone couldn't pay for the kind of expensive good taste that graced this particular rural retreat. The only note of incongruity was struck by an arrangement of framed Beatles album covers surrounding a signed photograph of the group which hung in pride of place above the fireplace.

'Pauline was very kind,' Susan continued. 'She introduced me around the village; made sure I was included in all the activities.

You know the sort of thing: helping out at the summer fête; coffee mornings for the NSPCC . . .'

'So she was involved in village life?'

'Yeah, I guess she was. And she knew a lot of folk around here through her job at the surgery.' She paused, thinking. 'She used to say she was still regarded as a newcomer – but I guess she just said that to make me feel better.'

Rachel, a farmer's daughter who knew all about the politics of village life, suspected that Pauline had been speaking the truth. In certain villages, though not all, it would take longer than a mere fifteen years to be accepted as a local.

'Tell me about her job.'

'She worked at the surgery in the village as a receptionist.'

'Did she have any problems at work that you knew of?' Susan shook her head. 'Was she well liked?'

'Oh, sure,' said Susan, almost indignantly. 'I told you, she was involved in all kinds of local activities.'

From Rachel's experience the two things didn't necessarily follow. The most active villager could be the most hated busybody. 'So she had lots of friends?'

Susan nodded.

'What about her family?'

'She said she had no family.'

'Any enemies? Anyone she didn't get on with?'

At this point Wesley came in with a tray. He put it down on the polished pine coffee table and sat by Rachel, looking at Susan expectantly.

Susan hesitated. 'Well, er . . . there was someone. Not someone from the village, you understand. A weekender.' She pursed her lips in disgust. 'Did you notice that place opposite? Worthy Court? It's a development of weekend and holiday cottages.'

Wesley had noticed. He had thought them rather tasteful: a small development around a central courtyard, cunningly disguised as a group of pastel-washed Devon thatched cottages. Very expensive.

'It was built a year ago,' Susan continued. There's an indoor swimming pool, a gym, a sauna, all sorts. The developers assured us it would be very select, and most of the people are very quiet, but . . .' She left the sentence unfinished and gave the two police officers a significant look. They understood. 'There's one man in particular and his wife . . . girlfriend, whatever. They arrive in this big Mercedes every Friday evening then they play loud music till all hours. Sometimes they bring friends with them and have parties,' she said disapprovingly. 'There was an unpleasant incident a couple of weeks back. The family from the end cottage have got two young kids. The little one was playing on his tricycle and this D'estry came speeding along in his Merc and almost hit him. Pauline saw it and told him he should drive more carefully when there were kids around. She was usually such a quiet person, but I guess . . .'

'If this sort of thing is a problem, Mrs Green, you can always call the police, you know,' Rachel suggested helpfully.

'What would be the use? People like that just don't care.'

'So what happened?'

'Pauline went over and spoke with him, as I said, but he gave her a mouthful of foul language.' Susan Green looked agitated; angry at the injustice of life. 'This used to be a peaceful village but I guess it's going to get worse. They're building another bigger development in the manor grounds. But local historians think it's a site of historical importance so the council have insisted on the site being dug up by archaeologists before the building goes ahead. The developers kicked up a fuss, of course, but they didn't have a choice,' she said with a satisfied smirk. 'I've heard that there are environmental protesters up there too 'cause they're going to destroy some ancient woodland.'

Rachel had a sudden vision of Mrs Green perched up a tree with a pair of unhygienic eco-warriors. Wesley sat forward. 'So they're doing a rescue dig? Where did you say it was?'

'On the main road on the left just before you get to the church. Don't you want to hear what that awful man said to Pauline? It might be why she killed herself. She'd been a bit quiet over the past few days . . . like there was something on her mind. People brood, don't they, bottle things up.' For the first time Susan Green was showing signs of grief for her dead neighbour. Her eyes became glassy with unshed tears. 'If only she'd said something . . . talked to me,' she added, her voice cracking with emotion.

Rachel looked at Wesley and raised her eyebrows. As neither of them had uttered the word 'murder', it was hardly surprising that Susan should assume it was a case of suicide.

'What did this man say to upset her, Susan?' Rachel prompted gently.

'He said she was a . . .' She hesitated. 'An interfering old bitch who should keep her nose out of other people's business, and he said . . .'

'Go on.' Wesley put his teacup down, listening intently.

Susan looked up, her eyes filled with anger. 'He said she'd better watch herself. He said he knew where to find her . . . and he knew how to deal with people like her.'

'And what did you take that to mean?'

'That he'd kill her, I guess.' At this point the tears began to flow in earnest.

Charles Stoke-Brown walked back to the mill, trying to look inconspicuous. The place was swarming with police. The young constable who had called on him that morning to investigate his break-in had mentioned nothing: whether this was from ignorance or discretion, Charles didn't know.

During his short visit to the village shop he had picked up more than a pint of semi-skimmed. The shop was the nerve centre of Stokeworthy's communications network. It had taken him all of five minutes to learn that Pauline had been found dead in the churchyard, the victim of some bizarre satanic ritual the details of which were too horrifying for even Mrs Weekes from the council bungalows to broadcast. The older villagers of Stokeworthy never let the facts get in the way of a good story.

Charles, of course, had not been asked to contribute to the conversation, being a newcomer. But he had taken it all in, every spicy detail. The police presence was at its most noticeable near the church. Scenes-of-crime officers in white overalls were crawling over the ground among the tombs like giant white maggots seeking out the dead. He suppressed a shudder and hurried on, hoping he could escape the notice of the law by returning quietly to his studio.

Something made him take the long route back, past Pauline's cottage. There was a police car parked outside, which was only to be expected, but no other signs of activity.

When he arrived back at the studio, still feeling that what he had witnessed in the village was somewhat unreal, he let himself in with his key. He had hoped that Stokeworthy would be the kind of place where you could leave doors unlocked, but the locals had put him right on this point when he'd first arrived: the smug, secret smiles over pints of best bitter in the Ring o' Bells mocking his naïveté.

As he shut the door behind him, blocking out the outside world, he recalled the previous night's encounter with the two youths. They'd spoken of an angel – presumably Pauline in her white mac flying from the yew tree. But would they describe Pauline as an angel? Maybe. He had thought so himself once. He bent down and picked up a canvas from the back of a pile of pictures propped up against the wall. He stroked the image, his hands feeling the texture of the oil paint, and considered what his next move should be.

Julian D'estry's Mercedes wasn't parked in the central courtyard. And there was no answer to Wesley's persistent ringing on his highly polished brass doorbell. He was out.

'Shall we see who else lives here?' he suggested to Rachel, who stood beside him, deep in thought.

'Nobody actually lives here, Wes. They stay here for weekends or holidays. They live somewhere else.' Their eyes met and she smiled.

'You don't approve?'

'No. They should be building places local people can afford.'

Wesley nodded. He had heard the arguments before from his wife, bemoaning the death of villages as the families and young people moved out and the wealthy weekenders moved in. As Pam, his wife, was a teacher with a vested interest in the health of the district's village primary schools, she was particularly passionate in the defence of 'proper village life' as she saw it. Wesley, born and bred in a well-heeled London suburb and educated in a private school sheltered from the winds of demographic change, felt unqualified to judge – but his instincts told him that Pam and Rachel had a point.

He rephrased his question. 'Shall we see if anyone else is here?'

The cottages were arranged around three sides of the square courtyard, accessed by an archway leading from the road. The accommodation seemed to consist of traditional thatched cottages, tastefully washed in pastel shades of blue, pink and cream. The far range opposite the archway was, in startling contrast, a modern wall of gleaming glass through which could be seen an indoor swimming pool and, on the floor above the pool, a gym filled with equipment that looked suitable for a latter-day inquisition. They knocked on several doors before one was opened.

The first thing Wesley noticed about the woman who answered the door of number seven was her hair. Long and auburn, gently waving almost down to her waist, the sort of hair immortalised in pre-Raphaelite paintings. The face matched the hair – beautiful, the lips full and sensuous. She was probably in her mid thirties, her build tall and athletic: Rachel assumed she made use of the gym facilities above the pool. A small girl clung to the woman's skirt and an older boy, aged about seven, stood behind, watchful. She looked almost defiant when Wesley showed his warrant card.

'If you've come about last night, I really wouldn't believe a word he says. You'd better come in.' Her voice was well bred – dead posh, Gerry Heffernan would have called it. She introduced herself as Jane Wills and led them into the living room, which was a luxurious pastiche of a country cottage; some fashionable London designer's idea of what bucolic living should be ... with all modern conveniences. A glass display cabinet full of fossils stood in the corner looking strangely out of place.

'Now, Mrs Wills,' said Wesley, formally. 'Can you tell me in your own words what happened last night?' He might as well get things clear from the start.

The children sat on either side of their mother, staring at Wesley with solemn fascination.

'I suppose he's made a complaint.'

'Who, madam?'

'That vulgar little man, D'estry. Who else?'

'It might help if you started from the beginning.' Wesley glanced at Rachel, who looked as puzzled as he felt.

Jane Wills took a deep breath. 'It's been going on for months, ever since D'estry and that woman bought number three. They come down here most weekends ... for the water sports, I believe,' she said with distaste. 'They play loud music, have friends down for parties in the pool. We bought this place because we thought it would be quiet ... select. Last night was just the last straw. They were playing that awful music at full blast after midnight. The children had gone to bed and we were playing a game and having a quiet drink. Then this noise started and we couldn't hear ourselves think. The couple in number ten, Mr and Mrs Bentley, knocked on our door. They were furious. Mrs Bentley's a formidable lady ... a former magistrate, I believe. They asked if we'd go over with them to complain, so I went with my father-in-law, who has the cottage next door. We went over to the pool and the noise was echoing in there; it was deafening. Mrs Bentley picked up his portable hi-fi and threw it in the water. We'd all had enough. And do you know what that pair were wearing?' She looked at Wesley defiantly. 'Nothing.'

Wesley tried hard not to smile. 'What time was this?'

'About twenty past midnight.'

'So what happened then?'

'Nothing. I think D'estry and his girlfriend were too shocked to do anything,' she said with satisfaction. 'Mrs Bentley might be getting on in years but she's more than capable of sorting out the likes of D'estry. So what did D'estry say? I can imagine him playing the injured party. Did you know he threatened some of the local people who've complained about his behaviour? That's the kind of man ...'

Wesley didn't give her the chance to finish her sentence. It was time to broach matters more serious than noisy nude bathing. 'Have you heard that there's been a suspicious death in the village?' He suddenly remembered the children, sitting in solemn silence on either side of their mother. There was something subdued, almost Victorian, about these youngsters. Wesley was sure that, despite a strict upbringing, he and his sister would have preferred getting up to mischief to sitting seriously listening to the questions of a stranger. 'Perhaps you'd rather the children didn't, er ...'

'We don't believe in shielding our children from the unpleasantness of life, Sergeant. I've seen police cars around, of course, but I don't know what was going on.'

'A woman was found dead in the churchyard last night. She lived in the middle cottage on the other side of the road, just opposite here. Her name was Pauline Brent. Did you know her?'

Jane Wills shook her auburn curls, avoiding Wesley's eyes.

'The threats Mr D'estry is alleged to have made: do you know if it was Miss Brent he threatened?'

25

'I couldn't say. It was common knowledge he'd threatened somebody in the village. I didn't know the details.'

'Did you see anything suspicious last night? Or did you see a middle-aged, fair-haired woman in a white mac at any time during the evening?'

'No, Sergeant. We arrived for the weekend just after six o'clock. My husband went out to a function in Bloxham and didn't get back till after midnight, but the rest of us – that's my parents-in-law, the children and myself – spent the evening together,' she said with finality.

There was nothing more to be discovered. Wesley stood up, and Rachel, in complete agreement, did the same. As Jane Wills showed them to the front door, leaving her two silent children on the sofa, Rachel turned and caught a glimpse of an elderly woman watching them intently from the top of the polished wooden staircase.

There was no reply from the other residents of Worthy Court: either the cottages were as yet unsold or their weekend occupants were elsewhere on a sunny Saturday morning. Wesley would organise someone to call round and take statements later.

He felt in his jacket pocket for the spare key to Pauline Brent's cottage, given them by Susan Green.

'I think it's time we looked through her things.'

Rachel nodded. They walked across the road in amicable silence, and Wesley turned the key in the lock. The hallway smelled of potpourri; watercolours of local scenes decorated the walls. Wesley stepped into the low-beamed living room. The furnishings and décor were solid, unexcitingly beige. Pauline had lacked Mrs Green's flair for interior design.

They agreed that Rachel should look upstairs while Wesley dealt with the lower floor. He was looking through the contents of a dark wooden letter rack when he heard Rachel's footsteps on the stairs. She appeared in the doorway and shook her head. 'Nothing much up there. Only clothes, make-up. Have you found anything interesting?'

'Nothing much,' he said, looking around. 'The only letters she seemed to get were official ones: electric bills, water bills, unremarkable bank statements. Nothing personal at all, from what I can see.' He produced a cheap piece of writing paper. 'There's a note here from a Dot Matherley to say could she come on Wednesday instead of Tuesday. Who is she, I wonder? Friend? Cleaner? That's all. No love letters upstairs, then?'

'Nothing.'

'She doesn't seem to have a telephone.'

Rachel looked around. 'You're right. That's a bit odd in this day and age, especially out in the country.'

'Perhaps she doesn't know anyone outside the village.'

Rachel shrugged. 'No car either. I wouldn't like to have to rely on the buses round here. Her clothes were quite good. She seemed to favour Marks and Spencer's.' Rachel paused, thinking. 'Have you found a passport, birth certificate, anything like that?'

'No. She might have hidden them away somewhere. We'll have to organise a thorough search.'

'Where to now, Sarge?'

'I've got to get back to Tradmouth for the post-mortem.'

'Rather you than me. Good luck.' She gave his arm a gentle, encouraging touch as they shut the front door of Pauline Brent's empty cottage behind them. 'You can give me a lift to the station, then.'

Rachel and Wesley drove down Worthy Lane, out of the village.

'Nice place,' Wesley commented, making conversation. Rachel didn't reply. 'How's Dave? Where's he living now?' Rachel's Australian boyfriend had recently moved out of the holiday apartment on her family's farm, where he had been allowed to spend the winter. The apartment was needed now for the holiday-makers who added more to the Tracey family's bank account during the summer than the sale of their new lambs.

'He's working in a hotel bar in Morbay, living in.'

Wesley didn't pry further. The fact that Dave was still in the area told him that Rachel held more attraction for the young Australian backpacker than the travelling life he had planned. He looked at her, concentrating on her driving. Her expression gave nothing away. He couldn't tell whether or not Dave's constancy pleased her.

They turned right by the Ring o' Bells, a thatched pub of picture postcard appearance, onto the main road. The ancient stone parish church with its extensive graveyard lay to the right and a high stone wall to the left. 'What's behind that wall?' Wesley asked.

27

Rachel was the fount of all local knowledge, having spent her childhood in the area. 'Stokeworthy Manor. It's owned by that Philip Thewlis. He's head of some big company ... he does that TV programme, *Popular Business*, and he's just been appointed to some government committee or other. Has his fat fingers in all sorts of pies.'

Wesley nodded. He, along with a good proportion of the population, knew Philip Thewlis by reputation.

'I wonder if we'll need to interview him,' pondered Rachel.

'If he's here. He probably has homes all over. He might have a flag flying when he's in residence, like the Queen.'

'Oh, no. I think he's here most of the time. He likes to play lord of the manor, apparently.'

There was a large gap in the wall nearly opposite the church. A sizable section had been demolished and replaced with high wire fencing topped with what looked like razor wire: vicious.

'Can we stop here, Rach?'

'Why?' She put her foot on the brake and brought the car to a halt on the wide verge next to the wire. 'What time's your post-mortem?'

'Won't be a minute.'

'Don't be,' she said firmly.

Wesley got out of the car and stepped up to the fence, peering through it like a visitor at a zoo looking for some particularly shy creature concealed among the foliage. The ground had been cleared beyond the wire. Mechanical diggers stood some way off like predators ready to pounce when the time was right.

A large area of soil lay bare. Here and there he could see embryonic trenches which had been dug not by machine but painstakingly, by hand. Wesley was on familiar territory: he recognised an archaeological dig when he saw it. A young man of his own age, long-haired with disreputable jeans and a filthy T-shirt, was deep in discussion with an overweight, middle-aged man who wore a yellow hard hat and a suit as smart as Wesley's own. The two parted. From the yellow-hatted man's expression of annoyance, the discussion hadn't been amicable.

'Neil,' Wesley called, and the young man looked up. A sudden grin lit his face. The pair of them, friends since their first term at university, had a lot to catch up on.

'Hi, Wes. Wasn't expecting the forces of law and order around

28

here just yet. Not after our protesters, are you?'

'No way. How many have you got?'

'Just a few up to now, up in the trees over there.' Wesley looked but could see nothing that gave away the protesters' presence. 'We're expecting more later when the diggers move in,' Neil Watson added with satisfaction.

'I've heard about the development. When's it due to start?'

'When we've finished ... whenever that'll be,' Neil said mischievously. 'So what are you doing here?'

'There's been a murder in the village. Heard about it?'

Neil shook his head. Once his mind was focused on a dig he noticed very little about the outside world. The parade of patrol cars through the village and the yards of blue-and-white tape sealing off the churchyard would have gone quite unremarked.

'Found anything yet?' said Wesley, surveying the half-dug trenches.

'We've only been here since Thursday. The local historical society have evidence that the village extended this way until the fourteenth century. Then the village population changed – black death, at a guess – and the lord of the manor added this bit to his land. There are strange tales about this particular site which are best told over a pint or two. How's Pam? And Michael?'

'They're both doing fine. Pam mentioned you the other day, wondered how you were.'

Neil's expression softened. He had gone out with Pam in their first year at university, until she had transferred her affections to Wesley. 'If you're not doing anything tonight we'll be in the Tradmouth Arms. Bring Pam along.'

There spoke a man without children. 'Baby-sitters aren't easy to get but we'll see what we can do. And it depends how this case goes.'

'What happened, then? Who was murdered?'

'A woman was found hanging from that big yew tree in the churchyard.'

'Know who did it yet?'

'Not yet. Early days.'

Rachel sounded the car horn impatiently.

'Is that the lovely Rachel you've got with you?' asked Neil suggestively, bending to peer through the car window.

'Yes, and we've got to be off. The post-mortem's at half past.'

Neil wrinkled his nose in disgust. 'I'll stick to dry bones, thanks.' He turned, then swung back as though he'd just remembered something. 'That big yew in the churchyard,' he began. 'According to local legend it was used for public executions. It was known as the hanging tree.'

Chapter Three

14 March 1475
The jury state that John Fleccer did trespass upon the Lord's
woodland. Fined 6d and given over to the care of his father for
guarantee of his good behaviour.

Indictment of Marjory Snow for keeping a common ale house
of ill repute, where there was frequent drunkenness, cutting of
purses and divers common whores. Fined 12d.

From the Court Rolls of Stokeworthy Manor

Dot Matherley picked up her plastic box full of polishes and
dusters and walked slowly up the great oak staircase of
Stokeworthy Manor. The staircase, Dot knew, was four hundred
years old . . . and there were times she felt that old herself. This
morning her arthritis was playing up again and she could still feel
the morning stiffness in her leg muscles. It was good of Mr
Thewlis to keep her on at her age There were a lot who wouldn't.
And there were a lot of people in the village who called him a
ruthless bastard, but to Dot he had been consideration itself . . . if
it wasn't for that business with Gemma she would have quite liked
the man.

Dot started on the children's bedrooms. Two children: Amanda
and Guy. Such sweet little things and such nice manners . . . no
thanks to that so-called nanny of theirs. They were out on their
ponies now with Mrs Thewlis: a real lady, a cut above her
husband socially.

The children's bedrooms done, Dot braced herself for the
stiffest test of her skills: the master bedroom. There were oak
panels from floor to elaborately plastered ceiling which had to be

polished until they gleamed. And there was the fine four-poster bed to make – not as easy to deal with as a modern divan. The bed had reputedly been slept in by Queen Elizabeth I herself, but it was now Mr and Mrs Thewlis's nuptial bed. Nuptial bed – Dot liked those words: they spoke of harmony, contentment, like Dot's own marriage before her Ted had passed over.

After checking that she had the right cleaning equipment (Dot liked to be well prepared) she pushed at the heavy oak door. At first she couldn't quite place the noises that came from the room: the rhythmic creaking of the bed and the soft groans. As the door opened wider Dot stepped across the threshold and the scene revealed before her seemed unreal, dreamlike. The young woman was naked, kneeling upright astride the man who lay on the bed. The man grabbed the white sheet and swiftly covered his head before Dot could identify him. The young woman, little more than a girl, turned slowly, a smile playing on her lips, her expression impudent, challenging. She looked Dot directly in the eyes and gave her a wide grin of triumph. Then she began to laugh, resuming her rhythmical gyrations astride her hidden partner.

Dot clutched at her chest as her heart began to pound uncontrollably and backed out of the room, leaving the door wide open. As she hurried across the landing and down the staircase she could hear the girl's tinkling, mocking laughter in her ears.

'Nanny,' mumbled Dot, her hands shaking. 'Calls herself a nanny. A common little whore more like.'

It was then that the baize door leading to the kitchens opened and the children rushed into the hall, breathless with excitement. Their mother, Caroline Thewlis, followed closely behind, taking off her riding hat.

'What's the matter, Dot? Is everything all right?' Caroline asked, her accent well-bred county.

Dot took a deep breath. 'Oh yes, madam. Everything's fine.'

Wesley Peterson was from a medical family. His parents had both come over from Trinidad to study medicine in London. Now his father was a consultant heart surgeon, his mother a GP and his younger sister, Maritia, an overworked junior doctor at the John Radcliffe Hospital in Oxford. But as Wesley stood watching Colin Bowman make the Y-shaped incision down the front of Pauline Brent's naked body, he felt some relief that he had not kept up the family tradition. The medical gene must have passed him by.

'Come over here and have a look at this.' Gerry Heffernan obeyed Colin Bowman's hearty command. Colin looked up and saw Wesley hesitating in the background. 'Come on, Wesley. You too. It's very interesting.'

Wesley took a deep breath of formaldehyde-laden air and followed his boss.

Bowman was leaning over the corpse's neck. 'See here. There are two marks. The mark made by the hanging . . . classic inverted V shape. See?' The two policemen nodded in unison. The rope had cut deep into Pauline's neck as she had hung from the yew tree, her body weight dragging downward and carving the pattern of the rope into the soft flesh. 'Now look here.' He pointed to faint red bruises encircling the neck below the more pronounced marks of death. 'It's as I suspected last night,' Colin continued. 'Full marks to Dr Palmer for spotting it. Someone strangled her first then hung her from the tree to make it look like suicide. I can't tell yet whether she was dead or just unconscious when she was hung up there. I don't suppose whoever killed her was too bothered.'

Wesley turned away as Bowman casually put his hands into the body and pulled out the vital organs for weighing, as someone washing dishes pulls crockery from the kitchen sink. Gerry Heffernan scratched his unruly curls and watched the procedure comparatively unmoved. But Wesley couldn't watch: only yesterday this had been a living, breathing woman with feelings, likes, dislikes, achievements, family and friends. He spent the rest of the post-mortem studying his shoes.

'She wasn't a virgin. But she'd never had a child,' said Colin conversationally. Wesley had to add lovers to his list of the things in Pauline's life . . . but not children.

'She was in fairly good shape for her age. Late forties, early fifties, I should say. No signs of serious illness. I'll let you have the toxicology and stomach contents results as soon as I get them, but at this stage I'd say this was death by strangulation. Murder by person or persons unknown.'

'So it's definitely not suicide?' asked Heffernan. He was a man who liked to know what he was dealing with.

'Definitely not. Sorry to add to your workload with the tourist season almost upon us.'

Gerry Heffernan gave his sergeant a hearty slap on the back.

'Right, then, Wes. Back to Stokeworthy. I think I'd like a word with those two lasses who found her. I'd better take you and not Steve Carstairs: I wouldn't trust him with a pair of teenage girls. Just imagine the comments.'

'About taking down more than their statements.' Wesley grinned. He had heard it all before. He himself had been on the receiving end of DC Carstairs' racist wisecracks when he had first arrived in Tradmouth. Although Wesley was now accepted by most of those at the station who had once shared Steve's jibes at his expense, and was now a popular member of the team – the man to be consulted about crossword clues and pub quiz answers – Steve still kept his distance.

Wesley drove back to Stokeworthy. Gerry Heffernan didn't drive, not on dry land. He saved his navigational skills for his boat, the *Rosie May*, caring for her as much as any classic car enthusiast cares for the object of his passion.

This time they passed the church and turned into a small cul-de-sac of council houses. Some of the expansive front gardens were impressive: a display of colour worthy of any French Impressionist's canvas against the dull cream council stucco.

But one of the gardens let the side down. The only flowers visible among the overgrown grass and rusty car parts were a few pioneering blooms on a pair of ageing unpruned rosebushes. Even the birds that sang so merrily in the neighbouring gardens thought this one beneath their attention. Heffernan pushed open the wooden gate and marched down the cracked concrete garden path.

Wesley saw the greying net curtains twitch. They were being watched. Heffernan beat a tattoo on the front door, loud enough to wake the dead. They waited. He was about to knock again when the door opened.

The woman stood in the doorway, her chubby arms folded. Wesley found it hard to guess her age. Like that of many overweight people her skin was smooth, her plump face almost babylike. Her small eyes regarded the newcomers with suspicion, particularly Wesley. 'We're C of E,' she announced belligerently.

'So am I, love. Police.' Heffernan thrust his warrant card in her face. 'Can we come in for a quick word, or do you want a reference from me vicar?'

The woman held the door open resentfully. 'I thought you were them Jehovah's Witnesses,' she explained defiantly, looking Wesley up and down.

'Sorry to disappoint you, love. I'm Detective Inspector Heffernan and this is Detective Sergeant Peterson. We'd like a word with your Joanne. Nothing to worry about: just routine.'

The woman made no comment. She led them through the cluttered hall into the sitting room. Here, as in the rest of the house, the pattern on the carpet was camouflaged by a layer of dirt. On a grubby Dralon sofa, which seemed to dominate the small room, sat two girls, aged about fifteen, scantily dressed to titillate the Steve Carstairses of this world: their midriffs were bare, their navels pierced by matching gold rings; and their skirts were short to the point of indecency. If Heffernan's daughter, Rosie, had attempted to dress like that when she was their age, he would have ordered her upstairs to put on something decent.

'Mind if we have a word about last night, love? Nothing to worry about. Just a few questions.' The two girls stared at him indifferently. 'Are you Leanne Matherley, by any chance?' he asked the slimmer of the pair. Joanne Talbot bore such a resemblance to her mother that he didn't have to ask which one she was. Leanne nodded. Neither of the girls seemed particularly traumatised by the events of the previous night.

Heffernan nodded to Wesley. He'd let him deal with these two for the moment. 'Can you tell us what you were doing in the churchyard last night?' Wesley leaned forward, expecting a nervous answer. To his surprise the girls caught each other's eye and began to giggle.

'A woman was murdered,' said Heffernan. 'It's nothing to laugh about. Just answer the question.'

'We were doing this ritual.'

The two policemen looked at each other. This was one the tabloids would love to get their hands on: midnight rituals in churchyards below the body of a hanging woman. They could see the headlines now.

'What kind of ritual?'

The girls at last had the good grace to look sheepish. What had seemed amusing at the time now looked somewhat pathetic. 'It was something my gran told us about,' said Leanne. 'She did it when she was young. You scatter some seeds on the church path

35

at midnight and you're supposed to see your true love. We thought it'd be a laugh, you know.'

Heffernan nodded. He did know. He'd done a lot of daft things when he was a lad in Liverpool, and he recalled some of them now with a blush.

'So what happened? Take your time,' coaxed Wesley. 'I'm assuming your true loves didn't put in an appearance?'

The girls shook their heads solemnly. 'We'd done the ritual, like,' Jo began. 'Then we turned round and saw her up there in the tree. The moon was bright and we could see her face: it was all . . .' Leanne nodded in agreement. 'Then I screamed.'

'What happened then?'

'There were some people we knew – neighbours – on their way back from the Ring o' Bells. One of them went to fetch my mum and they rang the police. That's it really.'

'Did you know the dead woman?'

'I knew who she was: the receptionist at the doctor's. But I'd never spoken to her, like.'

'What about you, Leanne?'

'The same. I seen her at the doctor's and round the village.'

'Did you see anyone else last night? When you first went into the churchyard was there anyone about? Anyone at all?'

The girls shook their heads, but from the sly look they exchanged Heffernan could tell they were lying.

The Ring o' Bells was the obvious choice for lunch. It was a pretty pub, thatched and pink-washed, which practised strict segregation: locals in the nicotine-stained public bar; tourists, weekenders and the educated classes in the low-beamed comfort of the lounge.

All Wesley's instincts told him to head for the lounge as the prospect of being stared at and their conversation being taken down and used in evidence all over the village didn't appeal. Gerry Heffernan had to admit that his sergeant had a point. They found a table by a tiny leaded window and settled down.

Heffernan had consumed half a bacon baguette and was halfway through his first pint of best bitter before he spoke. 'Those two lasses were lying through their teeth. They saw someone all right.'

Wesley nodded and took a sip of orange juice. 'It must be

someone they want to protect. A friend? Member of the family? Boyfriend?'

'We could get Rachel to have a word. She might get something out of them – the big-sister touch. As long as she doesn't take DC Carstairs with her. That pair'd fuel his Lolita fantasies. Did you see how they were dressed . . . or rather undressed? Would you let any daughter of yours go round like that? I know I wouldn't.'

'They want to follow fashion at that age. I can remember my father stopping my sister going to a school disco because he thought her dress was too revealing.'

'Did you agree with him?'

Wesley shrugged. 'I said I did. Anything to get one over on my sister – the old sibling rivalry. We get on fine now, though.' He bit into his tuna sandwich and changed the subject. 'So what have we got so far, sir?'

Gerry Heffernan sat back, pint in hand. 'Pauline Brent, spinster of this and probably every other parish, came here fifteen years ago. She made no enemies that we know of among the locals but received threats from one Julian D'estry. Our first priority is to hear what this D'estry character has to say for himself, and our second is to find out more about Pauline. Who were her friends? Was there a man in her life? That sort of thing.'

'Rachel and I looked through her things but we didn't find anything of interest. In fact it was strange.' He paused for a moment, deep in thought. 'There wasn't anything personal at all. No letters, no address book . . .'

'The doctor she worked for's away for the weekend. We'll talk to him first thing on Monday, see if he can tell us anything about her.' Heffernan sighed. 'There might be things going on under the surface in this village that we don't know about yet. In the old days every village'd have a police house and the village constable'd know exactly who had a grudge against who and why, going back a few generations. Now they're all based in Neston and Tradmouth and just whizz through in their patrol cars. Not the same, is it? No in-depth local knowledge – until a recordable crime's committed they haven't a clue what's going on.'

Wesley nodded in agreement. 'Have we managed to find ourselves an incident room?'

'Village hall. They're putting in the phone lines now.' He looked round the horse-brass-covered walls of the Ring o' Bells' lounge. Across the bar he could see the sparsely populated public bar where a few men were playing pool. 'At least this place serves a good pint.'

Wesley tried to make his next announcement sound casual. 'Neil Watson's doing a dig in the manor grounds.'

Heffernan looked up sharply. 'That mate of yours follows us around like a bad smell. Has he dug up anything interesting yet?'

'It's early days. Apparently the lord of the manor's building a holiday place on a bit of his land near the road . . . like those flashy cottages opposite the dead woman's house, only much bigger. According to local historians the site's supposed to be of some interest, so the planners are letting Neil see what he can find before the concrete's poured in.' He drained his pint of orange juice. 'Not everybody thinks the new development's a good idea. There are some protesters up there already. I'd better not tell Pam or she'd be up there in the trees with them.'

'I didn't know your wife had revolutionary tendencies, Wes.'

'She has her moments.' He sighed.

Heffernan finished his pint and looked at his empty glass with appreciation. 'Not a bad pint that.' He stood up. 'I'm going to take a look round the churchyard . . . I'll have a butcher's at the church and all if it's open: might give us some divine inspiration. Coming?'

Wesley nodded enthusiastically. His boss's love of wandering round old churches had surprised him at first, but now he considered it an asset that his inspector's taste in this particular matter matched his own.

The churchyard was still cordoned off, although the SOCOs seemed to have finished their work. Heffernan looked up at the great yew tree. The ladder still stood against it, dusty with fingerprint powder. 'Why did they always plant yews in churchyards, Wes? Were they sacred or what?'

'Nothing so mystical. They were poisonous so they were planted where cattle couldn't get at them. They used the wood for longbows, too . . . and the leaves for palms on Palm Sunday.'

'You're a mine of useless information, Wesley. Is that what they taught you at that university of yours? Come on, let's see if the church is open.'

There was a spotty young constable standing guard at the

church door. He drew himself to attention when he saw the inspector approaching.

'Hello, Johnson. All quiet?'

'Yes, sir. SOCOs say they've finished now.' He hesitated, weighing up whether or not his next piece of information was important enough to relay to a senior officer. He decided to be on the safe side. 'A couple of lads were here half an hour ago, sort of hanging around the gate.'

'Being nosey?'

Johnson put his head on one side, considering the question. 'No. They looked sort of ... furtive, if you know what I mean. One had very short blond hair, probably dyed. They other was taller with a ponytail.'

'Thanks. If you see these two arch-criminals again, let us know, won't you.'

'Do you think it's important?' Wesley asked quietly as they stepped into the church porch.

'No idea. Probably just being nosey. A murder's a bit of excitement to brighten up their dull little lives. Still, it gives Johnson something to do.' Gerry Heffernan pushed at the battered oak door, half expecting, in these days of high crime and scant respect, to find it locked. But it swung open with an ear-splitting creek.

'Oh, I forgot to tell you, sir,' a voice called from outside the porch. 'The vicar's in there.'

Heffernan turned. 'Thanks, Johnson. We'll make sure we mind our language.'

Heffernan and Wesley stepped inside the cool church, their eyes adjusting to the gloom after the bright June sunshine outside. A man stood by the altar. He was in his late thirties, tall, over six foot, with dark hair, glasses and the face of an earnest rodent. He wore a T-shirt and flawless jeans. He looked like an off-duty chartered accountant.

'Good afternoon,' he began nervously. 'I'm sorry, but I don't think the police are letting anyone into the ...'

'We are the police. DI Heffernan and DS Peterson. Are you the vicar, by any chance?'

The man nodded. 'The Reverend Twotrees ... Brian. Pleased to meet you.' He strode up to them and shook hands heartily. 'It's an awful business. Tragic.'

'Did you know Miss Brent?'

'Yes. She wasn't one of our leading lights, you understand: not one to push herself forward. A quiet woman. A nice woman, I'd say.'

'Can you tell us anything else about her?' asked Wesley. 'Did she give you any indication that anything was wrong? Did she seem worried about anything?'

'I must admit I haven't seen her for a couple of weeks. She wasn't in church last Sunday and I live in the village of Welton, three miles away. I'm responsible for three parishes, you understand.'

Heffernan understood all right. Like those of the police, the rural clergy's modern-day arrangements weren't as conducive to local knowledge as they had been in the past.

'Did she come to church every week?'

'Not every week.'

'So it wasn't unusual for her to miss the service last Sunday?'

'No, not at all.'

'Was she popular?'

'I think so. Yes. As I said, she was a quiet woman, not the sort to make enemies. I'm sorry I can't be more help.'

Gerry Heffernan nodded. 'That's okay, Vicar. We'll just take a look around your church if we may.' He saw that the vicar looked mildly alarmed. 'Not a professional look ... just out of interest,' he assured him.

The Rev. Twotrees' face lit up. 'You're interested in old churches, then?' he asked with some disbelief, looking them up and down.

'Oh, aye, always have been. And Sergeant Peterson here's got a degree in archaeology, so he's almost a professional.'

'Really?' The vicar looked at Wesley with new eyes. 'So how did you end up in the police force, Sergeant?'

'A grandfather who was a senior detective back in Trinidad and a taste for reading too much Sherlock Holmes in my formative years,' answered Wesley with a modest smile.

'That really is amazing,' said the vicar, genuinely interested. Wesley hoped he wouldn't be the subject of the reverend's next sermon. 'Come on. I'll show you around.'

The vicar did the guided tour, revealing with appropriate modesty that he was an Oxford man. Wesley soon found himself chatting about his sister, Maritia, who had read medicine at Oxford, and his own days at Exeter University.

Gerry Heffernan, who had never got further than his local technical college in Liverpool to study navigation, began to feel left out. 'Nice rood screen,' he commented, feeling that he had to show these two academics that at least he knew what the thing was called. He studied the elaborately carved edifice which separated the chancel from the nave. It was coloured in faded, subtle, medieval pigments and carved with breathtaking intricacy: a thing of true beauty.

'It's reputedly one of the finest in Devon,' said the vicar proudly.

'That's what they all say,' replied Heffernan with a cheeky grin.

Wesley's mind turned to the case he'd been working on before Pauline Brent's death. 'Have you heard about the things that have been going missing from churches round here?'

'Yes. It's quite a talking point among the local clergy. It amazes everyone that the items are actually returned. Our only real treasure as far as I know is a rather nice silver chalice, and I keep that in the vestry safe.'

'Good. The thieves haven't resorted to safe-cracking yet.'

'Give 'em time,' said Gerry Heffernan wearily, looking around the church.

Then he spotted it. On the south wall was a great stone framework, growing from floor level like flush-carved scaffolding, a stained-glass window inserted cheekily in its centre. At first Heffernan took it for wood, a strange patch of half-timbering on a white plastered wall. But on closer inspection it was mellow, golden stone, punctuated by holes as if once, in some forgotten time, it had, like a tree, been burdened with some strange fruit. But now only the framework remained, its original purpose forgotten. 'What's that?' Gerry pointed and Wesley and the vicar swung round.

'I was coming to that,' said the vicar smoothly. 'It's what's left of our Jesse tree. Very rare. There's only a handful of examples in the country, and none have remained intact. Our ancestors considered them a symbol of Catholic superstition: graven images and all that.'

'So what was it?'

41

Wesley took over. 'There was a figure of Jesse, the father of King David, in the centre at the base.' He strolled over to the south wall and gently touched the hacked stone. 'This must have been where Jesse was: this big stone panel beneath the window. The carving has been removed but it looks as though the panel behind it was painted.'

Heffernan bent down to look. 'So it was. Looks a bit of a mess. Someone's had a go at it . . .' He reached out, preparing to scratch off the offending paint.

Wesley acted quickly, grabbing his boss's arm before he could do any damage. 'That paint's the original. It's medieval.'

'About 1490, actually.' The vicar shot Wesley a grateful glance.

'So what are all them holes?'

'The reclining figure of Jesse had a tree sprouting from his groin.'

'Painful,' Heffernan uttered under his breath.

'And the holes supported statues of Jesse's descendants, culminating in Christ in glory right up at the top above the window.'

'A sort of family tree?'

'If you like. Yes.'

'So who was there right at the bottom?'

'Jesse's always at the base.'

'No he's not, Wes. Look.'

Wesley respected his inspector's talents as a detective, but medieval religious sculpture was definitely not his forte. With an effort of patience he looked where Heffernan was pointing.

'If that was Jesse there on that big slab under the window, who was down here near the floor? The poor relations?'

Wesley looked round at the vicar for inspiration.

'I have wondered about those holes down there myself.' Brian Twotrees bent to examine them. 'I've been told that it's most unusual to have anyone below the Jesse figure. After all, the point of the whole thing is to show Christ's descent from Jesse as prophesied in the Old Testament. "There shall come forth a shoot from the stump of Jesse and a branch shall grow out of his roots" – Isaiah chapter eleven, verse one,' he quoted helpfully.

'So what happened to all the figures?' asked Heffernan naïvely.

'The Reformation happened,' said the vicar cheerfully. 'All

statues and images were swept from the churches and smashed up or burned. Archbishop Cranmer called them "jolly musters".' He sounded rather enthusiastic about all this destruction.

'Sounds like that cultural revolution they had in China,' said Heffernan with disbelief.

'Oh, it was, Inspector. Very like. The old order was destroyed . . . and was seen to be destroyed.'

'How could they have just smashed up all that art? There must have been some beautiful stuff.'

'Of course, whether you approve or not depends on where you stand theologically.' The vicar leaned towards Wesley confidentially. 'I'm inclined towards plainer forms of worship myself.'

'So what happened to the Jesse carvings from here?' asked Wesley.

'There are accounts of churches in this area being visited and lists of what was destroyed, but apparently there's no mention of our Jesse tree in any of the commissioners' records.' He sighed. Wesley suspected that Brian Twotrees would have been glad to see the beautiful thing that the Jesse tree must have been smashed into dust by the iconoclasts' hammers. 'Actually,' he continued, 'the fate of the Jesse tree is the subject of local legend. Some say it was dismantled by the villagers and stored in the cellars of the Manor; others say it was thrown into Knot Creek. It's all a bit of a mystery, really.'

'It's not the only thing that's a mystery around here,' said Gerry Heffernan as his mind returned to Pauline Brent's hanging body.

Neil Watson returned from his meeting with Philip Thewlis up at the Manor feeling pleased with himself. He'd say one thing for Thewlis – he was thorough. He had wanted to know exactly how long the excavations would take; how many archaeologists would be involved; exactly where the trenches would be dug; and, most importantly, when the diggers could move in and begin work on the construction. But he'd met his match with Neil, who had patiently explained that the time the dig would take depended on what they found. If, he had said tongue in cheek, they were to find, say, an important Roman villa, then an alternative site might have to be found for the development. This had been a piece of mischief Neil couldn't resist. There was no suggestion that the

43

Roman empire had ever shown much interest in Stokeworthy. But it had been worth being a little economical with history to see Thewlis's face redden dangerously.

'Neil,' a voice called from the trees.

Neil looked up. A man with the face of an innocent elf looked down at him. He was probably in his thirties but, from his manner, seemed much younger. He wore an embroidered Peruvian cap over his long matted hair and his summer uniform of disintegrating tie-dyed T-shirt and filthy surfing shorts. 'Hi, Squirrel. How are you doing?'

'You know that murder? The old bird in the churchyard?'

'Yeah. What about it?'

'I saw her – last night. Should I let the pigs know? What do you think? I don't want to give 'em a chance to get me down from here.'

Neil smiled. 'No worries. There's no way they'll get you down. I know just the man . . . mate of mine. Trust me.' He extracted his mobile phone from the pocket of his jeans.

'Tell your mate I saw that woman going towards the Manor.'

'Will do,' said Neil as he waited for Wesley to answer his phone.

Chapter Four

14 March 1475

Elizabeth Pirie is a woman of ill fame and unfit to be amongst honest people. Alice de Neston did tell the jury that she did see her with John Fleccer, the blacksmith's son in the churchyard, and she being a married woman and twice his age.

Order: it is agreed by the Steward and jury that if any under-tenant is presented to be of ill fame and does not reform then four honest persons, with the Steward's consent, may expel such persons from the village.

From the Court Rolls of Stokeworthy Manor

Jo and Leanne, recovered from their ordeal of the night before, had taken up their usual Saturday afternoon post at the bus shelter opposite the village hall. This Saturday was more eventful than most as the village hall had been transformed into an *ad hoc* police station. Stokeworthy had been all but abandoned by the local bus operator, who grudgingly allowed the village two buses a day into Tradmouth, so the girls had the shelter to themselves. Leanne nudged Jo when she spotted a dark-haired young man getting out of an Escort XR3i. He wore an expensive leather jacket in defiance of the heat.

'He's not bad,' Leanne whispered as Steve Carstairs turned to look at them and gave them a knowing wink. Emboldened by this encouragement, Leanne called out, 'Hey. You a copper?'

Steve sauntered towards the girls, looking them up and down, his eyes coming to rest on their exposed bellies. 'Might be. Why do you ask?'

'We found the body.'

45

'Oh, aye?' The girls were interested, he could tell. Just longing to be chatted up.

Then suddenly Jo took Leanne's arm, her gaze focused beyond Steve's face. 'We've got to go.'

Leanne shook off her companion's hand. 'Why?' She was annoyed with Jo. Why did she have to ruin things just when she had attracted the attentions of a good-looking member of the opposite sex . . . and one with a decent car at that. He was a bit old, mid-twenties probably, but then Leanne preferred the more mature man: better than the acned specimens that hung around the village.

Jo tried again, her eyes checking the passage at the side of the village shop where she could see Lee and Gaz waiting, watching her talking to the pigs. Somehow she had to get Leanne away. 'Leanne. Come on. We've got to meet Lee. Remember?'

To Steve Carstairs' disappointment, Jo's tactic worked. 'See you around, then,' Leanne said casually before walking off. As the girls sauntered away, he watched them appreciatively. He would keep an eye out for them around the village. Stokeworthy might yet have its compensations.

The girls waited for Steve to disappear safely into the village hall before approaching their quarry. Two lads, one with dyed blond hair, the other wearing his long greasy locks in a ponytail, lounged against the side wall of the village shop, waiting for the girls to join them. They greeted them with studied indifference. Then the blond boy spoke. 'Were you talking to one of them pigs? The one in the leather jacket who reckoned he was flash?'

Jo got in first. 'It was Leanne. She fancied him. I thought he was a wanker,' she assured the lads proudly: she would never let the side down.

'I can handle him,' Leanne said, nonchalant.

'Bet you can. Bet that's what he's after . . . you handling him.' The ponytailed boy leered unpleasantly. 'That right, Gaz? Do you reckon he wants to give her one?'

'Piss off.' Leanne turned away, blushing.

'You heard what happened last night?'

''Course we heard. We saw her, flying up in the tree. We were stoned. You thought she was an angel, didn't you, Gaz? An angel on the Christmas tree.'

'You must have seen her before us, then. We found her. Gave us a right turn.'

'Don't remember much about it.' Lee shook his head, grinning. 'It was a fucking good trip. Amazing.'

Leanne turned back and looked at them. She felt uneasy. Was murder, death, really a thing to be taken that lightly? 'Have you told the pigs what you saw?'

Gaz snorted. 'Get real. We were stoned. Besides . . . ' Lee and Gaz exchanged looks. There was something else.

'Besides what?' Leanne said, challenging.

'Promise you won't tell that pig? Even if he gets his leg over?'

'Don't be pathetic. Come on. What is it?'

'We did one of them artists' places . . . in the old water mill. We saw the bloke go out and we broke in. Dead easy.'

Leanne looked away. She didn't want to hear. Jo was looking at Gaz with terrified admiration. This was dangerous. This was real.

'Did you get much?'

'Bit of cash. And I found this.' He delved into the back pocket of his jeans, drew out a photograph and handed it to Leanne. 'What do you reckon? That's her, isn't it? The doctor's receptionist? The one who topped herself?'

Jo snatched the photograph from Leanne's hand and stared at it. It was a recent picture of Pauline Brent, and Jo had to acknowledge that she'd been in very good shape for her age. After all, there's no hiding lumps, bumps and wrinkles when you are photographed stark naked.

'Steve.' Gerry Heffernan looked at his watch. 'Nice of you to call in.'

Steve Carstairs took his leather jacket off and draped it casually over one shoulder. He could do without the boss's sarcastic comments. He was still suffering from the effects of the eight pints of lager he had consumed in a club in Morbay the previous evening. He had felt temporarily better when that young girl had given him the come-on outside the village hall, but now his thumping headache had returned with a vengeance.

The incident room was taking shape. Phones and computers had been installed; desks littered the splintery parquet floor. At one end, by the rickety stage, stood a large notice-board decorated with photographs of Pauline Brent: Pauline hanging from the yew tree; Pauline cut down and lying on the churchyard grass; a picture of Pauline in life smiling outside her cottage, acquired by Wesley and Rachel during their search of her home.

Gerry Heffernan's voice boomed out as he called his team together. Steve wished he wouldn't shout so loud. When the inspector had finished recapping on the case so far and assigned everyone to their tasks, Steve discovered with some satisfaction that he and Rachel Tracey had been teamed up to visit the old water mill at the end of Worthy Lane, now home to a colony of artists – if colony was the right word. Steve searched for an appropriate collective noun: a layabout of artists; a scrounge of artists. He had a low opinion of anyone who pursued what he considered to be a namby-pamby occupation. He felt someone tap his shoulder firmly and swung round. It was Rachel.

'Come on. The boss says you're with me. I'm driving.'

As Rachel left the incident room, Steve following behind, his eyes downcast in appreciation of her calves, the telephone range on Wesley Peterson's desk and he rushed over to answer it.

'Where have you been? I've been trying to ring you.' Neil Watson sounded quite indignant on the other end of the line.

'Sorry. Been busy. What is it?'

'Just a juicy bit of information for you. One of our protesters here saw that murdered woman going up to the Manor last night. Thought you might be interested.'

'I'll come round right away. Is he still there, this protester?'

'Silly question, Wes. He's not budging till he's forced out.'

'What's his name?'

'Squirrel.'

'Up a tree, is he?'

'You guessed it.'

Wesley replaced the receiver with a smile and went over to where Gerry Heffernan was sorting through witness statements. 'Sir, I've had a call from Neil Watson. He says the dead woman was seen last night visiting the Manor.'

Heffernan looked at his sergeant with sudden interest. 'What time was this?'

'He didn't say. But the witness who saw her is there with Neil now. Shall we go and have a word?'

'Certainly. We can call in on our way to see this D'estry character. Who is it, this witness?'

Wesley grinned widely. 'A squirrel, sir.'

Heffernan began to laugh. 'There's no answer to that. Come on, then. Let's get going before this squirrel runs off to hide his nuts.'

The old water mill at the end of Worthy Lane was the last building in Stokeworthy before the landscape changed to open farmland. A small but spirited brook, hurtling down towards Knot Creek, had provided power for the mill in its working days. Now, passing by the side of the building, it gurgled picturesquely, a thing of leisure rather than industry.

There were three apartments in all, each comprising a large studio and living accommodation, and Rachel and Steve found the three artists at home. The first two, an elderly man with a mane of steel-grey hair and a mouse-haired woman with an other worldly manner, had seen nothing. They had stayed in last night and did not know Pauline Brent.

The third apartment was on the ground floor and belonged to a man called Charles Stoke-Brown. He opened his door, a worried expression on his lined but still handsome face, and stood aside meekly to admit them. He was a tall man with even, tanned features and a full head of grey hair worn in a neat ponytail. Rachel thought he must have been quite something in his youth . . . was still quite something, in fact.

He led them into his studio, which was littered with paintings in various stages of completion. A large canvas dominated the far wall; on it was painted what looked like a coat of arms, a golden eagle flying above an ancient ship.

Rachel noticed the broken pane of glass in the window. Some of the drawers stood open and their contents lay strewn on the floor, but the large desk in the corner of the room appeared undisturbed. Rachel's eyes were drawn to a small framed sketch of some sort of tree lying in the centre of the desk. Such delicate work. Charles Stoke-Brown was a talented man. He saw her looking at it and deftly made a show of tidying the desk, covering the picture with a piece of rag.

'I hope you don't mind me mentioning it, sir, but I couldn't help noticing that one of your windows is broken.'

'Er . . . yes. I had a break-in last night. Just kids probably,' he said, awkwardly.

'Did you report it?'

'Er, yes ... one has to, for the insurance company. A local constable came round this morning. Nothing much was taken, just some cash. And a small painting ... not one of my best. It's more of a nuisance than anything.' He fixed her with a charming smile. The subject was closed.

'If we can just ask a few questions, sir,' Steve began. 'Have you heard that a woman was found murdered in the churchyard last night? Hanged,' he added with relish. 'Here's a photo of her.' He handed Charles Stoke-Brown the picture of Pauline outside her cottage. 'Her name was Pauline Brent. She worked at the doctor's surgery. Did you know her at all?'

Something was bothering Stoke-Brown. Rachel could tell. He took a deep breath, his face impassive. 'I know her,' he said simply. 'But I didn't see her last night. Sorry I can't be more help.' He poured himself a drink from a half-full bottle of whisky and drank it down in one.

'Where were you last night, sir?'

'I was visiting my ex-wife in Plymouth.'

'There's been some trouble at Worthy Court, I believe,' Rachel stated innocently. 'Do you know anything about it? Do you know a man called D'estry?'

'Sorry. That place is far enough away not to bother us here. Is that all?'

Rachel looked around the studio. There was a pile of paintings propped up near the door. She went over to them and bent down to admire a landscape at the front. 'This is lovely, sir. Knot Creek, is it?'

'That's right.' Was it Rachel's imagination or did he sound nervous?

She reached out a hand, intending to look at the canvases stacked at the back. Stoke-Brown leaped forward. 'I'd rather you didn't .... er, some of them aren't very good. Really.' Rachel straightened up and encountered that charming smile again.

Steve, looking around at the other canvases, all attractive, shrugged. 'They're a darned sight better than anything I could do.'

The artist was now only too keen to get rid of them after his unexpected show of modesty. 'If you'll excuse me, I must get on. Sorry I can't be more help.'

As they stepped outside into the sunshine, Steve was the first to speak. 'I think those pictures were bloody good.'

'Yes, they were. But there were some he didn't want me to see. And from the expression on his face when we asked him about Pauline, I'd say there was something he wasn't telling us.'

Steve shrugged his shoulders again.

'Do you know, Steve, this village gives me the creeps. There's an atmosphere, don't you think?' Steve, an unimaginative soul, gave another shrug. 'I don't like this place,' Rachel announced with finality as she got into the driving seat of the police car.

The dig had begun in earnest. Neil was squatting in the largest trench, watched by a small group of serious-faced students. Wesley recognised Neil's colleagues, Matt and Jane, supervising the proceedings in two other trenches, answering the questions of the second-year students assigned to them. For a few moments he experienced a longing to join them, but the voice of Gerry Heffernan focused his thoughts on the matter in hand. 'There's your mate, Wes. Go on. Get him over here. I'm not breaking me neck climbing over this lot.'

Neil straightened himself up and grinned. 'You were quick. I'll give Squirrel a shout.'

'Found anything yet?' Wesley couldn't resist the question.

'Bit of medieval pottery. Give us a chance. We've only just started.'

'Have you got the geophysics results?'

Neil nodded. 'Yeah. They're quite interesting. There are some strange signals which could be a collapsed stone building or a piece of natural rock.' He indicated the trench nearest the road where an attractive young woman in a snowy-white T-shirt was instructing her students in the techniques of her profession.

'Found any evidence of the village extending this way?' Wesley glanced over at the inspector, who was standing watching Jane working in the trench.

'Yeah, there are some earthworks over that way.' Neil pointed east. 'Among the trees. But we're tackling the area nearest the road first . . . see if we can turn up anything interesting. Will you make it to the Tradmouth Arms tonight?'

'If I can.' He looked over again at his boss, who was starting to show signs of impatience.

'I'll tell you all about it then.'

'All about what?'

'The local stories about this site. There used to be a road just over there leading to the Manor. Later on in the eighteenth century the new drive was built and the old road fell into disrepair and got overgrown.' He grinned, a sinister gleam in his eye, like one telling a ghost story to a terrified audience. 'This was a crossroads.'

At this point Heffernan's patience snapped. 'Come on, Wes. Where's this squirrel? If there's any tree-climbing to be done, you're doing it. Right? My legs aren't what they were.'

Neil turned and shouted. 'Squirrel. You there?'

There was a great rustling in one of the trees fringing the site, and after a few moments a face appeared. The Peruvian cap made Squirrel look like some ancient tree spirit, a guardian of the woodland . . . which, after all, was what he had appointed himself to be.

'Come on down, Squirrel. My mate's here . . . the one I told you about.'

Another great rustling, then Squirrel, agile and wiry, climbed like a monkey out of the branches and landed on the soft earth beneath his tree.

'Squirrel, meet Wes. He was at uni with me. He's with the police but he's not interested in getting you off the site, only in the murder of that woman you saw. Okay?'

Squirrel nodded, eyeing the smartly dressed Wesley suspiciously.

'Neil's right,' Wesley began. 'We're only interested in what you saw last night.' Gerry Heffernan was making his way carefully over the bumpy terrain. Having decided that Squirrel was unlikely to come to him, he would have to make the effort to approach the timid creature.

'Who's that?' Squirrel swung round as he saw the inspector approaching.

'Don't worry.' Wesley held a hand up: a sign of peace. 'It's my boss. He just wants to know what you saw last night. It could be important. It could help us catch whoever killed her.'

Squirrel was no fool. He knew the information he held might not only help the police but his own cause. 'Okay. I'll tell you what I saw.' He shuffled his feet, thinking a while before beginning. 'It was still light. This woman with fair hair came walking round the corner past the Ring o' Bells. I was in one of the trees over by the road . . . just watching what was going on in the village. I've got a good view from up there.'

'What was she wearing?' asked Wesley.

'Sort of white mac . . . couldn't miss her. It had been warm but it had turned a bit chilly by then. She walked straight past my tree. She looked sort of . . . I don't know, sort of determined.'

'You were close enough to see?'

'I got binoculars, haven't I,' Squirrel said proudly. 'My early warning system.'

'So where did she go? Did you see?'

Squirrel nodded. 'Oh yes. I saw. She turned into the drive and walked up towards the Manor.'

'What time was this?'

Squirrel put his head on one side, thinking. 'I've not got a watch but I guess it was after half nine. I'd heard the church bells chime about five minutes before and the Ring o' Bells was filling up nicely.'

'Not tempted to pay a visit there yourself?' asked Gerry mischievously.

Squirrel looked disdainful. 'I'm teetotal . . . and a vegan,' he added proudly.

Heffernan, with an effort of self-control, passed no comment on Squirrel's exemplary lifestyle.

'Did you see her call at the Manor?'

'No. I lost sight of her halfway down the path.'

'Did you see her come out again?'

Squirrel shook his head. 'I gave up watching soon after that, went off to get something to eat with the others.'

'Does the drive only lead to the Manor?'

'There's a path leading off it which goes down to Knot Creek. It's a public footpath . . . well kept.'

There spoke a man, thought Wesley, who had studied the lie of the land.

'It's no use going to see Thewlis now,' Squirrel continued. 'He's out. I saw him go out in his bloatedcapitalistmobile this morning . . . not come back yet.'

'Who else lives up there?'

'His missus . . . couple of kids. But they were with him. They're all out.'

'Anyone else?'

'There's the nanny,' said Neil. 'About nineteen. Dark-haired. Not bad. And there's a couple of cleaners and a cook who come up from the village – and a secretary who drives up every day. Come to think of it, the nanny's the only one who actually lives in.'

Heffernan turned to Squirrel. 'Thanks for your help ... er, Squirrel. Keep up the good work.' He started to walk off in the direction of the drive. 'You coming, Wes, or what?'

Neil stood gaping. 'Well, I'll say this for your boss, Wes, he's got hidden depths. Keep up the good work? What's that supposed to mean?'

'Perhaps he's a bit of an eco-warrior on the sly. But he'll have to go on a diet or he'll never make it up into those trees. Best be off, Neil. See you later, I hope.'

Squirrel watched as the policemen disappeared, thinking with some satisfaction that support sometimes came from the most unexpected quarters.

Gemma Matherley was glad to have some time to herself. She relished every spare hour when she could pass on responsibility for Amanda and Guy to their idle bitch of a mother. But however obnoxious the kids were, however viciously they fought each other, it was better to have her job looking after their ever-increasing demands than to be stuck at home with her mum and Leanne, her stupid bitch of a sister.

Gemma began to paint her nails, smiling to herself as she remembered her encounter with her grandmother that morning. How she'd given the old cow a turn when she'd come in to clean the master bedroom. Her smile turned to a bubble of laughter. Queen Elizabeth's bed. Gemma had spent her school history lessons inscribing the names of pop stars on her pencil case, but even with her paltry amount of historical knowledge, she knew that Elizabeth had been known as the Virgin Queen. She must be turning in her grave, Gemma thought with glee, at what had gone on in her bed that morning when the kids and Mrs Thewlis were out riding.

And that interfering Brent woman was dead: killed herself, so they said. Gemma couldn't pretend she was sorry: that would be hypocritical and Gemma wasn't that. It still riled her that her grandmother had asked Pauline Brent to speak to Mr Thewlis. The cheek of it. She recalled her grandmother's discovery that morning with a further glow of satisfaction. That would teach her to mind her own business.

Gemma finished her nails and held them out in front of her for inspection. Then she got up and walked about the room, waving her hands about to dry the pale blue varnish. She strolled over to the window, bored. Her room was at the top of the house, in what had once been the servants' quarters. She had a good view of the drive and she could see two men approaching. One was young, dark-skinned and smartly dressed; rather good-looking. The other was overweight, middle-aged and scruffy with unruly greying curls. An incongruous pair. They were walking up the drive, deep in discussion. Then they turned off to follow the footpath to the creek.

Could they be the police? Gemma turned away from the window. Even if they found her, even if they came to question her, she would keep quiet about what she had seen last night.

'Aren't we calling at the Manor, sir?' Wesley was puzzled by his boss's sudden change of route.

'You heard what Squirrel said. There's nobody at home.'

'There's the nanny.'

'She can wait. So can the others. We'll pay them a visit tomorrow when they're off their guard after the Sunday roast. I wonder if Rachel and Steve have turned up anything with those artists.'

'Did Pauline Brent strike you as the type to mix with artists?'

'That's the point, Wes. We don't really know much about her, do we? She was the doctor's receptionist. She helped out at village functions but kept in the background. She was a quiet woman, according to the vicar. Not the sort to make enemies. You've talked to Mrs Green. What about her other neighbours?'

'The other cottage in that row belongs to a local family with two young kids. They didn't see or hear anything unusual last night.' Wesley changed the subject. 'Why are we heading down here, sir? Where does this lead?'

'Knot Creek. I fancied having a quick look. If she wasn't going to the Manor, this is where she could have been heading.'

The path, shaded by trees, was well maintained and smooth: no hacking through the undergrowth here. At least, Wesley thought,

Philip Thewlis took his obligation to maintain the public footpath that ran through his land seriously.

'Do you think Pauline was meeting somebody?'

'Well, our friend Squirrel said she looked determined. It's a good bet she was going to have it out with someone.'

'But she wasn't the battle-axe type. If she was the village busybody, always out for confrontation, I could understand it.'

'She stood up to D'estry and got threatened for her pains. We'll stroll up to Worthy Court when we've finished here and see if he's back.'

The path leading down to the creek became sandy as it emerged from the trees. Then it dropped away steeply to form a bank, full of exposed roots and stones.

Knot Creek, an inlet off the River Trad, was a picturesque spot. On the far bank stood cottages behind their rickety boathouses. Small boats bobbed in the channel of water down the centre of the creek. The tide was out and a wide area of muddy sand lay exposed and strewn with seaweed. A small, sleek cabin cruiser, the *Pride of de Stoke*, lay helpless on its side on the wet sand, waiting to be floated back to life when the tide returned. The bleached wooden skeleton of a large vessel also lay on its side some way away, a relic of the days when the River Trad and its inlets had buzzed with commercial traffic. Now the boat's remains had acquired a more romantic look: the wreck of an old pirate ship; the hull of an ancient war craft – anything the imagination of a child or a romantically inclined adult could manufacture.

There were a couple of rowing boats pulled up on the sand near the end of the footpath, probably there for the use of the Manor's occupants, thought Gerry Heffernan. 'This place hasn't changed much since I was last here,' he commented, seeing Wesley looking around.

'It's a lovely spot.'

'You're right there, Wes. Very peaceful. We had a picnic here once,' he said wistfully, 'when the kids were small. Kathy used to say it was one of the good things about living round here – lots of places for picnics.'

'We've not reached that stage yet. When Michael's a bit older ... ' Wesley paused. 'Actually, I've been meaning to ask you. Er ... it's Michael's christening at the end of next month.

We ... er, Pam and I wondered if you'd like to come. Two o'clock ... Sunday the 28th.'

Gerry Heffernan's face lit up with a wide, delighted smile.

'My parents are coming from London,' Wesley continued. 'And my sister's booked some time off duty; she's coming over from Oxford. It won't be a big do, but ... '

'Just try and keep me away. St Margaret's, is it?'

Wesley nodded. 'We were there last week sitting near the back.' He smiled. 'The choir were very good.'

Each Sunday morning Gerry Heffernan was to be found in the choir stalls of the parish church of St Margaret's, Tradmouth, singing his heart out. Wesley had heard rumours that he had an excellent voice, but last Sunday had been his first opportunity to confirm this for himself.

'I didn't know you'd started to come to St Margaret's, Wes. Why didn't you say?'

'It was a condition of getting Michael christened. I had a bit of trouble getting Pam there – she wasn't brought up with it like I was. In our house Sunday meant church and Sunday school.'

Gerry Heffernan nodded, his mind wandering back to his own days as a choirboy in the huge red sandstone church in the Liverpool suburbs where he had read comics and given cheek to the verger between anthems and evensong.

Wesley looked around again. 'Nothing here, sir. Where to now?'

'Worthy Court. Was this D'estry character really skinny-dipping in the pool there?'

'Apparently. In front of a former magistrate too.' Wesley grinned.

'Well then, Wes, I think it's about time we paid a little call on Mr Julian D'estry. Let's hope he's found himself something to wear.'

Chapter Five

14 March 1475
John Fleccer while drunk did cause disturbance to Marjorie
Snow at the hour of midnight and did, by his noise, affright
Master Snow's horse and cause it to bolt. Fine 12d.

Felicia de Monte is a scandal monger and a great provoker
of discord. She did strike her son, Thomas the stonecarver,
when she came upon him talking with Alice de Neston and did
call the said Alice a common whore. Alice doth plead that she
hath been sorely slandered. Felicia de Monte is fined 2d.

Ralph de Neston pays the lord 3s as fine and relief for Alice,
his daughter, to receive the inheritance of her mother
Matilda's land.

From the Court Rolls of Stokeworthy Manor

Julian D'estry's Mercedes was parked in its allocated space,
gleaming, shiny as a bullet.

'Looks like he's home. What about the other places here?'

'They should all have been seen by now. Rachel and I spoke to
the people in number seven ourselves. They couldn't tell us
anything.'

'Surprise, surprise.' Heffernan looked around the courtyard.
'Posh, isn't it.'

'Very.'

'Look at that swimming pool. Where do people get the sort of
money to buy places like this just as second homes, eh?'

'Crime?' suggested Wesley with a grin.

'It wouldn't surprise me.'

It took Julian D'estry several minutes to answer the door, and when he did so he appeared in a dressing gown with no hint of anything underneath. In spite of his sartorial disadvantage, he stood aside to let them in with a confident, even cocky, air.

A slender blonde wafted out of the bedroom dressed in a swimsuit made decent by the addition of a brightly coloured sarong. D'estry introduced her as Monica, his partner.

They sat down. D'estry lay full length on the white leather sofa, propping himself up like a Roman emperor contemplating an orgy. Monica hovered behind the sofa. If D'estry was displaying no sign of nerves, she was.

'Now, Mr D'estry.' Heffernan decided to do the talking. 'I don't know if you're aware that one of your neighbours has been found dead in the churchyard and that we're treating her death as suspicious.'

'I heard something. What's it got to do with us?' His accent was East End cockney. Somewhere along life's precarious path, D'estry had made a steep financial ascent.

'The dead woman's name was Pauline Brent. Did you know her?'

''Course I didn't. We don't mix with the yokels round here.' He smirked unpleasantly.

'What about you . . . er, Monica? Have you met Pauline Brent?'

Monica shrugged and shook her head. Then she sat down by Julian D'estry's feet, her sarong falling open to reveal bronzed and slender legs. Wesley averted his eyes.

Heffernan put on his puzzled 'thick copper' expression. Wesley had seen it before. He knew exactly what he was up to. 'They must have got it wrong, then.'

D'estry fell for the bait. 'Got what wrong?'

'The people who heard you threatening Miss Brent. What is it they said?' He nudged Wesley, who, playing along with the act, made a great show of consulting his notebook.

'That she was an interfering old bitch who should keep her nose out of other people's business. You knew where to find her and you knew how to deal with people like her.'

Heffernan leaned forward, his eyes narrowed. No longer the amiable Mr Plod. 'So how did you deal with her, Mr D'estry?'

'I don't have to talk to you without my solicitor.'

'Right, then. You call him and we'll go down to the station in Tradmouth.'

His bluff called, Julian D'estry backed down. 'I didn't do anything. It was just something I said to put the wind up the old cow. I didn't even know her name ... when you mentioned it before it didn't click. I didn't mean anything by it. I never touched her.'

'How about telling us what happened in your own words ... sir,' Wesley suggested, trying to be polite. He didn't like D'estry, and he knew exactly what the beautiful neighbour Jane Wills had meant when she had described him as a vulgar little man.

'We was down a couple of Saturdays back ... me and Monica and a few mates from the smoke. We went into Neston to get some booze and we was driving back when this kid runs out into the road. I nearly hit him but it weren't my fault. Then this woman comes across yelling that I was driving too fast ... said I could have killed the brat. She threatened to call your lot out.'

'Was she alone?'

'At first. Then the kid's mum comes out of one of the cottages, and another old bird ... short dark hair. I drove off before they could put their two-penn'orth in,' he said with satisfaction.

'Do you deny using the words my sergeant read out ... about dealing with people like her?'

'I might have said something like that. Can't remember.' D'estry was beginning to look uncomfortable. 'I didn't mean anything by it. I wouldn't hurt a fly. Monica'll tell you ...'

'It's not flies we're discussing, Mr D'estry. Where were you last night?'

'I was here. Monica'll tell you. We was having a swim. That old bag from number ten'll tell you. She chucked my CD player into the pool. And that husband of hers was there watching ... and that red-headed bint from number seven was there and all with an old geezer. And her husband's supposed to be a bloody lawyer ... standing for Parliament. Now I could report them for ...'

'I wouldn't bother, sir. There is such a thing as causing a disturbance, you know.' Heffernan looked him in the eye, challenging. 'What time did this lady throw your CD player in the pool?'

'After midnight. Why?'

'Thank you, Mr D'estry ... madam. I think that's all for now. You'll let my sergeant have details of when you plan to return to London ... and your permanent address.'

D'estry turned towards Wesley and looked him up and down with disdain. 'Long as he calls me Bwana.' He smirked unpleasantly.

Wesley and his boss exchanged looks. 'If you'll just give me the details, sir,' Wesley said calmly.

D'estry, sensing that he was pushing things a bit far, recited his London address with surprising obedience and added that they planned to stay down until late on Sunday to indulge in some jet-skiing. Heffernan grunted with disapproval. As a serious sailor, he hated the noisy things.

'Tell me, Mr D'estry,' he said, 'what is it you do for a living?'

'I'm in the City ... dealer,' D'estry said with satisfaction, hoping he'd impressed.

'I'd like to lock that toerag up and throw away the key,' Heffernan said softly to Wesley as they left. 'He's bound to have committed some offence. How about "being in possession of an obnoxious personality"?'

'That's not a crime, sir.' Wesley smiled.

'Then it should be. What do you reckon? Do you see him as our murderer?'

'Just because the man's thoroughly unpleasant doesn't make him guilty.'

'He's not got an alibi ... only the bimbo, and she'd back him up whatever he said. The irate neighbour didn't do her bit for peace and quiet till after midnight.'

'I think he's all mouth,' said Wesley. 'I can't really see him murdering Pauline then stringing her up. His type would just have a go at her verbally – make life unpleasant. Actually I see him more as a victim than a perpetrator: there must be a lot of people in this village – and probably in London – who'd like him out of the way.'

'Well, he's not exactly endeared himself to us, has he? Check him out on the PNC when we get back to the incident room.'

Wesley nodded and looked at his watch. Half past four. He hadn't realised it was so late. They drove back to the village hall, windows down. The car interior was like an oven and they wished they had chosen the healthy option and walked.

The village hall was bathed in sunshine. Nearby, outside the small village shop, Leanne and Jo sat on a wall, swigging from cans of cola, watching the comings and goings from the incident room. This was probably the most exciting thing to happen in Stokeworthy for a fair number of years, and the girls were determined to make the most of it.

Once inside, Wesley found Rachel writing up reports. He perched himself on the edge of her desk. She looked up at him and smiled. 'Did you manage to see D'estry?'

Wesley nodded. 'Lovely man. We got on like a house on fire.' He began to laugh.

'Telling lies to police officers is never advisable, Wesley.'

'Okay, okay. The truth is that he was an unpleasant little prat and anyone unfortunate enough to be his neighbour has my deepest sympathy.'

'Did he do it?'

'We've no evidence and, much as I dislike the man, I'm not jumping to any hasty conclusions. Any progress at the mill?'

'One of the studios there was broken into last night.'

'Anything taken?'

'Just some cash. But the man who lives there was very nervous about something.'

'Worth another visit?'

Rachel nodded earnestly. 'I think so. His name's Charles Stoke-Brown and he claims he was visiting his ex-wife in Plymouth last night. I'd like to check it out. I'll get on to . . .'

'Sergeant Peterson. Can I have a word?' Heffernan's voice boomed through the village hall. Wesley left Rachel sorting through statements and made his way to where the inspector sat in a partitioned-off area near the stage. He peeped round the partition and Heffernan, seeing him, beckoned frantically. 'Come in, Wes, and show me what to do with this thing.' He indicated the computer which squatted malevolently on his desk.

Wesley said nothing but leaned across the desk to switch the machine on. 'Shall we see if D'estry's got any form?'

'Great idea. Go on. You do it.'

'I really think you should get some practice in, sir.'

'No, no . . . I might break it, and you know what the Chief Super's like about his budgets. You do it.'

Wesley obliged, making a mental note to leave details of computer courses operated by Tradmouth College in a strategic place on his boss's desk. Surely even Gerry Heffernan had to give in eventually and accept that they lived in the age of technology ... but Wesley wasn't holding his breath.

The information flickered up on the screen. Julian Destry – without the apostrophe – had been done twice for actual bodily harm. Once for a fight outside a West End pub, and once for an affray outside Chelsea's football ground. He'd been fined and bound over on both occasions.

'It proves he's a man with a temper,' said Heffernan.

'A punch-up outside a football ground or a pub is hardly the same as strangling a woman.'

'Still, Wes, I don't think we can dismiss him out of hand.' Heffernan sat back and his chair creaked dangerously below him. He looked at his watch. 'Half five. I don't think there's much more we can do tonight. We'll visit the Manor tomorrow and catch Philip Thewlis over his Sunday lunch.'

'Rachel tells me there was a burglary last night at the water mill on the edge of the village ... it's converted into artists' studios. She said the victim seemed nervous about something.'

'Well, put his name into the infernal machine, then,' said the inspector, pointing at the computer. 'What's the use of having these new toys if we don't play with them?'

Wesley obliged, typing in the name of Charles Stoke-Brown, but came up with a blank. 'Nothing under that name.'

'He's a law-abiding citizen, then. But if Rachel thinks he's worth another visit, we'd better drop in for a cup of tea. And we mustn't forget Pauline's work first thing on Monday. Are you at St Margaret's in the morning?'

Wesley nodded. 'I hope you're in good voice.'

Heffernan blushed modestly. 'How about a drink at the Ring o' Bells?'

'I'd better get back. Pam'll be expecting me. I'm going to see if one of the neighbours'll baby-sit so we can go out for a drink with Neil later.'

Heffernan sat up, interested. 'Where are you going?'

Wesley's heart sank. He knew his boss had been desperately lonely since the death of his wife but Gerry Heffernan hardly fitted into their social circle, the circle of old student friends and professional archaeologists. But then his parents' and Sunday school's dictates about befriending the lonely came flooding back and made it impossible for him to utter a lie. 'The Tradmouth

Arms . . . your local,' he said, forcing himself to smile.

'I was thinking of going in myself tonight. I might see you there.'

'Great.' Wesley Peterson forced himself to sound enthusiastic. Then he took his leave, wondering if they'd be able to get a baby-sitter at such short notice.

The smell hit Wesley as he walked into the living room. He put his hand to his nose. 'Do you have to do that in here?'

Pam, who had been bending over the plastic changing mat on the floor, looked round, defensive. 'What do you mean?'

'It stinks.' He opened a window.

'Well, that's what babies do. Put this in the bin outside, will you?' She handed her husband a folded-up disposable nappy.

'Do you realise the amount of pollution these things cause? My mother says she always used real ones. They're far more environmentally friendly. I thought you were into things like that.'

'Fine if I had the time. I'll be back at work soon. Your mother didn't go back till you were older.'

'She did a couple of clinics when we were small . . . to keep her hand in.'

'Hardly the same as teaching full time,' Pam snorted resentfully.

'Then go part time. We could manage. I know Gerry's recommended me for promotion, so . . .'

'Come on, Wesley. Live in the real world. How would we pay the mortgage?'

'Okay,' he sighed. 'Any chance of getting a baby-sitter tonight for a couple of hours?'

Pam looked up at him, tired. Little Michael, clean and fresh in his new nappy, kicked happily on the mat; a healthy, handsome child with golden brown skin and a shock of straight black hair. 'Where are you thinking of going?'

'Neil said he'd be in the Tradmouth Arms . . .'

'Neil?' She raised her eyebrows but made no further comment. She thought for a moment. 'I'll ask Gaynor down the road.'

'She's only fifteen. Will he be okay with her?'

'Don't be so fussy. He'll be fine. Lots of teenage girls baby-sit for a bit of extra pocket money. How's your murder going? Arrested anyone yet?'

'It's early days.' Wesley didn't like talking shop at home. 'What have you been doing today?'

'Mixing in high society,' Pam said mysteriously. 'Someone I met at antenatal class suggested we had a get-together. I went round to her house and we talked babies for ages . . . pretty boring. Then she asked me about going back to work and had I chosen a childminder and we got talking about nannies – the live-in sort. You should hear what they charge . . . and some of them expect their own car and self-contained flat.'

'Out of our league. You shouldn't have married a policeman: you should have held out for a millionaire.'

Pam, whose boyfriends had never been the sort of which millionaires are made, shrugged. 'From what this woman said, her friends don't trust their nannies very much.'

Wesley was starting to lose interest in all this baby talk. The colour supplement from that day's newspaper lay open on the coffee table, and a large coloured photograph on the exposed page caught his eye. It was a familiar face: one often seen on the television screen spouting opinions on the world of business and social policy. Philip Thewlis, proud owner of Stokeworthy Manor, posed in his oak-panelled office, looking every inch the captain of industry. Wesley read the caption underneath.

Philip Thewlis, the man chosen to head the government's new National Children's Welfare Council, photographed here in his office at his lovely Devon home, Stokeworthy Manor. The office was used as a courtroom in the Middle Ages, Philip told our reporter, and he has renovated the entire house sympathetically, using local craftsmen to restore the many ancient features of the Grade One listed building. Philip (tipped by many to receive a peerage in the next Honours List) said that, as a devoted father of two young children, he was delighted at his new appointment and hopes to achieve much for the young people of the nation.

Wesley looked up and realised that he still had the nappy in his hand. He wrinkled his nose. 'I'll just go and get rid of this.'

'Okay. I'll pop round to Gaynor's. I'll take Michael with me.' She picked up the baby and kissed him. 'She won't be able to resist a date with him.'

Two hours later the baby-sitter, a plump, sensible girl, was safely installed with a supply of crisps and cola. Wesley and Pam walked arm in arm down the steep narrow streets to the centre of the town. They could tell that the tourist season was beginning. Holidaymakers – mostly young couples and the elderly as the schools hadn't yet finished for the summer – promenaded along the quayside and stood staring at menus in restaurant windows. The evening was warm, and Pam wore a long sleeveless dress, a cardigan draped round her shoulders. She looked good, Wesley thought; better than she had done since Michael's birth.

'How is Neil?' she asked as the Tradmouth Arms came into view.

'Fine. He's doing a dig in the village where our body was found.'

She rolled her eyes to heaven. 'I should have known. And I suppose you plan to give him a hand?'

Wesley opened his mouth to protest but Pam got in first. 'It's always the same when Neil's around. As if police work wasn't bad enough.'

She looked round at her husband, who stood by the pub entrance, crestfallen. 'Don't worry, I won't spoil the evening. God knows I get out little enough these days,' she said in martyred tones. Wesley didn't reply.

They found Neil installed in a corner opposite the bar with Matt and Jane. The Tradmouth Arms, dark and cosy with a nautical flavour and famed for its crab sandwiches, was a pleasant pub which stood in a commanding corner position in Tradmouth's older quarter, just next to Baynard's Quay, the small stretch of cobbled quayside with a small defensive castle at one end and Gerry Heffernan's whitewashed cottage at the other. In fact Heffernan and the Tradmouth Arms were virtually next-door neighbours. Wesley found himself watching the door, anticipating his boss's appearance.

The place was filling up, mostly with locals and members of the weekend yachting fraternity, some of whom were braying loudly by the bar. Neil stood up and gave Pam a kiss on the cheek. Matt and Jane raised a hand in greeting. Wesley, feeling more relaxed, bought a round of drinks, and when he returned from the bar he found Pam sitting next to Neil, listening intently as he spoke.

'Well, legend has it,' Neil was saying. 'that a young woman

was hanged on the yew in the churchyard; the same one that body was found hanging from last night.'

'I never talk shop out of working hours,' Wesley rebuked gently.

'I'm not talking your shop, Wes, I'm talking my shop. I'm telling Pam about the site we're excavating.'

'I thought it was a DMV, or a section of one.'

'What's a DMV?' asked Pam.

'A deserted medieval village,' Matt recited pedantically.

'Well,' Neil continued, 'the section of the village that extended out that way was abandoned as the population shrank – probably in 1348 with the Black Death – then later the village expanded again elsewhere, further from the lord's lands. But there are some interesting tales about the site. They say that a young woman was hanged then buried at what was then the crossroads – our site or thereabouts. That's why that yew's known to the locals as the hanging tree.'

'When was this?'

Neil shrugged. 'Could have been any time before the eighteenth century when the new drive was built. These old stories get lost in the mists of time.'

At this point Wesley felt a hearty slap on his back. 'Hi, Wes. Mind if I join you?'

Gerry Heffernan beamed round the assembled company. 'Hi, Pam. How are you? How's young Mike? Let you out for the evening, has he? Any room for a little one? Shift up, Wes.' The inspector inserted his bulk next to Wesley as Jane and Matt exchanged glances. 'Now then, what's this about hanging trees? This lot withholding evidence, are they, Wes?'

'Apparently, sir . . .'

'Oh, call me Gerry when we're off duty.'

Wesley tried to suppress a smile. He began again. 'Apparently there's a legend that a young woman was hanged on the old yew tree in the churchyard and that she's buried near the site of the dig.'

'She might turn up, then. It'll make the Chief Constable think we're being kept busy if we get two bodies for the price of one.' He nudged Wesley, who nearly spilled the beer he was raising to his lips. 'What I want to know is . . .' Heffernan paused. Then, seeing he had the group's full attention, he continued. 'If this woman was hanged there must be some record of it. Is that right, Wes? What was police paperwork like in those days?'

Neil sat up. 'There might be court records ... if we knew where they were. The fact that she was condemned in a village and not in some assize court in a larger town indicates that it's very early ... possibly some medieval manorial court with additional powers. I'll see what I can find. Thanks for giving me the idea ... er, Gerry. Nice one.'

Gerry Heffernan beamed all over his plump face. Wesley could tell that he was enjoying himself. He saw many more evenings ahead when the inspector would join them in the Tradmouth Arms, Neil's favoured watering-hole, and there would be no escape from reminders of the day's labours.

'And another thing,' Heffernan continued, his enthusiasm fired. 'What happened to that Jesse tree? It must be somewhere.' He sat back, waiting for a reaction.

'What Jesse tree's this?' Jane, the attractive blonde, spoke for the first time, her voice soft and well bred. She leaned towards Gerry expectantly.

'It will have been smashed to pieces during the Reformation,' Wesley said, pouring cold water on the proceedings. 'Not many carvings from that period have survived, believe me.'

Heffernan looked disappointed, like a child who had just been deprived of a newly given toy. 'Oh well, Wes. You're the expert,' he said, draining his glass. 'If you're getting the drinks in, mine's a pint.'

There was an hour to go until closing time. Lee hung about the side entrance to the public bar of the Ring o' Bells, shifting awkwardly from foot to foot. Gaz had gone in to get some lager to take out; of the two of them he was reckoned to look the older. Lee needed the drink, even though he had downed four pints already. The stuff he had taken last night had left him thirsty, restless. He kept seeing things, flashing back to the previous night; seeing the body hanging from the tree, the flat in the old mill they had broken into in a fit of chemically induced bravado. He felt lousy. The lager might, just might, make him feel better.

Gaz was taking a long time. Too long. Lee could hear footsteps approaching on the gravel path that ran down the side of the pub to the beer garden at the back: the beer garden that was always filled with bloody tourists and their screaming kids during the summer months. But not tonight. It was too early in the season, and there was a chill in the air that didn't encourage outdoor drinking. Lee was alone. Then the footsteps crunching on the gravel drew nearer. Lee turned round.

'You,' he gasped. Pictures flashed in his mind, pictures from the previous night. For the first time Lee was beginning to make sense of their significance. 'Last night . . . you were there . . .'

When Gaz emerged from the door of the public bar five minutes later carrying a six-pack of Continental lager, there was no sign of Lee. Gaz called his name a few times but received no answer. There was no one about; no one to ask if they'd seen his mate. For the want of anything better to do, Gaz made his way home, drank a can of lager by himself in his bedroom, and hid the rest of the cans under his bed: they would do for another day.

That night Gaz found it hard to get off to sleep. When he did finally drop off he had a vivid, horrifying dream. In this dream he saw Lee, hanging from the yew tree in the churchyard, a rope around his neck.

Chapter Six

21 March 1475
Felicia de Monte accuses Elizabeth Webster for dallying with charms and sorceries contrary to good faith and calling herself a wise woman. Felicia de Monte states that the said Elizabeth Webster did cause her babe to fall sick and die with a spell.

John Fleccer did break and enter the dwelling house of Matthew Watts and did steal a candlestick. Fined 5s and Master Fleccer, the blacksmith, doth give surety for his son's good behaviour.

From the Court Rolls of Stokeworthy Manor

Pamela Peterson sat in the uncomfortable oak pew in St Margaret's church cradling Michael in her arms and hoping he wouldn't cry. It was all right for Wesley: church had been part of his upbringing, of his family's life. But Pam's mother, a strong-minded sociology lecturer, hadn't believed in organised religion, although she had had a brief flirtation with Buddhism some years back. Pam listened to the service and attempted self-consciously to mouth the unfamiliar hymns; whereas her husband, standing next to her, seemed completely at home. She tried to peer through the richly carved and painted rood screen to see Gerry Heffernan, but he was just out of her line of vision. She had to admit that the choir was quite good, and she found herself positively enjoying the Rutter anthem which they sang with remarkable panache.

As she walked out of the cool stone church, she felt relieved that it was over and that Michael had stayed obligingly asleep. The real ordeal would come in a few weeks' time: the christening service with Wesley's family there *en masse*.

Gerry Heffernan, minus his surplice, met them outside. As Pam put Michael in the pram she'd left in the church porch, he drew Wesley to one side. Pam knew that murder didn't stick to office hours, but she felt a stab of resentment that work would take her husband away from home on a beautiful June Sunday. She thought of the places they could have gone: a picnic would have been nice. But there was no point making plans when you were married to a policeman.

As his wife pushed the pram up the hilly streets to their modern detached home above the town, Wesley drove his boss to Stokeworthy, where they looked in at the incident room. Rachel had got there an hour or so before them and was sifting through statements. Gerry Heffernan tried to sneak past, but Rachel wasn't going to let him get away that easily.

'Sir, I've just been going through these house-to-house statements. Nobody saw anything that night. They were all either tucked up at home or in the Ring o' Bells till closing time. It seems the murderer knew that the village would be quiet around ten thirty.'

'Local knowledge, then. Anything else?'

'Lots of people seemed to know her . . . not well, but enough to pass the time of day. Nobody's said a bad word about her. It seems she was well liked. She's usually described as a nice woman who always had a word for the kiddies, that sort of thing.'

'So she wasn't the traditional doctor's receptionist . . . the dragon at the gates of the quack's lair?'

'Apparently not. She used to make a special effort with the kids. And everyone said she took part in village activities but wasn't regarded as a busybody. She seemed a nice woman.'

'So why didn't she marry?'

Rachel shot him a look, bristling with anger. 'Women these days don't have to be tied to a man to justify their existence . . .'

Wesley, seeing Rachel's feminist hackles rising, stepped in to calm the situation. 'I think what the boss means is that she didn't have a high-flying career; she lived in a village; she appeared to like children. To me she seemed like the marrying kind.'

'Maybe she never found anyone suitable or the love of her life left her,' said Rachel, calming down. 'There was some mention of a boyfriend.' She began to search through the pile of statements. 'Here we are. The statement from her cleaning lady, a Mrs Dot

Matherley. Remember, Wesley, we found a note from her in Pauline's cottage?'

'Leanne's mum?'

'Gran, more likely. She's over sixty but she cleans for quite a few people in the village . . . even up at the Manor. Anyway, this Mrs Matherley thinks Pauline had a boyfriend although she couldn't say who. It was all kept very low key, she said. Discreet.'

'Could it have been this Matherley woman's imagination . . . or wishful thinking?'

'Possibly. She seemed to think very highly of Miss Brent. But I suppose the man could have been married or had a good reason for keeping the relationship secret.'

'Did she say anything else interesting?'

Rachel scanned the statement and shook her head. 'No. Nothing in particular.'

'So why did this nice popular woman, friend to little kiddies, leader of a blameless life, get herself murdered, eh?' Gerry Heffernan asked rhetorically. 'Come on, Wesley. I think it's about time you and me paid a visit to the Manor. Do you still have to pull your forelock when you meet his lordship?'

'I wouldn't, sir,' grinned Wesley. 'Just be polite and mind your p's and q's.'

'I think I can manage that.'

Wesley looked sceptical. They left the village hall only to find Steve Carstairs, complete with sunglasses and what looked like an Armani suit over a snowy white T-shirt, leaning casually against his Escort XR3i chatting up the two girls who had found the body. They seemed to be hanging on Steve's every word, and the body language told Wesley that if Steve didn't watch himself they would get him into hot water.

The inspector saw what was going on and shouted over. 'Steve, put 'em down and get on with some flamin' work, will you.'

Steve jumped to it and disappeared into the village hall, leaving his fan club gazing adoringly at his disappearing back.

'I'll have a word if it gets out of hand,' Heffernan assured Wesley as they set off down the road.

They had to pass the dig on the way to the Manor and Wesley couldn't resist a quick look, just to see how things were going. To his surprise it was Gerry Heffernan who took the lead, striding

72

confidently between the trenches towards Neil, who was bent double, deep in concentration, scraping away with his trowel.

'Hello, Neil,' he called, causing the students busy in the other trenches to look up. 'How's it going, mate?'

'Hi, Gerry. No villains to catch today, or don't they work on Sundays?'

'Our villains are very industrious. They work every day. Is Mr Thewlis in, do you know?'

'I think so, but he doesn't tell me all his movements,' replied Neil.

'Found anything yet?'

Neil straightened himself up and thrust a plastic box full of finds, mainly broken pottery and a few animal bones, at Wesley. 'That's all so far, but there's a bloody great geophysics signal from this trench . . . just a matter of digging down a bit deeper.'

'You might find that Roman villa yet.'

'We can but dream.' Neil laughed mischievously. 'But I don't think there's much chance.'

'Pity,' said Wesley with sympathy. 'What's Thewlis like?'

'Mid-forties. Sharp. He's chairman of Thewall Holdings. They've got a finger in every lucrative pie: retail; property. I've heard talk he's about to take charge of some government quango . . . and there are rumours of a seat in the Lords and all.'

'And he's settled here?'

'In this age of electronic communications you can run a business empire from anywhere. He also likes to dabble in the local economy – put something back into the community by helping to create jobs, he says. There's this holiday development, that place in Worthy Lane; and I've heard he's got a stake in those medieval banquets held in Tradington Hall once a month. God knows what they're like,' Neil added with the derision of the professional historian. 'All jesters with microphones and serving wenches chewing gum with their bra straps showing. We've been offered free tickets: I reckon it's a bribe.'

'If you don't find anything valuable, you get to fondle a few buxom wenches.' Gerry Heffernan sniggered. He turned to his sergeant. 'Come along, Wes. Time we were off.' He began to make for the trees. 'We'll take a short cut.'

'He's a laugh, that boss of yours,' said Neil to Wesley as the inspector disappeared into the wood.

Wesley rolled his eyes. 'Tell me about it. I'll see you later, Neil.'

He soon caught up with the inspector, and they strolled in the dappled sunlight that penetrated the small but ancient wood.

'And he wants to tear all this lot down, does he?' said Heffernan with disbelief. 'They're right when they say the worst criminals are the ones wearing posh suits.'

'I didn't know you were an eco-warrior on the quiet, sir.'

Before Heffernan could answer, a disembodied voice greeted them from above.

'Hi, pigs.'

Heffernan looked up. 'How are you doing, Squirrel?'

'Not bad. Forces of oppression ready for a confrontation yet?'

'Not us, mate. If it was up to me, I'd keep the trees. Do you see most of the comings and goings round here?'

'Depends where I am. We move about. Why?'

'On Friday night did you see anyone else come up the drive apart from the murdered woman? Think carefully.'

'No ... but then I wasn't watching the drive all evening.' He hesitated. 'Hang on, there was someone else. A couple of lads just hanging round ... coming and going all evening. One had a ponytail, the other had dyed his hair blond. I've seen them before. They often hang around.'

'How many of you are, er ... up the trees, like?'

'That'd be giving away strategic information.'

'Well, can you ask around? See if anyone else saw anything?'

Squirrel tilted his head to one side, a gesture that made him look even more pixie-like, and thought for a while. 'Okay. I'll ask around.' With a rustle of foliage, he disappeared from view.

'Still thinking of joining him, sir?' Wesley teased.

'If I was thirty years younger, who knows.'

They had reached the gravelled drive, and as they emerged from the trees the Manor came into view. Wesley stopped.

Stokeworthy Manor was no flashy stately home, likely to be full of ornate French furniture and marble pillars. To Wesley it was something far more desirable: a low, stone-built medieval manor house. The original great hall stood in the centre, with huge oriel windows to let the sunlight flood in. The stone additions to each side appeared to have grown organically from their central root over a couple of centuries. The Georgians hadn't got their tasteful hands on it; neither had the Victorians added their over-the-top Gothic fussiness. It was perfect. If Wesley could have chosen his ideal house to live in, this would, most certainly, have been it.

'Nice,' said Heffernan. 'Not too grand. Just right.' His taste in architecture matched his sergeant's. 'Lucky old Thewlis.'

Heffernan stood beneath a great carved coat of arms – an eagle flying above a ship – and hammered on the ancient oak front door. It was answered by a tall woman in her thirties: her clothes were fashioned with elegant simplicity, her long, horsey face made attractive by a skilful hairdresser and the expert application of make up. She looked them up and down, wary but not hostile.

Heffernan flashed his warrant card. 'Police, madam.' He recited their names. 'Mrs Thewlis, is it?' The woman nodded. 'We'd like a word with your husband, if he's free.'

The inspector was certainly on his best behaviour, Wesley thought. 'Madam' instead of 'love' was virtually unprecedented. Caroline Thewlis opened the door wide to let them in. Philip Thewlis, if rumours about his humble origins were true, had certainly married above himself socially: his wife had true class; that was something money could buy, but only up to a point. She asked them politely if they'd mind waiting in the great hall. Wesley thanked her. He was longing to have a good look at the place.

Wesley had seen grander great halls, larger and more elaborately decorated, but Stokeworthy Manor's was a gem. The great beamed roof rose above them, with a vent in the centre to take out the smoke once produced by the hearth in the middle of the floor. Rich tapestries hung from the walls; the floor was stone, worn over the centuries, covered here and there with antique Persian rugs. The furniture was lovingly polished oak, either several hundred years old or extremely good reproductions. The effect was one of richness and light, the latter provided by the huge oriel window in the corner, a pillar of sunlight reaching up to the roof.

'Please, gentlemen, sit down.' The newcomer indicated a pair of comfortably worn sofas arranged to face the great Tudor fireplace set in the south wall. He was a short man who reminded Wesley somewhat of the portraits of Napoleon Bonaparte in his later years – another enterprising man with designs on more than a business empire. Like Napoleon, Philip Thewlis wore his thinning hair swept forward to hide the ravages of time. 'How can I help you?'

Gerry Heffernan found himself sinking into the sofa; he hoisted himself upright. 'We're investigating the death of a woman called Pauline Brent. She lived in the village . . .'

Thewlis held up a hand to stop him. 'I think I know what this is about, Inspector. A lady of that name paid me a visit on Friday night. Not being privy to village gossip, I've only just found out about her unfortunate death. I was going to get in touch with you later today.'

'Why did she visit you?'

'To accuse me of seducing my children's nanny – quite an unjustified accusation, as it happens. I really don't know how she got hold of the idea . . . it's quite ridiculous.' He sat back, relaxed, no hint of nervousness in his manner. To Wesley he looked like a man innocent of the charge; but then he had to remember that intelligence and guile are required for success in business.

'Can you tell us in your own words what happened, sir?'

'Certainly. I made no secret of it, even to my wife. Miss, er . . . Brent turned up at the front door at about nine thirty. She asked if she could have a private word with me.'

'How did she seem?'

Philip Thewlis considered the question. 'Calm . . . but angry under the surface, I should say. Brimming with righteous indignation. My family were in the drawing room. I saw her in here. She sat where the sergeant's sitting now.' He smiled at Wesley. 'I must say she was reasonable . . . no hysterics or anything like that. She just said she'd heard from a reliable source that I was having an affair with our nanny, Gemma, and that Gemma's family were very worried. She gave me a lecture on how vulnerable young girls in Gemma's position are. She made me feel quite guilty, even though I'd done nothing. I can assure you, I've never touched the girl.' Another charming smile. 'Of course, I told her very politely that she was mistaken. She'd been misinformed by somebody. Then I told her how commendable it was that someone should be so concerned about a young girl's welfare . . . very rare nowadays.'

'Did you mean it?'

He shrugged. 'It seemed to keep her happy. By the time she left

76

she couldn't apologise enough. I asked her if she wanted to confirm my version of events with Gemma herself, but she assured me that there was no need. She seemed perfectly happy when she left.'

Wesley looked at Thewlis, who was smiling benignly. 'Did anyone else witness your conversation?'

'No. But I told my wife what had happened as soon as she'd left. We laughed about it.'

'Did you mention this to Gemma?'

'I didn't think it necessary. I felt it might have embarrassed her.'

'How long did Miss Brent stay?'

'Half an hour at the most ... probably less. As soon as she found she'd made a mistake, she was only too anxious to get away.'

'Did you see her go?'

'Yes. I saw her to the door and she walked off down the drive.'

'Will your wife confirm all this?'

'Of course. Do you want to see her?' He stood up, ready to summon her.

Heffernan realised that speaking to the woman would be a waste of time. From her husband's calm manner, he guessed that, should anything untoward need covering up, Caroline Thewlis had been well briefed. 'No, sir. That won't be necessary just now. If we could talk to Gemma ... find out how these stories got about ...'

'I'm afraid she's somewhere out in the grounds with the children at the moment. But if you'd like to telephone some time, I'll make sure she's available to speak to you,' Thewlis said, charming and reasonable himself.

'Thank you, sir,' said Wesley. 'Congratulations on your new appointment, by the way. I read about it in the paper.'

Thewlis smiled modestly. 'Thank you, Sergeant. One likes to make a contribution to the country ... give something back,' he said with apparent sincerity.

Heffernan stood up to go. 'Having a bit of trouble with those protesters in your woods, are you, sir?' he asked casually.

Thewlis's lips tightened. 'They'll be no trouble. Once this damned dig's finished we'll get rid of them easily enough.'

'I get the impression this development's not popular in the village,' Heffernan said innocently.

'What some people don't realise is that I'm boosting the local economy, creating jobs . . .'

Wesley and Heffernan exchanged looks. Thewlis's charming manner had disappeared and had been replaced by something far harder. Heffernan opened his mouth to speak.

'Quite, sir,' said Wesley with finality before his boss said something regrettable that would be reported to the Chief Constable over dinner. 'Thank you very much. We'll see ourselves out.'

'What did you make of him?' Wesley asked as they crunched their way down the gravel drive.

'Smarmy bugger. How many jobs do a few holiday cottages create? The builders'll come in from some big city and the types that buy these places hardly use the village shop, do they? And what was all that about a new appointment?'

'He's going to be head of some government council . . . something to do with children.'

Heffernan made no comment. 'Do you think he's having it off with the nanny?'

'Wouldn't put it past him. And we've only got his word for it that Pauline left here alive.'

'I think we should have a word with this Gemma. He said she was in the grounds.'

'It's a big place. She could be anywhere.'

By good fortune they heard the sound of a child shouting. 'No, no . . . get away. I hate you . . . Gemma, he hit me . . . he hit me . . .' The voice was spoilt, whinging.

'Oh, shut up, you bloody little brat. Just behave or I'll tell your mum about before.' A young woman's exasperated voice drifted over from the trees at the side of the drive . . . a young woman bored and at the end of her tether. Heffernan smiled triumphantly. They had found Gemma Matherley.

She emerged from the trees, the children in her wake engaged in what looked like a wrestling match. She turned to them. 'Stop that, will you. Amanda, get up. Look at the state of your bloody dress.'

Her words seemed to have little effect on the children, who continued their vicious battle. When she saw the two police officers she stopped. 'The grounds aren't open today. You'll have to go,' she said insolently, chewing gum while she spoke.

'Police, love. We're here enquiring about the murder of a Pauline Brent. Her body was found in the churchyard on Friday night. You're Gemma Matherley, I presume?'

'Yeah.' The girl turned to her charges, who were now engaged in a tug-of-war using the little girl's cardigan as the rope. 'Look, I can't be long. I've got the kids . . .'

'We just want to ask a few questions, that's all. Nothing to worry about,' said Wesley over Amanda's screams.

'Did you know Pauline Brent?'

'I wouldn't say I knew her. My gran cleaned for her and I've seen her at the doctor's. That's all.'

'Did you know she came here on Friday night before she died? She came to discuss your affair with Mr Thewlis.'

'What?' The girl looked horrified, oblivious to the violent punches young Guy was inflicting on his screaming sister. 'I don't know what you mean. I'm not having no affair with Philip . . . nothing like that.' She spoke with sincerity. Wesley was inclined to believe her. 'Where did she get that one from? There was nothing going on, I swear it.' She paused, thinking. 'I bet it was my gran, the old bitch. She's got hold of the wrong end of the stick. She cleans here and she cleans . . . cleaned . . . for Miss Brent. I bet she's told her some half-baked story and the old . . .' She hesitated, thinking better of slandering the dead. 'Miss Brent thought she'd stick her nose in. But she got it all wrong. There's nothing going on between me and Philip . . . honest.'

'Were you at the house when Miss Brent called on Friday?'

'I'd have been in my room once the kids were in bed. But nobody mentioned she'd been.'

'So you didn't see her at all that night?'

Gemma shook her head.

'Where is your room, Miss Matherley?' asked Wesley innocently.

'At the top of the house. Why?'

'Overlooking the drive?'

It may have been his imagination but Wesley thought he detected a change in Gemma's manner. She became more wary; on her guard.

'Yeah. Why? What are you getting at?'

'It's just that if you happened to look out of your window you might have seen Miss Brent leave. Did you?'

'No.'

'Can you hear if someone's at the front door from your room?'

'Er . . . not really.' She turned to the children, who were, by now, both in tears, the worst of the battle over. 'I've got to get back . . . clean these two up before their mum sees them.' She turned to the children. 'Come on. Get up off the bloody floor, will you. Look at the state of you. What have you done with that cardigan? Look at it, all stretched.'

'Thank you, Miss Matherley. You've been most helpful,' said Wesley as the nanny pulled her charges roughly to their feet.

As she disappeared towards the house, dragging the whinging pair behind her, Wesley turned to the inspector. 'I reckon she was lying about seeing Pauline on Friday night.'

'Seemed pretty straight to me. But you never can tell.'

'No, you can't,' said Wesley thoughtfully.

'A Mrs Telford's been in,' said Rachel as soon as they returned to the incident room. 'Her son, Lee, didn't come home last night. He doesn't make a habit of that sort of thing apparently. She looked pretty worried.'

'How old is he?' asked Heffernan. This was all they needed. As if they didn't have enough to do with a murder investigation on their hands.

'Seventeen, sir. He went out with his friend last night. The friend went into the Ring o' Bells for some cans of lager to take out – Lee was supposed to wait for him outside. When he came out Lee was gone. No sign of him. He'd disappeared.'

Heffernan looked at Rachel, suddenly concerned. This didn't sound like the usual story of a disaffected teenager leaving home for a few days after a row. 'Where was this Lee on the night of Pauline's death? Did you ask?'

'Of course.' Heffernan knew that Rachel could always be relied on. He really would have to think about recommending her for promotion. 'He was out with this friend, Gaz, wandering round the village apparently. Gaz was a bit cagey when I spoke to him. I asked him if he and Lee ever took drugs and he clammed up. He's certainly hiding something.'

'And you suspect it's bit of cannabis round the back of the village shop, do you?'

'It wouldn't surprise me. I asked him if he'd seen Pauline at any point during the evening but he said he couldn't remember. He'd had a lot to drink, he said.'

'Ah, the follies of youth.' Heffernan sighed. 'Circulate Lee's description, will you. And interview his other mates. He's probably crashed out on someone's floor.' He looked round. 'Wesley?'

Peterson, who was at the filing cabinet looking up Dot Matherley's address, turned. 'I thought we might have a word with Pauline's cleaner, Mrs Matherley. If she confided to Pauline about her granddaughter's supposed affair with Philip Thewlis, she must have known her pretty well.'

'Good thinking, Wes. We'll go and pay her a visit, but first I'd like a quick word with Pauline's neighbour, Mrs Green. That okay?'

Wesley sighed, his fancy turning to thoughts of food. It was nearly midday and he was going to miss the pasta Pam usually prepared in lieu of Sunday lunch: she claimed that she never had time to make a roast dinner. He walked with Gerry Heffernan to Worthy Lane and stood surveying the row of three cottages, each with its small front garden.

Susan Green's was at one end, then Pauline's, then, at the other end of the terrace, the young family's, the Platts: theirs was the untidiest front garden, with a tricycle and a toy car cluttering the garden path. Mr and Mrs Platt had been interviewed twice and had been keen to stress that Pauline was a good neighbour but that they didn't know anything of her personal life. Being familiar with the strains of family life, Wesley had no difficulty in believing them. Those with young children are usually too preoccupied to pry into their neighbours' business.

'This Mrs Green might be able to throw some light on Pauline's phantom lover . . . and Pauline might have mentioned the Gemma Matherley affair. You never know your luck.'

Before Wesley could reply, his boss was rapping loudly on Susan Green's front door. It was answered swiftly. Susan saw Wesley and gave a tentative smile, holding the door open with a mumbled 'Come in'.

Wesley introduced his boss and Susan invited them to sit down, asking them whether they preferred tea or coffee. He noticed Heffernan's eyes following her as she walked to the kitchen.

'Nice woman,' Heffernan whispered to his sergeant as he ran

his fingers through his unruly hair in an attempt to tidy himself up.

'It's nothing to worry about, Mrs Green,' Wesley assured her as she gave him his coffee. 'We'd just like to ask you a few more questions about Miss Brent.'

'Sure. Anything I can do to help.'

'Er . . . did she have any close friends that you knew of?' Gerry Heffernan asked softly, self-consciously. 'Any, er . . . gentleman friends, for instance?'

'Not that I know of, Inspector. We were good neighbours but she never confided in me about her emotional life.'

'So no close friends in the village . . . or any friends anywhere else she talked about?'

'She seemed to be on friendly terms with everyone . . . but no one in particular, I guess.'

'Did you see anyone call at her house regularly?'

'Really, Inspector, I don't spend my time spying on my neighbours.'

'Of course not,' the inspector said, uncharacteristically. Wesley looked at him, slightly puzzled.

'You've been here five years,' Wesley began. 'Do you know anything about Miss Brent's life before she came to the village?'

She appeared not to hear the question. 'It wasn't easy for me when I first came here. It was the second big disruption in my life. I moved here from the States when I met my late husband, then, when he died, I made a new start here in the countryside. Pauline was very good to me; introduced me to folk around here. Would you like a cookie, Sergeant . . . Inspector? They're home-made.'

Gerry Heffernan patted his stomach, then sat up straight, trying to hold it in. 'Go on, then, you've tempted me. Not often we get home-made biccies, is it, Sergeant?'

When she left the room Wesley noticed that his boss was sitting there with a bemused smile playing on his lips. Was it only Wesley who had noticed that she had evaded his last question with the skill of a senior politician? She returned with the biscuits, crisp and mouth-watering, and Gerry Heffernan set about praising her culinary skill with more enthusiasm than Wesley thought appropriate.

'Could you tell me,' Wesley said, 'if you've heard of a Gemma Matherley? She's a nanny up at the Manor.'

'I know the name Matherley, of course. They're an old village family. But I can't say I know a Gemma. Why?'

'Did Pauline know anyone up at the Manor . . . Philip Thewlis, for example?'

'Not that I'm aware.'

'She didn't mention to you that she planned to go up there and ask Mr Thewlis about an affair he was allegedly having with Gemma Matherley?'

Susan Green looked slightly shocked. 'No . . . no, she never mentioned anything like that.'

'Would something like that make her angry? A man in a position of power taking advantage of a young employee? Has she ever tackled anyone about anything like that in the past . . . some supposed injustice?'

Susan thought for a moment. 'She was certainly a woman who believed in justice . . . someone who thought about others. She tackled that man D'estry because he'd put one of the Platt children in danger.' She fluttered a smile at Gerry Heffernan, who was gazing at her with an apparent lack of professional suspicion.

Wesley finished his coffee and biscuit and gave his boss a nudge. 'I think that's all for now, Mrs Green. Thank you very much for the coffee . . . and the biscuits. They were very good.'

'I'm glad you liked them, Sergeant.' She looked directly at Gerry Heffernan. 'Please call again. It's nice to have one's cooking appreciated when one lives on one's own.'

'I know the feeling,' Heffernan said with some sincerity.

'You're not from Liverpool by any chance, are you, Inspector?'

'Yeah.' Gerry Heffernan nodded eagerly. 'How did you guess?'

'I recognised the accent. I don't suppose you knew the Beatles?'

'I went to the same school as Paul and George . . . but they were a few years ahead of me.'

Mrs Green looked impressed 'You must tell me about it some time. I'm a big fan of theirs.'

'I noticed.' He nodded at the album covers and photograph above the fireplace.

'I saw them in Shea Stadium when they toured the States . . . guess I've loved them ever since.' She smiled.

Wesley looked at his watch. 'Thank you, Mrs Green,' he said, breaking up the cosy scene. 'Sorry to have bothered you.'

'That's quite okay.' Her eyes and Heffernan's met, and Wesley stood by bemused. Then he stepped outside, the inspector following. Surely it had been his imagination . . . Gerry Heffernan just wasn't the type.

'She didn't answer that question about knowing what Pauline did before she came here. Did you notice?'

'Oh, no, Wes, she just didn't hear you. You'll have to speak up, you know. You speak too quietly sometimes. Nice woman, isn't she?'

Wesley sighed wearily. 'Yes, sir. Very nice.'

Matt and Jane approached Neil's trench, the focus of all the excitement. Without a word they dropped to their knees and began to work with their trowels and brushes, uncovering, bringing the thing into the light of the sunny late-twentieth-century day.

They dug in silence, hardly daring to breathe as it was revealed. A stone figure of a sad-faced, bearded man; about three foot tall. A scroll at the figure's base declared its name: Asa. The delicate carving was remarkably sharp and lifelike. From the figure's back protruded a peg, something to fix it to a frame.

'Medieval?' asked Matt.

Neil nodded solemnly. 'Looks like it.' He turned to the assembled crowd of students, who were watching open-mouthed. 'This explains the geophysics anomaly in this trench. Large pieces of stone give off a signal like that. I think there are more of them . . . it looks like they were buried in some sort of deep pit. There's the framework of a medieval Jesse tree in the parish church over the road, so I can only suppose that what we've got here is one of the carvings that belonged to it. This is a very important find . . . possibly of national importance.' A mumble of approval went round the students.

Then a shy voice, scarcely audible, said, 'Excuse me, we've found something in this trench over here.' Neil looked up at the speaker who was daring to deflect him from his moment of professional glory; a mousey girl with a ponytail and freckles who had been working in a smaller trench a few yards away.

'What is it?' he asked, mildly peeved at the distraction.

'It seems to be a grave-cut, and I think we've found a skull,' she said.

Neil climbed out of the large trench and followed her to where she had been working. He could see a bleached white orb protruding out of the dark soil in the bottom of the trench. Jane had got there before him. She examined the object and looked up. 'Looks human, Neil.'

Neil sighed. 'That's all we need,' he said. But he bowed to the inevitable, pulling out his mobile and dialling Wesley's number.

Chapter Seven

28 March 1475
6 yards of fine wool cloth and 4 yards of blue ribbon for the son
born to my lady upon the Feast of the Annunciation..............5.6
For hiring Felicia de Monte as wetnurse for the child......3.0
From the household accounts of Stokeworthy Manor

The food in the Ring o' Bells was remarkably good and, after roast beef and all the trimmings followed by home-made apple pie and custard, Wesley had to admit to himself that he had eaten better than he would have done at home ... although he would never have admitted this to Pam.

He had asked discreetly at the bar whether Pauline Brent was a regular customer but the landlord had shaken his head. He had never heard of her.

Plates cleared and glasses drained, the two policemen stood up to go. Then Wesley's mobile phone rang, causing the regulars to turn and stare. Wesley sat down again and tried to answer the call as inconspicuously as he could. It was the incident room. A Neil Watson had left a message for him to get in touch as soon as possible. Wesley thanked the constable on the other end and put his phone back in his pocket. Neil would have to wait.

'Right, Wes, let's pay Mrs Matherley a visit. But I want to look in at the incident room first. WPC Walton makes a wicked cup of tea.'

'I think that could be construed as sexist, sir. Don't let Rachel hear you saying that.'

'Saying what, Wes? I was merely stating a fact.'

'Then be careful who you state it to.' Wesley grinned.

There were two reports waiting for them back in the village hall. The first one concerned material found on the church path during the SOCOs' routine search. *Cannabis sativa.* Dried marijuana leaves. Scattered liberally up the path to the church door. When Leanne and Jo had talked about scattering seeds on the ground in their pathetic little ritual they had never been specific about what sort of plant matter they used. It had been obvious the girls were hiding something – now their secret was out.

The second report stated simply that there were signs of disturbance near the yew tree where Pauline's body was found, consistent with a struggle. There were matching traces of soil on Pauline's sandals. Gerry Heffernan looked at the report then threw it down in disgust. 'Oh, Wes, it's this Pauline Brent. She seems too good to be true. Nobody disliked her . . . but on the other hand nobody seemed to know her very well. She was friends with everyone, even stood up for people if she thought they were being taken advantage of, but she had no close friends. There were no personal letters or even addresses in her cottage. What do you make of it?'

Wesley shook his head. He was as puzzled about Pauline Brent as the inspector was. 'I wonder where she lived before she came to Stokeworthy. If she was here fifteen years that means she must have come when she was in her mid-thirties. What was she doing before then?'

'You think her past's caught up with her, do you? That the murderer isn't from the village at all?'

'He's got local knowledge . . . knew when the village was likely to be quiet.'

'A weekender?'

'Possibly.'

'What made Pauline Brent tick? Why didn't she have close friends? And what about this supposed boyfriend? Perhaps Dot Matherley'll throw some light on the matter. If there's one person who knows your secrets it's your cleaning lady . . . so I've heard. I've never had the luxury of one myself.'

The phone on Wesley's desk shrieked into life. He rushed over to answer it. After a couple of minutes he returned to Heffernan, an expression of eager anticipation on his face. 'That was Neil, sir . . .'

'Oh, what did he want? Doesn't he know we've got a murder case on? And this missing lad. Tell him you're busy.'

'I told him I'd go round to the dig. They've found a body. He's asked me to ring Colin Bowman.'

'Cheeky bugger.' Heffernan sighed deeply. 'I suppose we'd better drop in on our way to visit Mrs Matherley. Let's hope it doesn't add to our workload, eh.'

There was quite a crowd around the trench where the skeleton lay, half exposed against the sandy soil. Jane and Matt were working with trowels and brushes, carefully but quickly. A couple of trusted students were helping them, looking nervous about the responsibility. Neil stood on the side of the trench, chatting to Colin Bowman but shooting an occasional supervisory glance at his students. It seemed like an age before enough of the skeleton was exposed to allow Colin to make an initial assessment. By that time Wesley and Heffernan had arrived.

Gerry Heffernan led the way. 'What have we got, Colin?'

Colin Bowman looked up, an amiable smile on his face. 'Hello there, Gerry. Good to see you. In answer to your question, we appear to have another hanging . . .'

'Right, then. Let the dog see the rabbit. Excuse me. Police.' He pushed his way through the group of gaping students. Then, for the first time, he saw the object of all the attention. He turned to Wesley. 'I thought he said it was a body, not a ruddy skeleton.'

'It's a very well-preserved skeleton, Gerry,' said Dr Bowman from the trench. 'Fully articulated. She's been hanged . . . more professionally this time. Clean break to the neck. She's not been laid east to west, which indicates this wasn't a standard Christian burial. If she'd died accidentally, or been murdered, she would have been buried in the churchyard. As it was, she ended up in an unhallowed grave.'

'Where did you pick that one up from, Colin?' asked Heffernan, amazed at this piece of unscientific information coming from the pathologist's lips.

'Neil here. He says it's probably either a suicide or an execution. By the break to the neck I'd opt for the latter.'

'Neither were buried in consecrated ground,' Neil added helpfully. 'And as I said before, if you remember, this was a crossroads. Suicides and criminals were often buried at crossroads. I think we've found the woman in that old village legend . . . the one who gave the name to the hanging tree.'

'When was all this? How old is she?'

Wesley, who had been watching and listening, fascinated, spoke. 'It's hard to tell.'

Colin Bowman interrupted. 'If you want to know how old she was when she died, I'd say at a very rough guess she was pretty young . . . late teens, early twenties. I'll be able to tell you more when I've had a proper look at her.'

'No, I meant when was she hanged? How long ago? We're not looking at three years ago, anything like that, are we?'

'I don't think so,' said Wesley. 'Looks pretty old to me.'

'We'll do radiocarbon dating on the bones,' said Neil, helpfully. He picked up a plastic box and waved it in front of Wesley's nose. 'She was buried with this. Looks medieval.'

Wesley took the box. Inside was a small crucifix, delicately carved in marble, about twelve inches long. A thing of real beauty. 'Looks like she was buried holding it. Somebody thought enough of her to leave this in her grave. Wonder why.' Neil paused for a while, gazing down at the box, contemplating the mystery. Then he looked up at Wesley, fresh enthusiasm lighting up his face. 'In all the excitement about the body I haven't shown you our star find.' He led Wesley away from the crowd around the burial trench, over to the edge of the site where a couple of students were brushing earth off what looked like a statue lying on a length of plastic sheet. They brushed carefully, delicately, as if the thing would disintegrate like a cobweb if they used too much force. Neil said nothing but allowed his friend to examine it, awe-struck.

'Asa. It's off the Jesse tree . . . it must be.' Wesley could barely hide his excitement. 'Where did you find it?'

'Buried in the big trench, a couple of yards away from our skeleton. It's in remarkable condition and the carving's quite masterly. It wouldn't surprise me if this was made by someone who worked on one of the cathedrals or abbeys round here. It's high-quality stuff. We've just got to find the others now.'

Wesley looked up, eager. 'Others? You think there are more of these?'

'I'd say there were a load of them, buried in some sort of pit. It fits in with the geophysics findings, and Matt's started to uncover another one. It's my bet the locals dug a big hole and buried them so that Henry VIII's commissioners couldn't get them and smash them up.'

'Makes sense. It's absolutely amazing. If they could be restored in the church . . .'

'Hang on, Wes, we're looking at something quite unique here. I don't think a country church is really the place for something as important as this.'

Wesley shrugged and made no comment. 'Keep me posted, won't you. By the look of that framework in the church there must have been a dozen figures at least.'

Wesley turned to go. Heffernan was waiting impatiently near the huddle of students. Satisfied that the discovered corpse was probably outside his jurisdiction, he was anxious to be away. They had a cleaning lady to interview.

Neil muttered something about the Tradmouth Arms and waved Wesley goodbye regretfully.

The inspector said nothing as they trudged past the church and into the small council estate by the side of the main road, at the opposite end of the village to the dwellings of the more comfortably off and those who used Stokeworthy as a weekend retreat. The weekenders seldom ventured this way: the council estate was strictly locals only, some families going back many generations.

The Matherleys were just such a family. And Dot Matherley lived in a one-bedroomed bungalow in the next road to her son, daughter-in-law and granddaughter, Leanne. She opened the door to the two policemen at once, almost as if she'd been waiting for them.

Tea was offered . . . and accepted gratefully. After a decent interval it was Heffernan who began to ask the questions. 'What can you tell us about Pauline Brent?'

Mrs Matherley sat back, a benign smile on her face, preparing to eulogise the dead. 'She was a lovely lady. Couldn't do enough for you. So considerate . . . not like some I clean for.'

'Do you clean for many people in the village?'

'Oh, yes. There's them up at the Manor, Miss Brent, and two of them new places on Worthy Lane – Mrs Bentley and Mrs Wills. Though they're never there when I call . . . always leaves my money in an envelope, they do.'

'They must keep you busy,' said Wesley, pleasantly.

She looked at him with undisguised curiosity. 'Oh, they do that all right, my luvver. I'll have to look for someone else, mind, now Miss Brent's gone.' Her puffy eyes began to fill with tears. She took a clean white handkerchief from the pocket of her apron and dabbed them. 'Oh, it's awful what some folks do these days. Poor Miss Brent, such a nice lady . . . not an enemy in the world.'

'You confided in her, I believe. About your granddaughter, Gemma.'

Dot looked up sharply. 'How did you know that?'

Wesley didn't answer the question directly. 'You told Miss Brent that she was having an affair with the owner of the Manor. Is that right?'

'I've been worried out of my head. She's only nineteen . . . never been out of the village. Then this man old enough to be her father . . . Some folks think they can buy anything. And our Gemma was bought, like a common whore. Miss Brent was ever so good, really sympathetic. She said she'd go up and have a word with Mr Thewlis . . . seemed quite keen to help. She said she didn't like to see those in vulnerable positions taken advantage of, that was it. She was a saint, that woman . . . a saint.'

'Are you sure of your facts here, love?' Heffernan chipped in. 'Mr Thewlis denies everything.'

'Well, he would, wouldn't he.' She leaned forward. 'I've seen them . . . doing it. While his wife was out.' She nodded righteously.

'Actually seen them?' said Wesley, incredulous.

'Well, he covered himself up as soon as I got in the room, but she was shameless. When I think of what she was like before she went to that place. I'd have never . . .'

'It was definitely Mr Thewlis she was, er . . . with?'

'Who else would it be?' she said, as if the question were particularly naïve. 'And I bet that wife of his doesn't know . . . cut above him, she is. And her with those sweet little kiddies. The things I could tell about some of the people in this village . . .'

This was more like it. Heffernan sat forward, willing her to spill her secrets. 'What sort of things? Anything about Pauline Brent? Don't worry, love, you might know something that might help us catch whoever killed her.'

Dot thought about this for a moment and nodded. Never had gossip been in such a good cause. 'Well, I think she had a gentleman friend, if you know what I mean. Oh, she was very discreet . . . didn't say anything to anyone, but' – she leaned further forward and lowered her voice – 'I found a pair of men's underpants under the bed one day when I was cleaning.'

'And you've no idea who it could have been?'

Dot Matherley shook her head.

'She worked for the doctor. Any chance it could be him?'

Dot chuckled. 'Oh no, my luvver . . . not Dr Jenkins. He'd never wear underpants like that.' She seemed to find the idea irresistibly amusing, and it was a while before she stopped giggling like an elderly schoolgirl.

'There was no address book found in Miss Brent's house,' said Wesley, regaining control of the situation. 'Did she have one, do you know?'

'No. Come to think of it, she didn't. Bit odd that, isn't it?'

Wesley and Heffernan looked at one another. Each knew what the other was thinking. There was something missing in Pauline Brent's seemingly perfect life . . . and that something seemed to be a past.

Wesley looked at his watch. It was nearly four o'clock . . . another working Sunday for Pam to complain about. He contemplated ringing her but thought better of it. The inspector was charging ahead, making for the home of Gaz Sweeting, just two streets away from Dot Matherley's bungalow. 'I want a word with this Gaz. From his description, I bet he's one of the lads Squirrel saw hanging about on Friday night. And there's the small question of the cannabis on the church path and who supplied it. Could the two lads have been with the girls when they were doing this ritual thing? There was certainly something the girls weren't telling us.'

'Their true loves, you mean?' said Wesley with a wry smile.

'If they can't do better than that pair then heaven help 'em. I think even Steve Carstairs is a better bet . . . oh, I don't know, though. What number does this Gaz live at?'

Wesley consulted his notebook. 'Number nine.'

Heffernan marched down the neat front path of 9 Stoke Gardens and rapped firmly on the front door. A thin woman with dyed blonde hair answered, her figure and dress proclaiming that she was under twenty-five but the deep lines on her face giving the lie to this. She was forty if she was a day but didn't want to admit it. When they showed their warrant cards, Mrs Sweeting looked exasperated. 'I've got two of your lot here already. What is this? A raid?'

Heffernan looked puzzled. 'Can we come in, love? Nothing to worry about. We just want to ask your Gaz a few questions about his mate.'

'That's what they all say,' Mrs Sweeting mumbled bitterly as she led them through to the lounge, where they found Rachel and Steve perched on the settee sipping tea. Opposite them in an armchair, making a detailed study of his feet, was Gaz, his hair dyed to match his mother's. Wesley found himself wondering if they had cosy evenings in, doing each other's hair with a bottle of bleach. He dismissed this frivolous thought as Rachel stood up. Steve, he noticed, remained seated, and was staring at him with what looked like resentment.

'We thought we were dealing with this one,' Steve mumbled.

Heffernan, anxious to preserve a united police front in the presence of members of the public, spoke firmly. 'We're here about something else. Have you finished, then?'

'Yes, sir,' said Rachel firmly, giving Steve a nudge. 'We've quite finished.'

Wesley noticed that Rachel's gaze kept turning towards the mantelpiece where a small oil painting of a sailing boat stood in pride of place next to a plastic clock. It was a painting of quality, an original. It looked out of place among the tawdry modern ornaments that kept it company.

Rachel sat down again. 'I'd just like to ask one more question, if that's all right.' She looked to the inspector for approval and he nodded. 'Where did you get that painting on the mantelpiece, Gary?'

Gaz looked up, flustered. 'Can't remember. Me mum got it, didn't you, Mum.' He looked desperately at his mother for confirmation.

The loyal parent nodded. She knew the answer that was expected of her. 'Yeah. That's right. I bought it. Car boot sale. Okay?'

Sensing that it was useless to enquire further, Rachel stood up and glared at Steve. 'Thank you for your time, Mrs Sweeting, Gary. We'll let you know if there's any news of Lee . . . and you will let us know if you remember anything that might help us, won't you, Gary?'

Gaz nodded absent-mindedly. Steve moved himself slowly off the settee and followed Rachel into the hallway. Mrs Sweeting went with them to see them safely off the premises.

Gaz was seventeen; old enough to be interviewed without the presence of his mother. Wesley made a start. 'Gary, we've got a witness who saw you and Lee hanging round the village on the night Pauline Brent was killed. Were you near the churchyard?'

'Can't remember much about that night. We were out of our heads, me and Lee. Hey, you'll find Lee, won't you? I mean, he's my mate and . . .'

'What was it you were out of your heads on? Drink? Drugs?' Gaz stared at Wesley in defiant silence. 'All we're interested in is catching whoever killed Pauline Brent. And it would help if you told us the truth about where you were and what you saw. Okay?'

Gaz nodded. 'We were stoned . . . acid. We saw her hanging in the churchyard . . . all in white, like an angel.' He spoke quietly, the image returning to his mind.

'Did you see anyone else?'

Gaz put his head in his hands. 'Can't remember.'

'What about Lee? Did he see anyone else? Did you split up at all?'

'Yeah. We were hanging out round the village, then he went off to get the stuff.'

'The acid?'

'Yeah . . . and some grass. Some friends of ours wanted it . . .'

'Leanne and Joanne, for their little ritual. A quantity of cannabis was found scattered on the churchyard path.'

Gaz looked up in disbelief. 'What a waste.'

'Was it them?'

'I'm not saying.'

'So where did Lee go to get the stuff?'

'He had it at home. He'd bought it in Morbay last week.'

'Would he have passed the churchyard on his way home?'

Gaz nodded. 'Suppose so.'

'What time did you split up?'

'About ten. I don't know exactly.'

'And then Lee came back to meet you?'

'Yeah. That's right. I was with Leanne and Jo. He gave them the grass, then they went off home.'

'What did you do after that?'

'Just hung around. Got stoned.' Gaz was suddenly on his guard. Wesley had the feeling he was holding something back.

'When did you see Miss Brent's body hanging from the tree?'

'Not till later . . . about half eleven. She was dead by then,' he added helpfully.

'And you didn't think to tell anyone?'

'We were out of our heads . . . didn't know what was real and what wasn't.'

Wesley leaned forward. 'This could be very important, Gary. Pauline Brent was murdered at around half ten. Did you see anything suspicious? Or did Lee mention that he'd seen anything when he went off on his own? Please think. We're not concerned with your drug-taking activities at the moment. We just want to find this murderer . . . and find Lee.'

Mrs Sweeting chose that moment to re-enter the room. 'Hey, what's this about drug-taking?' She turned on the two policemen. 'What have you been asking him? He's not saying anything else without a lawyer present.' She had clearly been watching too much television.

Wesley tried to calm the situation. 'Your son's not under arrest. He's just answering a few questions. We can continue at Tradmouth police station with a solicitor present if you wish, but I can assure you there's no need.'

'That's right, love. There's no question of an arrest. Your son's just helping us with our inquiries,' said Gerry Heffernan, trying to be helpful.

'And we all know what that means,' Mrs Sweeting said, losing her enthusiasm for the fight. 'All right. But I'm staying here.' She sat down with firm defiance.

Wesley restated his last question, hoping Gaz's mood of co-operation hadn't passed. 'Did Lee mention to you that he'd seen anything suspicious . . . anything out of the ordinary?'

'He said he'd seen something . . . but he wouldn't tell me what it was. He said he wanted to keep it to himself, like.'

'Why?'

Gaz shrugged. 'I don't know. Lee never said. I thought he was just trying to make himself look important, like.'

'Can you remember exactly what he said?'

'Not really. Just something like he thought he'd seen the

murderer. I thought he was just bullshitting . . . didn't take much notice.'

Heffernan stood up. 'Thanks, er . . . Gaz. I think that's all for now. If you remember anything else, you'll let us know, won't you?'

Gaz nodded, relieved to be let off so lightly. His mother scowled at Heffernan, who took the hint. They left.

'So we have a possible witness to our murder who's disappeared,' Heffernan said thoughtfully as they walked back towards the incident room. 'I don't like it, Wes. I think it should be our top priority to find this Lee as soon as possible.'

'So you believe him? Gaz didn't and he was his friend.'

'I don't know . . . but I'm not willing to take the risk. And another thing that occurred to me. Don't you think that the whole thing about the hanging tree's a bit, er . . . theatrical. If she'd been found dumped in the creek, fair enough. But someone went to a great deal of trouble to hang her from that tree.'

'I've been thinking that myself. Unless the killer thought it was a handy way of covering up his crime . . . making it look like suicide.'

'That fits with Lee witnessing something. I've got a bad feeling about this one, Wes.' He looked at his watch. 'I think it's about time we got off home. Pam'll be thinking you've been kidnapped by the Vegans.'

Wesley groaned inwardly. That joke must have been festering in his boss's brain since their encounter with Squirrel.

'First thing tomorrow we'll pay a call on this Dr Jenkins . . . break the bad news and see what he's got to say about his late receptionist.'

'Let's hope he can throw some light on where she came from.'

'Yeah. At the moment it looks as if Pauline Brent landed here from outer space fifteen years ago with no friends, no family and no past. She's a model villager, kind and concerned about everyone . . . too good to be true. A sort of Stepford Spinster.'

'Apart from her lover, sir.'

'Whoever he was. And what do you reckon about this missing lad?'

'We'll find him, sir. Don't worry.' Wesley tried his best to sound confident as he made his way back to the village hall.

Chapter Eight

6 April 1475
Alice de Neston, being of good repute, is hired as nursemaid to
the son born to my lady of the Feast of the Annunciation.....3.0
*   For the wetnurse, Felicia de Monte...................................2.6*
*   For the grey pony for my lord's son, Simon.................£2.3.4*
*   For Thomas de Monte, the stonecarver to carve my lord's*
arms above the great door...£1.5.6
*   From the household accounts of Stokeworthy Manor*

Pamela Peterson had had an awful day. Michael had cried non-stop from noon to half past three. She'd rung her mother, who'd diagnosed colic. By the time Pam had weighed up in her mind whether to believe her mother or ring the doctor, Michael had gone to sleep. When Wesley returned home at six o'clock the baby was wide awake and gurgling happily, his previous bad behaviour forgotten. Angry with her husband, the police force and anything else that came to her mind at that moment, Pam slammed Wesley's meal down on the table, dislodging several pieces of pasta from the congealed pile on the plate so that they fell, staining the tablecloth tomato red.

'Your son's been a little monster today. Screamed non-stop for hours. Give me a class of thirty kids any day.'

Wesley knew he would have to tread carefully. 'Sorry I couldn't be here. But this murder ... A teenage boy's gone missing too, so ...'

'All right, all right. I know,' she said impatiently. She had known what to expect when she had married a police officer.

'Look, when it gets nearer the christening I'll try and help. I know it's bad timing but . . . I'll help. Promise.'

'You'd better,' she said, before sweeping from the room.

Wesley picked up the Sunday paper that was lying on the floor and began to flick through the pages absent-mindedly until a face caught his eye. He read the caption underneath. 'Timothy Wills, the new Labour parliamentary candidate who is to fight the forthcoming Bloxham by-election and his wife Jane.' Jane Wills smiled out at the camera, serene and beautiful, her long auburn hair tumbling almost to her waist, not the usual stuff of which politicians' wives are made. Wesley read the short article underneath, skimming through the politics. 'Timothy Wills,' it said, 'is keen to buy a house in Bloxham, his chosen constituency. In the meantime he is staying at his holiday home in the village of Stokeworthy with his wife Jane, his children, Jeremy and Sarah, and his parents. He loves this part of Devon, he says, and he would find nothing more rewarding than representing the people of Bloxham as their MP.'

Wesley put the paper down wearily. Too many brushes with the worst side of human nature had rendered him cynical about politicians and their motives. He closed his eyes, dozing until Pam returned a few minutes later, somewhat calmer.

'I've been invited to a coffee morning.' She said the last two words with heavy irony. 'If anyone had told me a couple of years ago I'd be going to coffee mornings, I wouldn't have believed them.'

'Don't knock it till you've tried it,' said Wesley, encouragingly. 'It'll be a chance to meet other people with babies, and . . .'

'And talk about brands of disposable nappies?'

'I'm sure it's not like that. Where is this great social event?'

'Other end of Tradmouth . . . some posh place near Battle Creek. Let's hope the house isn't too impressive or I'll never be able to invite them here.'

'I thought you wouldn't want to,' Wesley said sharply, sensing the contradiction.

'I'm keeping an open mind. Apparently tomorrow we're watching a video.'

'Nothing obscene, I hope.'

'Chance'd be a fine thing. To be honest I don't know what to expect.' Pam sat down, a small worried frown clouding her face.

Something was bothering her, Wesley could tell. He asked her what it was but she shook her head. 'Nothing,' she said unconvincingly. 'I rang one of the childminders on that list I was given.'

'Any luck?' asked Wesley, half listening.

'She said I could go round tomorrow, but ... well, she didn't sound too friendly and there was a dog barking in the background. I don't really think ...'

'It's early days yet,' Wesley said absent-mindedly, picking up the newspaper. 'You've got until September.'

Pam opened her mouth to speak but thought better of it.

At eight thirty precisely on Monday morning, Gerry Heffernan and Wesley Peterson stood at the door of Dr Jenkins's surgery, which occupied the ground floor of a small brick-built semi on the edge of the village. It stood in the no-man's-land between the older village and the council estate, this neutral position confirming that it served all villagers, rich or poor, as well as several surrounding communities. The doctor didn't live on the premises, and the top floor of the building was converted into a flat for the elderly couple who acted as caretakers.

When the police had telephoned Dr Jenkins, who lived on the outskirts of the ancient port of Tradmouth, they were told by his teenage daughter that the doctor and his wife were away for the weekend visiting relatives in Swansea. The teenager hadn't been told the reason for the call. Pauline Brent's death would come as a shock to her unprepared employer.

There was nobody at the surgery when they arrived. And when Dr Jenkins, a cheerful-faced Welshman in his late fifties, eventually turned up, he looked somewhat bewildered to see the two detectives waiting for him.

'Sorry about this. I can't understand why my receptionist isn't here to open up ... she's always here by now. New patients, are you?' His accent was strongly Welsh and lilting. He fumbled for his keys and opened the surgery door. 'Please, come along in. I shan't keep you long.'

Wesley decided it was time to put the doctor straight. He produced his warrant card and introduced himself. The doctor's expression changed to one of anxiety; but the anxiety that anticipates bad news rather than immediate arrest. He hurried the two men into his surgery and asked them to take a seat.

It was Wesley who broke the news, Gerry Heffernan sitting beside him, watching the doctor's reaction. Nothing, however, sounded any warning signals in Heffernan's brain, tuned as it was to detecting signs of guilt. The doctor expressed shock, then disbelief, then a seemingly sincere willingness to help the police catch whoever had deprived him of his receptionist. His own alibi was provided. At half past ten on Friday he and his wife had been at his mother's in Swansea, visiting for the weekend. They had set off straight after surgery finished at six o'clock. Pauline had been fine when he had left, had even wished him a good weekend.

'Has she seemed worried about anything recently?' asked Wesley.

'Now that you mention it, she has seemed a little preoccupied . . . but that could be my imagination,' the doctor said with a sad smile.

'So what was she like as an employee? As a person?'

'She was a very nice lady. Efficient, hard-working, good with people, which is very important in her job.'

'Did she ever clash with anybody? An irate patient wanting an appointment; somebody she thought wasn't ill enough to see you who later died – anything like that?' Wesley suggested, thinking of all the horror stories about a GP's life he'd heard from his mother.

'Nothing like that, nothing at all. She was very sympathetic . . . not the traditional dragon at the gate, I assure you. She knew most of the people in the village and, as far as I know, she was popular. She was a quiet, gentle woman, kept herself to herself; very fond of children. There were times when she'd persuade me to see a child as an emergency even though I knew there was nothing wrong that a bit of Calpol wouldn't cure. No, Sergeant, I can assure you she made no enemies through work. In fact I'd be surprised if she had any enemies at all.' He shrugged, as if mystified by the whole thing.

'Did she have a boyfriend, do you know?'

'She never confided in me if she did. But then she was a discreet woman; not the sort to . . .'

'Quite. How long has she worked for you, Dr Jenkins?'

'A long time.' The doctor paused, the reality of Pauline's death beginning to sink in. Theirs had been a long and contented working partnership. He began at that moment to contemplate the implications of her death. 'Fifteen years,' he said softly. 'She got the job when she first came to the village.'

'What happened? When she got the job, I mean. She must have had references and . . .'

'It's so long ago, it's all a bit hazy. I think I advertised in the local paper: that covers Neston and Tradmouth and all the surrounding villages. I had several applicants, some local women who, how shall I put it, might not have appreciated the need for complete confidentiality.' Wesley nodded knowingly. 'I interviewed and there was something about Pauline I liked . . . a sort of calm efficiency.'

'She must have said what she'd been doing before she came to Stokeworthy.'

'I really can't remember. She had office skills but I think she'd been looking after an ageing relative, something like that. Sorry I can't be more help.'

'Did she ever talk about her life before she came here?'

'No . . . no, come to think of it, she didn't.'

'You asked for references, I take it?'

'I must have done.' He held up a hand as if he'd just had an idea. 'It might be in the files. If you'll bear with me . . .'

Dr Jenkins disappeared into a back office where the practice paperwork had been neatly filed away by the dead woman. Her death could well throw the system into chaos, something the good doctor was only just beginning to realise. He returned holding what looked like a letter. 'There was this. A reference from a Rev. Geoffrey Willington up near Bromsgrove. He said she'd done some work for him and he'd found her efficient, pleasant and helpful. As I recall she gave me his address and I wrote to him . . . one can't be too careful if one doesn't know somebody.'

'Of course. Do you mind if we keep this, Doctor?'

'Help yourself.' The doctor sat in his swivel chair, looking suddenly lost. 'Oh dear, the patients will start to arrive in ten minutes.' He looked up at Wesley in desperation. 'I suppose my wife could fill in until I find someone. I'll have to ring her. This is all such a shock. She was hanged, you say?'

'Strangled, then hanged from the yew tree in the churchyard,' said Gerry Heffernan brutally. 'Not a nice death.'

The doctor, now lost for words, shook his head. The two

policemen exchanged looks. It was time to leave the amiable medical man contemplating mortality. They thanked him and politely took their leave.

'Tell you what, Wes,' said Gerry as they left, passing the first of Stokeworthy's sick and wounded to turn up in the waiting room, 'I wouldn't mind a word with this Rev. Willington. Where did he live again?'

'Bromsgrove, sir.'

'Ever been to Bromsgrove, Wes?'

'Can't say I have.'

'Well, they say travel broadens the mind,' the inspector said cryptically as they walked back to the village hall.

Coffee was incidental: Pam had found that out in the first ten minutes. Most of the women at Charlotte's coffee morning (Pam never discovered her surname) came from the well-heeled end of Tradmouth. The only other woman not sporting designer labels was a quiet, dark-haired librarian called Anne. She and Pam instinctively teamed up, each one recognising a likely kindred spirit. Anne's baby, Laura, wore, like Michael, an outfit that had been reduced in Mothercare's last sale; the other babies were colourfully kitted out by more exclusive establishments. Financial standing begins to be displayed at a very early age.

Pam and Anne were only starting to get to know each other – exchanging backgrounds and details of work to be returned to when their maternity leave had run its course – when Charlotte announced that the morning's entertainment would begin. A woman called Hattie, who owned Tradmouth's most exclusive designer boutique, held out a videotape in her beautifully manicured hand, saying that they should all see how idle and unreliable girls were nowadays. She'd sacked the girl, she said, as soon as she'd seen the tape and replaced her with an Austrian au pair who was lovely apart from a slight personal hygiene problem.

It wasn't until the tape had been running five minutes, accompanied by giggles and whispered shhh's from the small audience, that Pam understood the significance of Hattie's words. The tape showed a young girl who didn't look more than seventeen, sitting in a sumptuous lounge, her feet up on a gilded coffee table, reading a magazine. In the background a toddler scampered round the long, expensively draped curtains, playing a solitary game of hide-and-seek. The young woman was ignoring him, and the child's assaults on the curtains became steadily more violent. The child began to whine, then shout, but the girl merely threw out an unfocused 'Shut up' and returned to her magazine. Hattie then leaped forward to wind the video on, assuring the audience that 'It gets worse'.

The tape began again. This time the scene had changed to a large and luxurious kitchen, with units that Pam estimated would have cost her a full year's salary ... at least. The young woman was there again, this time spooning some glutinous substance into the mouth of a young baby sitting in a high chair. The toddler was once more clamouring for attention and knocked the spoon out of her hand. The girl responded by giving the child a sharp slap across the face, his shocked cries setting off his baby brother. The two bawled in harmony for half a minute before the girl, having had enough, left the room. Once alone, the toddler picked up the food-caked spoon from the floor and climbed up onto the kitchen table, from where he fed his brother inexpertly but with a touching display of sibling concern. Then the tape ran out.

'See what I mean?' said Hattie, indignant. 'If I'd known the way she treated them I'd have got rid of her ages ago. Thank goodness Chloe told me about the video surveillance.' She looked at another expensively dressed woman with studied gratitude.

'How did you arrange it?' Pam's curiosity gave her the courage to speak.

'A place in Morbay. They specialise in surveillance. They planted four hidden cameras around the house ... ever so tiny. Marvellous, really. Lets you know exactly what's going on when you're not there ... at a price, of course.'

'Of course.' Pam wondered what other sorts of surveillance were available, and whether the police were aware of this service. Maybe she would mention it to Wesley. 'Is it legal?' Was her next question.

'As far as I know. It's your own house, isn't it? An Englishman's home, and all that. Why? You're not married to a policeman, are you?' She laughed at the thought.

'As a matter of fact I am.' Something in Hattie's tone had made her hackles rise.

'So we'll have to watch what we say, will we?' Hattie looked round at the others for support.

It was at that moment that Michael began to cry, and for once Pam was grateful to her son for causing a disturbance. 'I should get him home. He's ready for his sleep.' She didn't feel comfortable: she wanted to get out of that room and its cloying atmosphere, a heady mixture of well-powdered babies and expensive perfumes.

'I must go too. I'll walk back with you.' It was Anne who spoke. Pam shot her a grateful look. Anne, by happy chance, lived just three roads away from the Petersons. Ten minutes later, the babies safely installed in their prams, the two women strolled back up the steep streets to the top of the town.

'Have you got anyone to look after Laura when you go back to work?'

'I'm back already part time. My eldest's just started school, so my childminder's taking Laura. She's a lovely lady ... very motherly. Only lives on Victoria Road. What about you?'

'I haven't started looking seriously yet. I suppose I should. I've been putting it off. Has your childminder got any vacancies?'

'Not that I know of ... but I'll ask for you.'

'Thanks. What did you think of the coffee morning?'

'I went to quite a few coffee mornings when I had my eldest and I used to enjoy them: I made some good friends. But that lot ...'

'I know what you mean. What about that video?'

'I know.' Anne turned to look at her. 'Is your husband really a policeman?'

'Yes. A detective sergeant. Why?'

'I thought you were just saying it to wind that Hattie up. Fancy coming back for lunch? Nothing fancy ... just a sandwich.'

'That'd be great.'

Pam walked with her new-found friend back through the narrow streets, their prams two abreast. But somehow – and she wouldn't admit this to Anne, not on such a short acquaintance – she couldn't get the sad images on the video out of her mind. She looked down at Michael, now sleeping innocently. Something, she told herself, would have to be done.

The first person Wesley Peterson encountered on his return to the incident room was Rachel. She was waiting impatiently for Steve Carstairs to finish a suggestive conversation with WPC Trish

Walton, who was perched on the edge of a desk showing a considerable amount of black-stockinged leg.

'How did you get on with the doctor?' she asked Wesley.

Wesley smiled. 'Same story. Pauline Brent was a nice lady with no enemies.'

'She had one . . . and he killed her,' said Rachel simply.

'Are we sure it was a he? On the other hand I can't see a woman setting up that hanging, can you?'

Rachel shook her head. She hated to admit, especially when Steve Carstairs was in the vicinity, that there was anything a man could do which a woman couldn't. But the sheer strength required to haul a body about would be beyond the average woman. 'Unless she had help, of course,' she said as Steve appeared round the corner, shooting a resentful look at Wesley. 'We're off to see Charles Stoke-Brown, the artist over at the old mill. I think that painting on the mantelpiece at the Sweetings' house is one of his. I recognised the style.'

Wesley looked impressed. 'I didn't know you were interested in art.' Their eyes met and she smiled shyly.

'Come on,' snapped Steve, impatient to be away.

Rachel said nothing more but walked out of the village hall behind Steve, turning to give Wesley a small smile of farewell.

Wesley returned to his desk and began to sort through the pile of paperwork – witness and house-to-house statements, pathology and forensic reports. He was looking for something – anything – that would refocus his mind on the death of Pauline Brent. Overnight several reports had come in of Lee Telford being sighted in the area. He had been seen in a nightclub in Morbay, a chip shop in Neston and aboard a yacht in Tradmouth harbour. The boy on the yacht later proved to be the owner's son, and the other sightings were inconclusive as the boys in question had disappeared before the uniformed officers turned up. As was normal in a missing-person case, there was a lot of activity that was leading nowhere.

Rachel and Steve found Charles Stoke-Brown in his studio wearing a paint-stained shirt, his grey hair tied back in a neat ponytail. He greeted Rachel with a charming smile but ignored Steve, who hovered in the background like a surly dog, growling the occasional question.

The artist confirmed that a small picture had indeed been stolen on Friday night. He gave a description of the oil painting which matched exactly the one that graced the Sweetings' mantelpiece. Gaz Sweeting had some more questions to answer.

They were about to leave when the artist touched Rachel gently on the shoulder. 'Do you know, yours is just the face I've been looking for ... to paint. It wouldn't take long ... just a couple of hours. Say you'll think about it.'

Rachel, for once lost for words, nodded. Charles Stoke-Brown gave her a dazzling smile. She found it difficult to maintain an expression of professional detachment ... but she just about managed it.

As they took their leave, however, Rachel noticed that an uneasiness, a subdued quietness, was clouding Stoke-Brown's charming amiability. Something was worrying him. She had a feeling that there was more to the matter than the simple theft of money and a small painting.

Gaz was in. His mother opened the door grudgingly, wearing a thin cheap satin dressing gown. Her son, she said, was still in bed. He didn't work ... couldn't get a job – there was nothing round here for a lad of his age. He had been on some youth training scheme, she explained, but hadn't worked since. 'There's nothing he fancies,' she stated indignantly. Rachel made no comment but wondered where the money for the drugs came from.

As Mrs Sweeting disappeared upstairs to wake her son, Rachel told Steve she proposed to take him back to Tradmouth for questioning. 'If they broke into Stoke-Brown's studio,' she explained, 'it might not be their first burglary. I think we might get a result here.'

Steve flexed his shoulders. Action at last. This is what he had joined the force for.

Half an hour later they were sitting in an interview room at Tradmouth police station. Rachel, to Steve's annoyance, had summoned Wesley over from Stokeworthy to conduct the interview with her. Steve had said nothing, but Rachel could tell what he was thinking. He returned to Stokeworthy, keeping a lookout for the two young girls who seemed to be showing such an interest in his charms.

Wesley and Rachel sat next to each other in the green-painted interview room, Gaz sitting opposite with the bored-looking duty solicitor, a tall, pale man in his late twenties who looked as if he'd rather be elsewhere.

'We know where this picture came from.' Wesley produced the small painting, now shrouded in plastic as it had become a piece of evidence. 'You broke into one of the studios at the old mill on Friday night, didn't you?'

'It weren't my idea . . . it was Lee. He said he knew the bloke – the painter – was out. He said it'd be easy.'

'And was it?'

Gaz nodded.

'How did Lee know this bloke was out?'

'Dunno. He never said.'

'What did you take?'

'Some cash . . . about forty quid. This painting. It was small, see, and I thought my mum'd like it.'

Even the worst villains, thought Rachel philosophically as she listened, were reputedly good to their mothers. 'Anything else?' she asked.

Gaz looked sheepish, as if making a decision of an embarrassing nature. After a few seconds' silence he spoke. 'There were some photographs. They were in a drawer near the money. They were of this woman with no clothes on.'

'And you took them?'

'Yeah . . . just for a laugh.'

'Where are they now?'

'Lee had them.'

'Did you recognise the woman?'

'Oh yeah. It was the one who was murdered . . . it was Pauline Brent.'

An hour later Gerry Heffernan stood at the door of Charles Stoke-Brown's studio, the bag containing the small painting clutched in his large hand. He looked at Wesley triumphantly. They were getting somewhere at last. The artist was quick to answer the door. He stood aside meekly to allow them in, almost as though he had been expecting them. Wesley looked around the studio, noticing the painted coat of arms that hung on the far wall. He had seen it somewhere before but he couldn't, for the moment, remember where.

'Recognise this, sir?' Heffernan showed the painting to Stoke-Brown.

'Yes. It was taken on Friday. Have you arrested someone?'

'That's right, sir. Young lad. He's confessed to your break-in. Do you mind if we ask a few more questions?'

Stoke-Brown led them through to the sitting room and invited them to sit down. But before they could begin their questions he started to speak. 'I've thought about it very carefully and I think it's time I told you the truth about my relationship with Pauline Brent.' He leaned forward, his manner frank and sincere. How much of this was real, Wesley wondered, and how much a skilled display of acting? 'I met Pauline when I went to see Dr Jenkins. I had an old rugger injury which needed treatment from time to time and she was very good about getting me appointments. Then I was painting up by Knot Creek. She was walking there. She said it was one of her favourite spots for just being alone and thinking. We met there often and . . . She had quite an interest in art: said she'd done some herself at one time.'

'Where?'

'I don't know. There was a lot about Pauline I didn't know. It didn't seem to matter at first, but if you feel someone's holding something back . . .' He stopped, examining his paint-stained fingers nervously.

'Go on,' Wesley coaxed.

'I had a broken marriage behind me. I told Pauline all about it . . . but she never said anything about her past. Yet she seemed keen on commitment . . . kept hinting at marriage.'

'Did you share her feelings?' asked Wesley quietly.

Charles shook his head. 'No. I'm not ready for that sort of thing.'

'Did you tell her?'

He shrugged. 'Why rock the boat? She would have realised eventually.'

'What about the photographs?'

'Oh, them. Have you found them?'

'No. Apparently they were in the possession of the boy who's disappeared.'

Stoke-Brown seemed uneasy about this. He began to explain. 'It's very hard to find anybody willing to be a model, as you can imagine. I told Pauline how keen I was on painting the human

108

form and she volunteered. I took a few snaps to work from but mostly she would come and pose for me here. I was worried when I found they were missing. You know what villages are like. If they got passed around among the local youth or fell into the wrong hands ...' He didn't finish his sentence. Gerry Heffernan knew exactly what he meant.

'Why didn't you tell my officers this before?'

'I don't know. It was stupid of me. One of your officers – a charming young lady – nearly discovered my paintings of Pauline, so I hid them. I didn't really want to ... to be asked a lot of questions, to come under suspicion. I realise it was stupid now but Pauline's death came as such a shock.'

Heffernan sat back in his chair and looked the artist directly in the eye. 'Your relationship wasn't well known in the village. Ashamed of her, were you?'

'Well, I didn't want Pauline to get the wrong idea: she was hinting at wedding bells as it was. Then there was my ex-wife. She's a neurotic woman: she slashed my clothes, damaged my car. She even ordered a hearse for me once. If she got an inkling there was someone else in my life, there's no knowing what she might have done.'

'Why did you break up?' Wesley asked, curious.

'I felt there was nothing more for me in the marriage. It was sterile, Sergeant. We went through the motions but there was no feeling there. I had to get out ...'

'Needed your own space?' asked Heffernan. He had heard all this before.

'That's right.'

'So Pauline had to put up with a clandestine affair. Didn't you think she might like to ...'

'As I said, I wasn't ready for commitment. Pauline seemed happy enough with the situation.'

'Did she say anything at all about her past?' asked Wesley. 'Anything you can remember, however small?'

Charles shook his head.

'Did you ever ask her?' asked Heffernan, coolly.

'Yes. When we first met ... but she was good at evading any direct questions.'

'Did she seem worried about anything ... or anyone?'

'Now you come to mention it, she did seem distracted,

preoccupied over the past couple of weeks. Of course, I might have been imagining it. Actually, she did say something strange a few days ago. She said there was something she had to sort out before we, er . . . made things legal.'

'What did you say to that?'

'I told her to slow down . . . see how things went. But as I said, I didn't want to rock the boat too much.'

'You had a nice, compliant girlfriend who was willing to pose in the raw for you. Why spoil things by telling her your intentions weren't honourable, eh?' said Heffernan with a smirk.

'Precisely, Inspector.'

'Where were you on Friday night?' Heffernan asked sharply, the smirk disappearing.

'Pauline normally came to the studio on a Friday and I'd cook a meal. But she said she couldn't see me; she was being very mysterious about it so I, er . . . went to visit my ex-wife. I'd been a bit worried about her . . . her state of mind. I was there until about eleven thirty then I drove back. That was when I discovered the break-in and phoned the police. A young constable came round who looked as though he was on work experience.' He laughed nervously at his joke. 'That's all that happened. I'm sorry I can't be more help.'

'Will your ex-wife verify this?'

'I should imagine so, yes,' Stoke-Brown said with brittle confidence before reciting her address reluctantly. Was the scorned wife so resentful, Wesley wondered, that she might lie to make life awkward for the man who had abandoned her?

'Pauline visited Philip Thewlis on Friday night. Did she mention this at all?'

Stoke-Brown shook his head, genuinely puzzled. 'I'd no idea she moved in such exalted circles. Why did she visit him? Do you know?'

'To accuse him of having an affair with his nanny. Do you know anything about it?'

'No . . . no, I don't. It's a complete mystery to me. Sorry.'

'Apparently her cleaning lady, Mrs Matherley, is the nanny's grandmother and she told Pauline that she was concerned for the girl's welfare. Did she mention this to you at all?'

'No. She didn't.' Stoke-Brown looked unconcerned that she hadn't confided in him.

'It seems Pauline was a bit of a crusader when she thought some injustice was being done.'

'Yes. She complained that some yob had nearly killed a child at that new development in Worthy Lane.'

'She told you about that?'

'Yes. She said the man had threatened her. I told her not to take it seriously. I've seen the man in question . . . all big talk. Pauline seemed very gentle but she had a tough streak, you know. I can quite imagine her tackling even Philip Thewlis if she thought he was abusing some young girl. She seemed to feel strongly about things like that. I wonder . . .' He paused. Wesley waited in silence for him to speak again. 'I wonder if she went too far . . . got on the wrong side of someone.'

'It's certainly a possibility and one that we'll bear in mind.' Wesley looked at the inspector, who was studying a painting of the village church propped up against the wall. He looked up at Wesley and gave an almost imperceptible nod. 'Well, thank you, sir. We might have to ask you some more questions later on . . . and if you remember anything, anything at all that might help us . . .'

'Of course. I'd like to see the bastard who did this caught, I really would.' He looked Wesley straight in the eye. 'She didn't deserve anything like that.'

It was Gerry Heffernan who led the way out, anxious to be gone. 'What did you make of all that?' he said as soon as they were out of earshot.

'I suppose his story adds up, but I'd still like to know why he didn't come forward sooner to say he was involved with Pauline.'

'It's my guess that he was just stringing her along till something better came along. Hardly the reliable type, is he?'

'Maybe he knows we usually treat the husband or boyfriend of the deceased as the prime suspect.'

'All the more reason to establish his innocence by coming forward immediately, surely. Do you believe that she wanted to marry him? I would have thought he was the type for a more, er . . . artistic arrangement. What do they call it? An open relationship?'

'She obviously didn't realise that. It shows she was naïve for her age . . . but he is a bit of a charmer. Apparently he asked Rachel to pose for him.'

'Not . . .?'

'He only mentioned her face, sir.'

'Thank goodness for that. We'll have to check his alibi, of course.'

'I'll see to it when we get back. Do you mind if we make a detour?'

'Where to?'

'Worthy Court. I want another word with D'estry . . . see if he knows anything about this missing lad. And there's a Timothy Wills – he's standing in the Bloxham by-election. He was out and about on Friday night, according to his wife. He might have seen something.'

The visit to Worthy Court didn't take them far out of their way. Wesley noticed his boss sneaking surreptitious looks at Susan Green's cottage, as though tempted to call. He half expected him to suggest an impromptu bit of questioning, but he seemed content to follow the sergeant through the archway into Worthy Court. A couple of solemn-faced children were playing in the courtyard, some quiet game without a requirement for noise or laughter. Wesley recognised them as Jane Wills's children. He smiled at them and said hello, but they made no answer, merely rewarded him with a serious stare. Wesley went up to D'estry's door and rapped loudly. There was no answer.

'Probably jet-skiing – scaring the life out of the local jellyfish,' said Heffernan with disapproval.

'He'll wait,' said Wesley. 'Let's see if Mr Wills is at home, shall we?'

'You reckon he'll be here?'

'Those are his kids. He might have gone back to London but it's worth a try. I think his parents were down here as well.'

'Okay, then. Will you knock or shall I?'

The children watched in silence as Heffernan rapped on the door, loud enough to waken the dead. Jane Wills, still beautiful with her long pre-Raphaelite hair, opened the door looking mildly annoyed. When she recognised Wesley her expression changed to one of expectant co-operation. It would hardly be appropriate for a parliamentary candidate's wife to antagonise the local constabulary.

'Do come in,' she said politely after checking that the children were all right. 'If you've come to ask me more questions, I'm afraid I can't tell you any more than I did on Saturday.'

'Are you staying down for the week?'

'Yes. Then we're returning to London as my husband has a case there. Then we'll be back here for the by-election.'

'Is your husband here?'

'He's gone to the constituency office for a meeting. Did you want to see him?'

'Yes. We wanted a quick word ... just a formality, you understand. Have you been down here much recently?'

'Since my husband was adopted as candidate for Bloxham we've been coming down here on and off when his work permits. Of course, if he were to win the by-election, we'd have to get somewhere in Bloxham itself as well. But we'll always keep this place for holidays and weekends.'

'Wesley nodded. Mrs Wills was far friendlier, more forthcoming, than she had been when they had last met. 'Do you know many people round here?'

'Not many, I must admit. My parents-in-law have the cottage next door. They're not here at the moment. My mother-in-law had to go back to London for a hospital appointment. When we're down we tend to stay here as a family and keep ourselves to ourselves: we don't get to meet many local people,' she said without regret.

'Do you know Philip Thewlis?'

'My husband does. Contacts are so important in politics and business.'

'Does he visit him up at the Manor?'

'I believe he's there quite often, yes. We don't always come down here with him, you understand. He has so much to do and the children are at school and ...'

'But you're down here most weekends?'

'Yes ... most.'

'And you didn't know the dead woman, Pauline Brent? She lived in the cottages opposite.'

'No. I didn't know her. As I've said, Sergeant, we stay as a family. We value our time together.'

'So your husband doesn't mix with the locals much.'

'No. I wouldn't say so.'

'But surely, as a prospective MP ...'

'He mixes with the people in his constituency party, of course,

and any people who might be of use to him ...' The open
friendliness was beginning to tarnish a little.

'Like Mr Thewlis?'

'Yes. People like that.'

'Surely he has to go out and meet the people who might vote for
him?'

'He goes handshaking in Bloxham. He has no reason to do it
here: this isn't in the constituency. He is a busy man, you know.'

'And so are we, love,' Gerry Heffernan said with finality.
'Thanks very much for your time.'

'We would like a word with your husband. Just routine,' said
Wesley.

'If you could ring first ...' she said coolly.

'Of course.' The two policemen were on the threshold, about to
leave, when Wesley turned. 'By the way, were you in
Stokeworthy when Miss Brent was threatened by Julian D'estry?'

She looked uncomfortable. 'I was driving into the courtyard
here a couple of weeks ago. I saw D'estry arguing with a woman.
His car was slewed across the road and I had to avoid it. Why do
you ask?'

'What about your husband? Or your parents-in-law?'

'My in-laws would have been here: they are most weekends.
But I'm sure they knew nothing about it. As for my husband, I
don't think he was. Is it important?'

'Just looking for witnesses,' Wesley said unconvincingly,
before thanking her and taking his leave.

'What was all that about, Wes? You don't think they've got
anything to do with it, do you?'

'I don't know, sir. Perhaps it's just prejudice. Perhaps I don't
trust politicians.' He grinned.

'That's not prejudice, Wes. That's common sense. Come on,
let's get back to the incident room. I've got to ring a man about a
vicar.'

As it turned out, it wasn't a man that Gerry Heffernan spoke to but
a woman. The new vicar of St Matthew and St Luke's near
Bromsgrove was the Rev. Sandra Paulet, a friendly woman, only
too eager to be helpful. The Rev. Geoffrey Willington, she said,
had retired ten years ago and was in a nearby nursing home. Some
of her parishioners still visited him. He was crippled by arthritis,

she said; such a sad predicament for one who had lived such a healthy, useful life. Gerry Heffernan made sympathetic noises and took down the details.

Then he made another phone call and went off to find Wesley.

Steve Carstairs decided to take a detour of his own – to the village shop to buy himself something for lunch: a pork pie, a can of Coke and some crisps. Stokeworthy Stores had branched out in recent months and the sign outside boasted that it stocked local wine, cheeses, ice creams and fine cured bacon – all to tempt the weekenders. But none of these delights tempted Steve. The woman behind the counter served him enthusiastically. The police presence in the village was good for business and discouraged the louts who usually hung around outside her shop.

Steve didn't fancy eating his paltry rations in the incident room. He would go for a walk – get some fresh air. As he stepped outside into the daylight, nursing his resentment, a voice to his right made him jump.

'Your lunch-time is it?'

Steve turned to see Leanne Matherley sitting on a low wall, displaying an alarming quantity of leg as she had hitched up her denim miniskirt.

'Where's your friend?'

'School.'

'Shouldn't you be there?'

She looked mildly insulted. 'I'm on study leave. Haven't got to go in.'

'You in the sixth form, then?'

Leanne nodded, avoiding his eyes. 'Yeah. 'Course I am. Where's your car?'

'Parked round the back of the village hall. Why?'

'I've never been in an XR3i. How fast does it go?'

'Fast as you like. Fancy a drive?' Steve looked the girl up and down, noted her attractions and felt reckless.

'Thought you'd never ask.'

'Wait here. I'll bring the car round,' he said, not wishing to risk being seen by his colleagues. This was strictly pleasure.

Ten minutes later he was shooting down the high-hedged country lanes demonstrating the power of his vehicle. Leanne sat beside him, her bare legs stretched out, the seat belt obscuring the midriff that Steve knew was also exposed. He could hear her catch her breath as they rounded blind corners. The prospect of meeting another car didn't occur to him as the adrenalin pumped and he felt the sexual excitement of the situation. He glanced at his companion to see if she shared his exhilaration. He saw her eyes fixed ahead but failed to notice the gritted teeth and the hands clasping the seat belt, white-knuckled.

'Can we stop somewhere?' she said breathlessly as a slow-moving tractor loomed in front of them.

'Sure.' With a squeal of brakes, Steve turned the car down a lane, even narrower than the last. 'Do you know where this leads?' She wanted to stop. He was on to a good thing here.

'Down to the creek ... farther towards the river. It's a dead end.'

Steve smiled and checked his appearance in the rear-view mirror. It was his lucky day. The road ended, as Leanne had predicted, in a dead end near the water. He got out and walked slowly round the car to open the passenger door, anticipating, aware of the physical effects of his excitement. He helped Leanne out of the car and they walked, hand in hand, down to the creek, wider here than at Stokeworthy.

'Haven't you brought your lunch with you?' she asked tentatively.

'Why? There's better things to do than eat,' he said suggestively.

He looked at her. She was eyeing him nervously. They were alone. He stopped and put his arms round her. She stiffened, drawing away slightly. Taking her reluctance for preliminary nerves, he bent and whispered in her ear, 'It's all right. There's nobody about,' before kissing her on the lips, exploring her mouth with his tongue.

Leanne stood quite still. She hadn't expected this ... not so soon. He kissed her again, his hand creeping up towards her breast. Over his shoulder she could see the creek, the water lapping gently against the muddy sand at its edge. The tide was in.

As Steve's hands explored further, Leanne pushed him away half-heartedly. He whispered to her not to be a tease. She knew she shouldn't have come. She knew she shouldn't be there. As he kissed her again, more fiercely this time, and pressed his body against hers, she focused her eyes on the water that glistened behind him and watched what looked like a pile of clothes caught up in branches, floating near the shore. She put a hand up and shoved Steve away.

'What did you do that for?' he asked, indignant, threatening.

'Look.' She pointed to the shape in the water. 'It's a body . . .' She suddenly felt unsure. Perhaps it was something else, a log or a bundle of old rags.

Steve looked at her, weighing up the situation. Was she having him on? Teasing now when the messages she had been sending out had been crystal clear? He turned. Once he had reassured her that there was no body, everything would be all right.

He strolled down to the water's edge, his eyes fixed on the shape in the water. It was very near the shore, caught up in some branches that were growing out into the creek. He squatted down, shielding his eyes from the sunlight that sparkled on the water. It certainly looked like a body. He picked up a large branch lying nearby and reached out towards the shape, touching it so that it bobbed up and down. He could see that it was dressed in what looked like jeans and a dull orange T-shirt: long hair streamed out as the body moved. Steve stood up slowly and walked back to Leanne, who was watching him anxiously from farther up the bank.

He drew himself up, feeling important under her expectant gaze. 'It's a body, all right. I'll have to get back. Look, Leanne, I'll have to report this, but there's no need to mention, er . . .'

'No. Is it a man?'

'Can't tell . . . I think it's a woman.'

As he hurried her into his car, Steve thought he detected relief on Leanne's face.

Chapter Nine

12 April 1475
Ralph de Neston for not cleansing his ditch near the highway.
Fined 2d.

   Thomas de Monte, the stonecarver, is amerced for
trespassing upon the lord's woodland.

   Alice de Neston, nursemaid to my lord's son, spoke for him
to the jury saying it was on her request that he did meet her on
the lord's land.

                    From the Court Rolls of Stokeworthy Manor

It was a late lunch but Gerry Heffernan had used his questionable charms to persuade the barmaid at the Ring o' Bells to provide a couple of cheese and pickle sandwiches. The inspector sat back, holding his pint of best bitter, a satisfied smile on his face, while Wesley sipped at his orange juice.

'We'll set off about nine tomorrow. That okay with you?'

Wesley nodded. 'It'll take about three hours to get there, depending on the traffic. What did the matron say exactly?'

'That the Rev. Willington's all there ... crippled with arthritis and in a wheelchair but completely *compos mentis*. He's nearly eighty, she said.'

'That means he must have been sixty-five when he gave Pauline her glowing reference ... nearing retirement.'

'That's right.' Heffernan chuckled in anticipation. 'I can't wait to hear what he's got to say ... and there are bound to be other people who knew her up there in Bromsgrove. We're getting somewhere at last, Wes.'

'You don't see her artistic lover in the role of murderer, then?'

'Crime of passion? Doubt it. More likely he wanted to give her the heave-ho if she was getting too keen and hearing wedding bells . . . but I'm keeping an open mind.'

'What about D'estry? Any more thoughts on him?'

'All mouth. No, Wes, I'm sure this all has something to do with the lady's mysterious past, whatever it was. I mean, you've moved here from London but you still talk about living there: your family; the Met; people you knew. If you move to a different place you don't blank out your past . . . unless there's a very good reason.'

'Let's hope the Rev. Willington can shed some light on it.'

Wesley was about to take another drink when he heard a voice behind him. 'I've tried to ring you twice. Didn't you get my message?' Neil Watson sounded quite indignant that police work should be getting in the way of his concerns.

'Hi, Neil. Come and join us.' It was Gerry Heffernan who extended the invitation, cheerfully offering a drink and dispatching his sergeant to the bar to get it.

'What is it?' asked Wesley as he put the pint on the table in front of Neil.

'Just thought you'd want to know that we've found three more of those statues. They're turning up thick and fast. We've got Reheboam, Joram and King David himself complete with harp.' Neil could hardly contain his excitement. Wesley knew the feeling: he felt like this when a particularly obtuse murder case was unravelling itself. 'We've got a television crew coming this afternoon for an interview,' Neil continued. 'Although I think they might get more than they bargained for.'

'What do you mean?'

'Squirrel and his mates are hoping to get a few words in.'

'Don't you mind?'

'Mind what?'

'Your hour of glory being hijacked.'

Neil shrugged. He wasn't particularly bothered about glory. 'Philip Thewlis is whizzing in in his helicopter too to say a few words . . . about how exciting the finds are and all that, and how he'll be delighted to see them in the County Museum even though they were found on his land – you know the sort of crap. He's not really got much choice in the matter, but he'll make out it's his decision to grant these great treasures to the nation . . . I believe it's called good publicity. Are you coming to have a look, Wes?'

'Not got time. Sorry.'

'We've got a murderer to catch,' Gerry Heffernan chipped in. 'I don't suppose any of Squirrel's furry friends have come up with anything they saw on Friday night, have they?'

'No. Sorry.'

'Great,' said Wesley. 'There's never an eco-warrior about when you need one. Have you heard anything from Colin Bowman about that skeleton you found?'

'Yes. He came round this morning.' Gerry Heffernan raised his eyebrows. It seemed that Neil and his team were getting better service than the police, who generally had to visit Dr Bowman rather than the other way round. 'It was probably a hanging, either professional or very lucky. The neck was broken cleanly. She was aged about eighteen, hadn't had any children, and we've sent the bones away for radiocarbon dating, which takes ages. I'd say by the teeth she's old ... very old. There's no dental work and I'd say she had a medieval diet – nothing refined, nothing sweet. There's no evidence of disease either: she was a healthy specimen.'

'Not once she was strung up, she wasn't. What would they have hanged people for in those days?'

'That depends when we're talking about. You could be hanged for most things from the sixteenth century onward, but if she's medieval ...' Neil hesitated. 'I'd take a guess, and it's just a guess, that it could be murder ... and her hanging may have been a lynching of some kind as small manor courts rarely gave out death sentences. A murderer would usually have been tried before the magistrates at Neston or Tradmouth ... or at the assizes in Exeter. But don't take my word for it. I could be completely wrong, and it's still possible it was a suicide.'

Gerry Heffernan drained his glass and looked at his watch. 'This is all very interesting but we've got to get on.'

'Don't forget to watch me on telly tonight ... half past five, local news.'

'I'll even video it,' said Wesley, tongue in cheek.

As they left the pub they heard a helicopter overhead, the deafening chugging of its engines tearing through the quiet air of the village as it descended behind the trees to squat on the grassland in front of the Manor.

'There he goes,' said Heffernan with a sigh. 'Nothing like a bit of free publicity, is there?'

'Do you think we need a bit of publicity on this case, sir? Perhaps we should put out an appeal for anyone who knew Pauline Brent to come forward.'

'All in good time, Wes. I think our visit to Bromsgrove tomorrow might do the trick.'

It was then that Wesley's mobile phone rang.

Steve knew he should have stayed with the body and phoned for assistance. But there was the problem of Leanne. He decided to drive back and report it at the incident room. He could always make up some story about his mobile phone not working if anyone enquired too closely.

He dropped Leanne just outside the village. From the expression on her face he guessed she was annoyed. But it couldn't be helped. If they'd been seen together, it wouldn't have looked good.

The incident room was busy. Most of the officers assigned to the case were at their desks, sorting through piles of paperwork, tapping at computer keyboards or answering phones. Inspector Heffernan wasn't there; neither was Sergeant Peterson. Steve's eyes rested on Rachel, engrossed in some computerised task. She would have to do.

'Rachel.' He bent down behind her and whispered in her ear. 'I've found a body.'

Rachel didn't look up from her computer screen. 'Are you sure?'

Steve straightened himself up. Did she really think he didn't know a dead body when he saw one? 'Of course. It's in the creek. Do you know where the inspector is?'

'Ring o' Bells, he said ... working lunch. I've just rung him there. He's on his way back. Whose body is it?'

'A woman ... drowned.'

'You'd better get a car there right away. I'll tell the inspector when he gets back. Is anything wrong, Steve?' She looked at him, a half-smile playing on her lips.

'No. Why?'

'What were you doing down by the creek?'

'Having a walk ... thinking.'

'That makes a change,' she said, turning away to summon assistance before Steve could retaliate. It took her only a couple of minutes to organise a couple of uniformed officers to go with him to where he had found the body, and she promised to let the inspector know as soon as he came in. 'One thing, Steve,' she began as he was about to leave.

'Why didn't you ring for assistance from the creek?'

'My mobile's on the blink . . .battery . . .'

'It's nothing to do with that schoolgirl I saw you with, then?'

Steve's face turned an unhealthy shade of red as he hurried away, almost colliding with Gerry Heffernan, who had just arrived at the village hall. Steve hesitated, Rachel's comments having rendered him temporarily speechless, and stood there facing Heffernan and Wesley, his mouth opening and closing like that of a landed fish.

'Steve's just found a body in the creek, sir,' said Rachel, taking pity on him.

Steve nodded. 'Drowned . . . a woman . . .' He hoped his lack of coherence would be put down to shock.

'Right, then. You go with Johnson and Trish in the car. Wes, we'll follow.'

'There's been a call for you from the station at Plymouth, sir. It's about . . .'

'Okay, Rach. I'll call them later.' Heffernan hurried out. He had more on his mind than returning phone calls.

It wasn't long before, guided by Steve's directions, the patrol car, followed by Wesley's unmarked Ford, had reached the banks of the creek. Steve just hoped no questions would be asked. He would have to invent a new hobby such as bird-watching if necessary . . . in fact bird-watching might fit in very nicely.

PC Johnson waded out into the shallow water and hauled the body onto the bank, first unhooking it from the branches that had caught it and held it fast.

'Well, it's not a woman,' said Heffernan, observing the baggy long-sleeved T-shirt that clung to the skinny body. 'Turn him over, will you, Johnson.'

Johnson obliged. The long hair obscured the corpse's face before Johnson pushed it back. 'I recognise him, sir. It's one of the boys who was hanging round the church on Saturday.'

'Lee Telford,' said Wesley quietly. 'We'd better get Dr Bowman down.'

Heffernan nodded. 'One thing puzzles me. How on earth did Steve Carstairs mistake him for a woman? I would have thought he'd know the difference if anyone did.' He looked up at Steve, who was standing there trying to look inconspicuous. 'What did you say you were you doing here, Steve?'

'Bird-watching, sir.'

Heffernan caught Wesley's eye and shook his head. Was nothing certain in this world any more? Wesley took his mobile phone from his pocket and dialled Colin Bowman's number.

It would be a while before the pathologist arrived, but Heffernan was determined that they would fill the time usefully. Wesley organised a search of the area where the body had been found, but there was no sign of anything untoward apart from a couple of used condoms beneath a tree. If this place was used by courting couples, Wesley thought, there was a chance that someone might have seen something. A further examination of the scene, however, produced no evidence to link it with the death of Lee Telford: no sign of his clothing catching when he fell in; no sign of a struggle. 'It's my guess he went in somewhere else and was carried here by the current,' he said to Heffernan, who nodded.

'You're right, Wes. The currents in this creek are pretty powerful, so if he went in upstream near the shore then he'd be pulled along underwater till he got caught up in these branches.' He looked at Lee Telford's face. 'He looks a bit battered . . . but so would you if you'd been dragged along the river-bed. Looks like his mouth and nostrils are full of sand . . . poor kid.'

Gerry Heffernan was staring at what was left of Lee Telford, contemplating the fragility of existence, when Colin Bowman arrived, made a preliminary diagnosis of death by drowning, and obligingly arranged the post-mortem for early the next morning.

'Look forward to seeing you tomorrow, Wesley,' said Bowman cheerfully as he passed. 'Has Neil told you about our hanged lady?'

'The one at the crossroads? Yes. Did you know he's going to be on the local news tonight?'

'Really? I must watch it. It *was* a hanging, you know. Not a botched-up strangulation like that poor woman in the yew tree: a

123

real hanging . . . neck cleanly broken. I wonder what she did?'

'Neil thinks it might have been some sort of lynching . . . judicial hangings were usually carried out in towns.'

'Well, I'll look forward to hearing what he finds out. And what about these statues? Very interesting, all this archaeology, isn't it? Never know what you're going to turn up next.'

'A bit like police work,' said Wesley, glancing over at Lee Telford's body, which was now being carried to the waiting mortuary van.

Gerry Heffernan strolled over to join them. 'I suppose someone had better break the news to his mum. I'll ask Steve to go with Rachel. She's good at that sort of thing.'

Rachel was indeed good at that sort of thing, but Wesley knew she still hated this aspect of the job. When they returned to the incident room, Gerry Heffernan asked her to go to Mrs Telford's. She nodded with resignation. She'd do her best.

Wesley's telephone rang. He answered it absent-mindedly and heard Neil's voice, excited and positively triumphant. 'You know I wanted to find the records of Stokeworthy Manor Court to see why that woman was hanged? Well, I've been on to the County Museum. They know where the court rolls are.'

'Where?' Wesley hadn't got time for guessing games.

'At the Manor itself. They've never left.'

'So Thewlis has got them? What does he want with medieval court rolls?'

'I expect they were there when he bought the place. It's a good bet he doesn't even know they're there or what they are.'

'Then let's hope he hasn't put them out for the binmen.'

'I don't think he'd chance throwing out anything that looked old and might be worth a bit. He might be a bloody philistine but he's not completely stupid.'

'So what's so exciting?'

'I've got permission to search the Manor for them. He said so on telly . . . in front of thousands of witnesses. Fancy coming with me?'

'I've already visited him in my official capacity, Neil. I don't think it'd be appropriate . . .'

'Nonsense. Ask Gerry.'

'I'll think about it.'

Neil, bubbling with professional excitement, rang off. Wesley looked at his watch. Nearly five o'clock. The time had gone quickly. Gerry Heffernan emerged from behind his partition.

'I've got a suggestion, Wes. Why don't you go home and grab something to eat now. With this Lee Telford business it could be a long day. And Rachel mentioned something about a phone call from Plymouth. Will you see to it?'

Wesley nodded and grabbed his jacket from the back of his chair.

Wesley knew there was something worrying Pam. But he had no idea what it was.

He found her in the living room sorting through baby clothes, Michael peacefully asleep in his carrycot. He kissed her and she gave him a weak smile in return.

'You're back early.'

He explained . . . even offered to make the meal. 'How did your coffee morning go?'

'All right,' she said unenthusiastically. He could tell she was keeping something back. 'I had lunch with a librarian called Anne. She's a widow. Her husband died in a car accident last year . . . really sad. She's got a little girl of Michael's age. She's very nice.'

'Good,' was the only thing Wesley could think of to say. Pam still looked worried. 'Are you okay?'

'Of course I am.' She walked across to Michael's carrycot and gazed down at him pensively.

'Neil's on telly tonight. Half five. I'll record it.'

'Why's he on?'

'These statues they've found. They're very rare . . . possibly unique.'

Normally the prospect of a friend appearing on television, even on the local news, would be greeted with excitement. But tonight Pam seemed uninterested. 'You record it if you like,' she said.

Wesley made them an omelette each and settled down in front of the television, having set the video first. The news began with a story about EU fishing quotas and how they affected the fishermen of Bloxham. The scene flashed to Bloxham harbour, where each of the candidates in the forthcoming by-election was meeting the fishermen to assure them of their undying support. Wesley sat eating his omelette, impatient for Neil's five minutes of fame,

125

when a name flashed up on the screen under the face of a smooth-talking man in his mid to late thirties. Timothy Wills was, by any standards, a handsome man. His thick fair hair was worn fairly long; his suit was expensive and immaculate with the flamboyant touch of a red silk handkerchief spilling from the top pocket. His manner was confident, his assurances to the motley group of fishermen apparently sincere. So this was the husband of the beautiful Jane Wills: they certainly made a handsome couple. But Timothy Wills was a politician to his fingertips. Wesley wouldn't have trusted him an inch.

Wills was suddenly replaced on the screen by Neil Watson ... a stark contrast. Neil made no concession to the art of public relations, but his enthusiasm for his work and the treasures unearthed in Stokeworthy was infectious. After assuring the interviewer that the find was of national importance as so little English sculpture survived from that period, he went on to outline the mystery surrounding the find. The skeleton of a woman, apparently hanged, had been found near the sculptures with a carved crucifix that the experts assured him was in the same style as the larger carvings. The only chance Neil and his team had of solving the mystery was to examine the records of Stokeworthy Manor, which were currently in the possession of Mr Philip Thewlis. At this point Thewlis was brought on, trying to make the best of the situation. He promised the interviewer that he would do everything in his power to make the information available to the archaeological team, and made enthusiastic noises about this exciting new addition to the country's artistic heritage. The words came out right but somehow, Wesley thought, the eyes betrayed his true feelings. Neil and his team were a nuisance and were putting a block under the mighty wheels of commerce.

With a polite 'Thank you, Mr Thewlis, and thank you, Neil Watson: good luck with your research', the interviewer, an earnest young blonde, was about to hand back to the studio when there was a commotion in the background. The trees surrounding Neil's site seemed to come to life as figures shouted from their branches. Squirrel leaped to the ground accompanied by six or so similarly dressed companions. The interviewer looked round, assessing the situation, and the professional journalist in her took over as the cameras kept rolling. Neil stepped into the background, a smile playing on his lips. Thewlis stood, tight-lipped and furious, rooted to the spot.

Squirrel and his colleagues chanted, 'Save the trees, save the trees,' while Thewlis performed mental somersaults, trying to figure out the best way of coming out of the situation with his dignity and reputation intact. At that point, to Wesley's disappointment, the scene cut back to the studio. Whose decision had it been, he wondered, to spare Philip Thewlis potential embarrassment? Wesley also wondered whether the ubiquitous businessman held shares in the television company . . . or was it just that working for the police had made him cynical?

Pam had been watching from behind the sofa. 'Neil was good . . . came over well.'

'Yes. He did. He'll be standing for Parliament next.'

Pam didn't reply. She collected the dishes and began to walk towards the kitchen.

'What's wrong?'

'Nothing.' She walked out of the room. Not for the first time Wesley felt helpless. If she wouldn't even confide in him, there was nothing he could do. He looked at his watch. It was time to get back to Stokeworthy. There was a phone call to make.

Gerry Heffernan had still not returned. Neither had Rachel and Steve. Wesley guessed that they had taken Lee Telford's mother down to the hospital to identify her son's body. He shuddered. Fatherhood had made him feel differently about things that he would once have regarded as routine.

Pushing the thought from his mind, he picked up the telephone and dialled the number Rachel had left on his desk. He was soon talking to the sergeant at a police station in Plymouth. When the conversation was finished, Wesley Peterson sat back, turning over what he had just heard in his mind. When asked to provide an alibi for her ex-husband for the night of Pauline Brent's death, Charles Stoke-Brown's ex-wife had clearly told the constable who called on her that she hadn't seen Charles for three months.

Chapter Ten

21 April 1475
Randle Tandy and his wife Christina are common evil doers
and breakers of hedges as they did break down the hedge of
Ralph de Neston. Fined 6d.

The son of Robert the Minstrel did take a mallet from
Thomas de Monte then he, for fear of discovery, did return it.
Fined 2d.

The jury heard that John Fleccer made an assault upon the
priest and drew blood on him. It was ordered that he should
suffer three full days punishment of his body in such manner
and with such diet as the steward shall appoint.

From the Court Rolls of Stokeworthy Manor

Wesley averted his eyes as Colin Bowman delicately slit open Lee
Telford's naked body. A post-mortem was a rotten way to begin
the day. According to Rachel, Lee's mother was distraught,
inconsolable. Understandable. The body on the slab was skinny;
the ribs were visible. Lee Telford had been seventeen; lying there
dead, he looked younger.

Even Colin Bowman's normally genial face was serious as he
went about his work. 'Looks like drowning, Gerry,' he said when
his gruesome tasks were finished. 'But there's something else.
Look at this head injury.' He beckoned the two policemen over so
that they could get a better view. 'He's been hit with something
hard and possibly flat.' He looked puzzled. 'I can't tell what it
was.' He gazed at the wound for a minute. 'It looks a bit like one
of those big steam irons. But I've never seen an ironing fatality in
all my years as a pathologist, so it could well be something else.'

He grinned. 'It's my guess he was knocked out, then he fell into the water and drowned. Of course, there are further tests . . .'

'There always are, Colin. Could it have been an accident?'

'You mean did he fall and hit his head then slip into the water?' Bowman thought for a moment. 'I think it's unlikely. This head injury was made with some force, as if someone had a good swing at him. It's always possible it was an accident, though. You can never be sure until you find what caused the wound.' He stood back from the body and sighed. 'I think that's it for now, gentlemen. The rest's up to you.'

'Thanks, Colin. We'd better be off. We're going up to Bromsgrove to see a vicar.'

'I'll put everything in my report, then. Have a good journey.' The pathologist smiled and began to sew up his patient.

Relieved at his release from the post-mortem room, Wesley marched to the car, the inspector trailing behind.

'So what shall we tell the Plymouth force to do about Mrs Stoke-Brown?' Heffernan asked as they set off. The discovery of Lee Telford's body had been temporarily distracting them from yesterday's intriguing little discovery.

'I think we should pay her a visit.'

'Mmm. But if she's as neurotic as her ex made out, she could be lying to get him into trouble.'

'And if she's not?'

'Then we'll have to have another word with our artistic friend . . . see if he can paint us a few murals on our cell walls – brighten the place up a bit.'

But the former Mrs Stoke-Brown would have to wait until another time. Three and a quarter hours after they'd driven away from Tradmouth Hospital, they were sweeping up the drive leading to a large house. Smart white signs on the elaborate wrought-iron gates had proclaimed its name to be Cricketers Grange Private Residential Home. A logo beneath the name announced that the establishment was owned by Owlways Health Associates PLC . . . caring for the community. Caring for their shareholders more like, thought Wesley fleetingly.

The house itself was built of red brick in the Victorian Gothic style; rather ecclesiastical with its pointed windows and arched doorways. Perhaps the Rev. Willington would feel at home here after all.

The woman who greeted them was in her early twenties, plump, and smelled of cheap scent and cigarettes: her face was blank as she opened the door. Wesley's heart sank. In a split second he visualised the elderly vicar – an educated, fastidious man – being hauled about resentfully by this bored young woman whose only thought was to abandon him for a gossip and a cigarette at the first opportunity. Shorn of all dignity, all individuality, the reverend would exist in his private hell until released into a better world. Wesley felt distinctly depressed . . . until the woman opened her mouth to speak and her face became animated. He gave silent thanks that his first impression had been wrong.

'Oh, come in. I thought you might have been the laundry people. The reverend's expecting you.' The young woman's face lit up with a cheery smile. 'He's quite excited at helping the police with their enquiries. He loves detective novels, you know . . . the library can't keep up with him. I'm always looking out for new ones for him when I go down there. And when he's not reading he's on that computer of his. He gets in touch with all sorts of places with that Internet, you know. You'll want a cup of tea, I expect. Did you have a good journey?' Her voice, distinctly Midlands, was friendly rather than patronising, and Wesley felt a pang of guilt for having judged her so swiftly and so harshly.

She led them down a wide corridor, richly decorated in medieval blues and reds, and stopped at a magnificent Gothic door. Whoever had built this house had possessed the romantic Victorian view of how medieval life ought to have been . . . but never was in reality. The woman knocked on the door and called through. 'Reverend Willington. It's the police.'

It was a while before the door was answered. Then it opened slowly to reveal an elderly man in a wheelchair. The Rev. Geoffrey Willington had a shock of white hair and the face of an elderly angel. The bright blue eyes that weighed up the two policemen twinkled mischievously.

'Thank you, Maureen,' he said to the young woman. 'Come in, gentlemen. I must say I'm intrigued.' He manoeuvred his wheelchair so that they could enter the room, a large, airy chamber of magnificent proportions furnished with all the necessities of a comfortable life: a bed, a desk on which stood a flickering personal computer, several items of desirable antique furniture and, in the corner, a small *en suite* bathroom.

He saw them looking around. 'As you see, gentlemen, I live in style. And the ladies who work here couldn't be more helpful. I lost my wife ten years ago and then I lost the use of my legs, but I'm fortunate compared to many. Now, how can I help you? It must be something more than a motoring offence if it brings two members of the CID a hundred and fifty miles out of their way.' He tilted his head expectantly. 'I do hope you've not come to arrest me, as I assure you my conscience is clear. I've led a tediously blameless life.'

Heffernan nudged his sergeant. Wesley began. 'About fifteen years ago you provided a reference for a Miss Pauline Brent . . .'

'I've provided references for a lot of people in my time, Sergeant. It's an occupational hazard. But I'll try to remember. Jog my memory, if you will. What kind of reference was it?'

'A glowing one. She'd applied for a job as receptionist for a Dr Jenkins down in Devon . . . a village called Stokeworthy.'

The reverend nodded. 'I remember. Nice woman, attractive, mid-thirties?'

'That's right. What can you tell us about her?'

'There's nothing much to tell. She worked for me for a few months . . . filling in when my secretary was sick. She was a pleasant woman, good at her work. But, as I said, she only worked for me for a short time.'

'Did she tell you anything about her private life?'

'As far as I can remember she didn't discuss it. Mind you, it was a long time ago. She might have mentioned something which was too dull to remember.'

'How did she get the job with you?'

He thought for a while. 'I think it was George Weeks who recommended her . . . vicar of a neighbouring parish, you understand. He was always trying to find homes and jobs for his waifs and strays. He was even chaplain at an open prison a few miles from here, so what with his parishioners and his ex-cons . . .'

Gerry Heffernan was sitting up and taking notice. 'What was Pauline Brent? A parishioner or an ex-con?'

'George would never say. He believed very strongly that once somebody had paid the price for their crimes they should start off again with a clean slate. I never asked about Pauline's background . . . and even if I had, George wouldn't have told me. I presumed she was a parishioner fallen on hard times. She hardly seemed the ex-con type.'

'Do you know where she lived? Whether she lived alone? Anything about her at all?'

'I had an address for her, of course, some way away in George's parish ... but I don't remember it and all my old records went years ago. She never spoke of anyone else as far as I can remember. I'm sorry I can't be more help. I hope you don't mind my asking, but what exactly has she done?'

'I'm afraid she's dead. She was murdered.'

The Rev. Geoffrey Willington's face suddenly turned ashen. He shook his head. 'Terrible ... that's terrible ... poor woman ...'

'Our problem is that nobody in the village seems to have a motive for killing her. She was a popular woman. Our only thought is that there might have been something in her past ... something nobody knew about. That's why we've come to see you.'

'I see.' The Rev. Willington, lover of detective fiction, saw the sense in this. He screwed up his face, his brain working fast.

'Could we have a word with your friend George Weeks? Do you have his address?'

'I'm afraid George died last year. Cancer. Very sad.'

'What about his wife?' A wife might have held on to her late husband's papers ... even remembered some of the people he'd helped in the course of his career.

'He was unmarried, I'm afraid.'

That was that. Another dead end. As soon as Pauline Brent was beginning to come into tantalising focus, she disappeared again. Wesley had another idea. This open prison – was it a man's prison or ...'

'Oh no, Sergeant. It was a women's prison. We used to joke about George's fallen women ... bit naughty of us, I know.'

Wesley looked at his boss. Now they were getting somewhere. 'I think we should go and have a word with the governor, sir.'

'Sorry to dampen your enthusiasm, Sergeant,' said the reverend, 'but I'm afraid the prison closed down some years ago. It's now some kind of young offenders' institution. Of course, you could always ask George's curate. I still keep in touch with him, you know.' The old man's eyes lit up as he glanced over at his computer. 'I could e-mail him now. How about that?'

Gerry Heffernan shuddered inwardly at the mention of high technology. 'Would he remember Miss Brent, do you think?'

'He might, although I have the feeling that poor Pauline was rather a dull woman . . . easily forgotten, if you see what I mean. But it's worth a try.'

'Where does this curate live now?' asked Wesley.

'Down your way, as a matter of fact. Devon.'

'What's his name?'

'Twotrees . . . Brian Twotrees. Shall I e-mail him for you?'

'No need, sir. We know where he is.'

'Do you really? What an extraordinary coincidence.' The reverend's eyes were shining with excitement. 'If you see him, do give him my regards.'

'We will, sir.' Gerry Heffernan, anxious to be away, refused the offer of a medicinal sherry and bade the Rev. Geoffrey Willington a polite farewell.

'Not entirely a wasted journey, sir,' Wesley commented as they got into the car.

'Why didn't the old man put two and two together? Pauline working in Stokeworthy and Twotrees being vicar of Stokeworthy?'

'Twotrees lives in another parish . . . Welton. He's got three parishes to look after. Willington wouldn't have made the connection.'

'Come on, Wes, let's get back to where we came from.' He sighed loudly. 'Sometimes I think we're going round in ruddy circles with this case.'

There was a cryptic message from Neil waiting for Wesley when he got back – 'Have infiltrated behind enemy lines. Ring me.' Wesley looked at his boss who was talking animatedly on the phone. Neil would have to wait.

The first thing Gerry Heffernan had done on his return was ring the vicarage at Welton, only to be told that the Rev. Twotrees was out visiting a sick parishioner but would be calling in at Stokeworthy church later. One of the churchwardens there had found a picture missing from a side chapel: the local police had been called.

Heffernan began to pace up and down restlessly, impatient to talk to Twotrees, frustrated at the delay. Rachel, who knew his moods and generally disregarded them, reported to him that so far the house-to-house enquiries she'd organised regarding the death of Lee Telford had turned up nothing. The inspector nodded absent-mindedly. She wasn't going to get much sense out of him so she gave up and went over to where Wesley was sorting through some paperwork.

She perched on the edge of his desk. 'How was Bromsgrove?'

'It turns out that the vicar, Brian Twotrees, might have known Pauline before she came to Stokeworthy. That's what's eating the boss. He can't wait to get his hands on him, as it were. How's the house-to-house coming on?'

'I think everyone's blind and deaf in this village ... nobody's seen anything. It's just like it was with Pauline. Everyone's either in the Ring o' Bells or at home watching telly.'

'Stokeworthy's not exactly a hotbed of activity.'

'You don't know what goes on behind closed doors ...' She leaned forward and lowered her voice. 'And I know of one girl not a million miles away who's so desperate for a bit of excitement that she'll go for a drive with Steve Carstairs. Now that's what I call boredom.'

Their eyes met conspiratorially and Wesley tried not to laugh. 'Is that why he didn't phone from the creek when he found the body? Do you think he was with ...'

'I'd say there's no doubt about it. I had a look at his phone when he left it on his desk. There was nothing wrong with the battery and he hadn't had time to charge it.'

'You're not in CID for nothing. Are those girls sixteen?'

'If they are they're only just. I'll ask around.' Rachel sighed. 'He'll have to watch himself.'

'Any news from the creek?' Before they had left that morning the inspector had given orders for the banks upstream from where Lee's body had been found to be examined for signs of anything suspicious.

'No, but there's a lot of ground to cover. Do you think the two deaths are linked?'

'I'm certain of it. I think when Lee and Gaz split up that Friday night, Lee saw Pauline's murderer where he shouldn't have been. Whether the murderer saw him or whether Lee was stupid enough to let the killer know what he saw, I don't know. But I'm sure that's why he was killed.'

'Not an accident, then?'

'Colin Bowman said he was hit over the head. He went into that creek somewhere and if we can find out where . . .'

'Wes.' Gerry Heffernan's voice boomed across the room. The acoustics in the humble village hall were better than Wesley would have expected. 'Let's get down to the church. Come on.'

Wesley gave Rachel an apologetic smile and left.

They found a patrol car parked outside the church gate and the church door standing open. An elderly lady polishing brasses inside the gloomy building looked up with curiosity as they entered. She was used to visitors in the ancient church; usually middle-aged couples, families with National Trust membership or the curious from overseas. But this pair looked different, purposeful.

Heffernan flashed his warrant card. 'Is the vicar around, love?'

'There's one of your lot already here in the vestry,' the woman said crossly. 'Never see hide nor hair of a copper till summat goes missing, then they're queuing up when it's too late.' She looked them up and down with distaste, then, as if on cue, Constable Ian Merryweather appeared, ambling down the aisle. He greeted the two newcomers warily, wondering what had brought CID to the scene of the crime so swiftly.

'I believe there's been a theft,' said Wesley.

'Nothing much taken,' said the constable, mildly affronted. 'I could have dealt with it.'

'I'm sure you could,' said Wesley, smoothing ruffled pride. 'But we were here for something else anyway. What was taken?'

Merryweather, surprised by Wesley's sympathetic tone, opened up a little. 'Just a little picture. It was on the wall in the de Stoke chapel. No one noticed it was missing until today. It might have gone weeks ago, according to the vicar.'

'Valuable?'

'The vicar doesn't know. He'd never really noticed it. The churchwarden thinks it was a drawing of some sort of tree . . . very old.'

'The Jesse tree,' said Wesley, thinking aloud.

Merryweather looked at him blankly. The black graduate whizz kid from London wasn't what he had expected. 'It was quite small . . . about eight inches square with a tatty old frame. Hardly worth pinching.'

'A lot of small valuables have gone missing from churches

round here,' said Wesley, conversationally. 'They always turn up again after a few weeks.'

'Let's hope it does, then.' Merryweather's radio crackled into life. An affray at the travellers' caravan site outside Neston. Could he attend? 'Best be off, gentlemen,' he said, unhurried. 'Vicar's through there if you want a word.'

The constable nodded towards the vestry, and Wesley saw his boss's face light up with something verging on glee. He followed him past the frame of the Jesse tree. The hewn stone looked sturdy, expectant; ready to bear its exotic fruit once more . . . if the powers that be gave their permission.

The Rev. Brian Twotrees was at his desk in the cluttered vestry, reading through some paperwork. He looked up, mildly surprised at receiving another visit from the constabulary, and greeted the two policemen with a polite smile, just as he greeted his congregation at the church door.

'I've just told Constable Merryweather all I could about our missing picture. I really don't know much about it, I'm afraid . . . certainly not its value.' He smiled. It was clear that he wasn't prepared for Wesley's first question.

'Why didn't you tell us that you'd known Pauline Brent back in Bromsgrove?'

For a moment he sat silent, his mouth open. Then he gathered his thoughts. 'You never asked me, Sergeant. I would have told you if you'd asked me. It was a long time ago and I didn't know her well . . . hardly at all.'

'Tell us about her,' said Heffernan, perching his large frame on the edge of the vicar's desk, which gave a complaining creak.

'There's nothing much to tell.' Wesley looked at the clergyman's eyes. He wasn't telling the whole truth . . . and he was a pretty useless liar. 'I was curate at St Jude's near Bromsgrove and my vicar, George Weeks, had a lady working for him – just temporarily – while the parish secretary was away. When it was time for her to leave he found her another job with a vicar in a neighbouring parish. I hardly spoke to her . . .'

'But you recognised her?'

'Not at first. It was a long time ago and she'd changed the colour of her hair. When she began to help out with some church functions I heard her name and I recognised it. That's really all I can tell you.'

'Did she recognise you?'

The vicar looked embarrassed. 'Yes. I think she did. But she never said anything.'

'Why was that, do you think?'

The vicar shook his head.

'Did George Weeks tell you anything about her . . . about her background?'

Wesley knew he'd hit the jackpot. The vicar looked alarmed. There was something he didn't want to reveal.

'George always said it wasn't up to us to judge. If someone had paid for their sins and repented then it was our duty to help that person all we could to begin a new and useful life.' He hesitated. 'He told me that Pauline had just come out of the open prison nearby.'

Wesley and Heffernan looked at each other. 'Do you happen to know what she was in prison for?'

'It was George's policy never to mention a person's past. He wanted them to start with a clean slate. George Weeks was one of the most truly Christian men I've ever met. He taught me a lot.'

'I'm sure he did, Vicar,' said Heffernan, growing impatient. 'And I think he had a point. But in this particular case we need to find out everything we can about Pauline Brent's past. Discretion won't help her now, but if you know anything – anything at all – it might help us catch whoever killed her.'

Wesley looked at the inspector, admiring his uncharacteristic eloquence. He couldn't have put it better himself.

The vicar thought for a moment. 'There was something I remember. I'm not proud of this but I was looking for something on George's desk one day and I came across a letter from a charity – something to do with the resettlement of offenders. It was about Pauline and . . . I shouldn't have read it but . . .'

'Go on,' Wesley encouraged before Brian Twotrees's attack of conscience made him clam up altogether.

'It mentioned that her offence carried a stigma that made it difficult to integrate her into society again . . .'

'And what offence was that?' Heffernan said softly.

'Murder.' The vicar looked up at the inspector. 'Pauline Brent was a murderer.'

Chapter Eleven

21 April 1475
Robert the Minstrel is a common drunkard. Fined 6d.
   Christina Tandy, maidservant to my lady, is a liar and a listener under windows and did accuse Alice de Neston of fornication with Thomas de Monte while she was in my lord's service. Thomas de Monte stated that he visited Alice but once when he was working on my lord's arms above the great door. Christina Tandy stated that Alice de Neston did leave my lady's baby alone to meet Thomas de Monte. Alice did deny it. Master Fleccer, the blacksmith, did state that his son, John, is to leave the village for London and that his fines will be paid in full.
                        From the Court Rolls of Stokeworthy Manor

Gerry Heffernan disappeared behind his partition as soon as they arrived back at the incident room. He emerged again after a few minutes. 'I've rung the Home Office but they've all gone home. All right for some. I got some cleaner who said to ring again in the morning. Have we looked Pauline up on the PNC?'

'Of course. There's nothing.'

'Odd.'

'She might have changed her name, sir.'

'Hidden her identity, you mean?'

'It's possible.'

'Fancy a visit to the Ring o' Bells, Wes?'

'I keep getting these strange messages from Neil. I wanted to see if he's still at the dig.'

'We can kill two birds with one stone, then. Come on.' Gerry Heffernan led the way, revitalised by Brian Twotrees's revelation.

138

He felt, as did Wesley, that they were getting somewhere at last. The knowledge of Pauline's alleged crime opened up all kinds of new possibilities.

They walked swiftly past the church. The great yew tree that dominated the churchyard swayed in the warm breeze, a thing of nature and beauty rather than an instrument of death.

Opposite the Ring o' Bells the dig continued. Figures, deep in concentration, stood or kneeled in trenches, oblivious to the world on the other side of the road. Wesley screwed up his eyes against the sunlight and studied the scene. Neil wasn't there.

His first mission aborted, he followed the inspector into the pub. There, in a corner, sat Neil, talking to a small woman in late middle age. Her hair was grey and worn in a fluffy, flyaway bun, and when she had dressed that morning her mind had been on academic matters rather than her appearance. She looked up and spotted her former student.

'Wesley. How nice to see you. Neil told me you were in Stokeworthy. Another of your murders, is it?' Dr Daphne Parsons, Wesley's old tutor, spoke loudly. Drinkers at the bar looked round at the mention of murder.

'That's right, Daphne. Two murders, to be exact. Are you here to see Neil's Old Testament worthies?'

'The Jesse tree figures. Yes. It's so exciting.' She hugged herself like a child contemplating a particularly desirable Christmas present. 'It's quite the most exciting find I've been involved in for years. And to think they'd been buried all that time. I think the villagers must have taken them out of the church when all the local churches were being stripped of their treasures, dug a pit, buried them safely and waited for better times ... which never came. The unhallowed ground at the crossroads was a strange choice ... usually reserved for the burial of society's outcasts, as it were. I wonder if it has any significance.' She looked up at Wesley and smiled. 'To find the figures intact like that, and the inscriptions of their names are so sharp ... as if they were carved yesterday. Have you seen them all yet?'

Wesley shook his head. 'Only a couple. Neil whisks them off for conservation before I get a chance to have a look. What's the score, then, Neil?'

'Seven so far... a few to go. We're making sure there's

someone on the site day and night. We don't want any of Jesse's descendants to disappear, do we?'

'Who gets the graveyard shift?'

'Squirrel and his mates. He doesn't mind acting as unpaid caretaker. Did you get my message?'

'I got it but I didn't understand it,' said Wesley reproachfully.

Neil leaned forward, winking at Dr Parsons, who gave an excited giggle. 'I've got into the Manor . . . set myself up in the muniment room to go through all the old manor records. Thewlis didn't even know the stuff was there. There are account books going back to 1415, what looks like all the records of the manor court, letters . . . In fact there's so much I think I'll need some help. Fancy having a quick look now, Wes? In your job you'll be used to sifting through evidence.'

Wesley looked at his watch, then at Gerry Heffernan, who was looming towards them, laden with drinks from the bar. 'I don't think I've got time.'

'Time for what?' Heffernan had overheard.

'Going up to the Manor.'

'On the contrary, Wes. I think we should take every opportunity to get our feet under the table at that Manor.'

'Any particular reason?'

'It's just that it happens to be the last place Pauline Brent was seen alive. Let's not forget that.' Heffernan turned to Neil. 'Is Squirrel around?'

'He won't be far away.'

'Right. After we've drunk these we can pay him a visit. Then you, Wes, can go and see what Mr Thewlis has got to hide in that Manor of his.'

Wesley looked at his watch again. Quarter to six. Pam would not be pleased.

Squirrel sat on a low branch. Behind him was a thin, grubby girl, similarly dressed, her hair arranged in mousey dreadlocks. He introduced her as Earth. She stared at the two policemen with some hostility until it was explained to her that Wesley was a mate of Neil's and that they had no interest whatsoever in evicting them from their leafy perches.

'I've been wanting to talk to you,' said Squirrel, the good citizen. 'You know that lad . . . the one that disappeared. Well,

Earth here saw him on Saturday night.'

'What time was this?' asked Wesley gently, not wishing to alarm the timid creature.

Earth shrugged. 'It was dark by then but there was a good moon.' Her accent was unexpectedly Yorkshire. 'He had long hair tied back in a ponytail and he was wearing a T-shirt. I saw him walking past the site with someone else ... a man, or at least I think it was a man.'

'Can you describe the man he was with?'

'No. It was just a figure, wearing one of those weatherproof coats people wear for sailing ... dark-coloured ... had the hood up.'

'Was he tall ... short ... fat ... thin?'

'I couldn't tell. But the boy was trying to keep up with him ... he was walking fast.'

'Thanks, Earth. You've been very helpful.'

The girl nodded earnestly and disappeared into the foliage.

'I'm off back to the incident room,' Heffernan announced. 'You go and see the lie of the land at the Manor, Wes, then if I were you I'd get off home ... remind your Pam what you look like.'

The inspector lumbered off across the treacherous terrain of the dig, narrowly avoiding falling into a particularly deep trench. Groups of fresh-faced archaeology students watched him with undisguised curiosity. Wesley stood there beneath the trees, torn between a desire to explore the mysteries of the muniment room and his need to get home to Pam. Curiosity won. He turned to Neil. 'Are you going to show me this room, then?'

'No worries.' Neil chuckled. 'I reckon Thewlis thinks archaeologists are one step below dung beetles on the evolutionary ladder. I can see him gritting his teeth every time he passes me. At least you get to the muniment room from outside so we don't tread dirt into his precious antique rugs.'

'I think you're enjoying this,' Wesley observed. He knew Neil of old.

'Too right I am.'

The Manor came into view and Wesley admired it afresh. He hoped Philip Thewlis appreciated it: it was a house to be loved rather than treated as a financial investment. Neil led him round to the back, produced a large key and opened an ancient door set into a wall in what must have been the humbler domestic section of the house. He stepped inside, beckoning Wesley to follow. The muniment room was small and stone-lined, the only natural light coming from a small barred window. This had been a storeroom for the manor documents, not a room for everyday use. Large wooden cupboards punctuated the walls, some open to reveal books, papers and ledgers inside.

'This place is amazing,' said Neil earnestly. 'There are records here going back to when the house was built ... 1415 or thereabouts. There are all the accounts for any later building works, and the household accounts of the de Stoke family. There's stuff going back to the time of the Wars of the Roses. Look at all these. They're so well preserved.' He opened one of the cupboards; the door creaked dangerously. Inside were rolls of parchment, neatly laid in rows. 'I haven't had a good look at them yet. Know what they are?'

'Manorial court rolls. We had a look at some in the county archives when we were students, remember.'

Neil looked embarrassed. He sometimes forgot their shared studies now that Wesley was firmly established in the police force. 'I could really do with some help to go through them. There's so much here.'

'Don't look at me,' said Wesley, slightly alarmed. 'I've got two murders already, without a load of medieval misdemeanours to deal with.'

'But if we could find out about the woman who's buried at the crossroads ... Well, don't you want to know?' Neil asked challengingly.

Wesley sighed and nodded. He couldn't argue with that.

It was after half past eight when Wesley arrived home. He parked the car sheepishly in the drive and let himself into the house. Everything was quiet. Michael wasn't screaming and he couldn't smell his dinner burning in the oven. Maybe that was a good sign.

He could hear voices coming from the living room; women's voices. Intrigued, he pushed open the door. Pam was sitting talking to another, dark-haired, woman. They both turned round.

'Wesley, this is Anne. Anne, this is my husband, Wesley.'

Anne smiled, looking him up and down. 'Glad to meet you, Wesley. I've heard a lot about you. Archaeologist turned

142

policeman, I believe . . . Tradmouth's answer to Indiana Jones.'

Wesley laughed and assured Anne that there wasn't much call for Hollywood action antics in Tradmouth CID. He had taken an instant liking to Anne . . . and the fact that Pam was unlikely to scold him for his lateness in front of her added to the favourable impression. The two hours spent with Neil going through dusty parchments in the muniment room of Stokeworthy Manor had left him feeling hungry. Emboldened by Anne's presence, he asked if there was anything to eat and was told that his dinner was in the microwave.

As Wesley ate his lasagne in the kitchen, he felt a glow of domestic satisfaction. The baby wasn't howling and his wife was being understanding and cheerful: things were looking up . . . at least until Anne left. He joined the women in the living room with fresh confidence.

'I hear you're working in Stokeworthy at the moment, Wesley,' said Anne, making conversation.

'Yes. We've had a couple of suspicious deaths there. We've had to set up an incident room in the village hall.'

'The Manor was owned by the de Stoke family, wasn't it?'

Wesley looked up, surprised. 'That's right. A friend of mine is in charge of a dig there.'

'Pam was telling me,' said Anne with a meaningful look at Pam.

'He's discovered all sorts of old documents about the de Stokes in the muniment room of the Manor.'

Anne leaned forward. 'I work part time in Tradmouth library, and a man came in a few weeks ago asking if we had any of the old court records of Stokeworthy Manor.'

'Historian, was he?'

'No. He said he was doing some research into his family. Now what was his name? It was a double-barrelled name . . . Stoke-something.'

'Stoke-Brown? Charles Stoke-Brown?' suggested Wesley, suddenly interested.

'Yes. That's right. Charles Stoke-Brown.'

Michael Peterson had slept through the night, an unprecedented achievement. Wesley awoke refreshed, but Pam, as she put the breakfast cereal into bowls, looked as tired as she normally did.

She hadn't been able to sleep, she explained, but Wesley didn't question her further. Something was bothering her, but whatever it was there was little he could do. He had two murders to investigate.

When he reached the incident room he found Gerry Heffernan pacing up and down like a frustrated animal. 'They've got no record of her, Wes. I rang the Home Office and they've no record of anyone called Pauline Brent being in any prison at any time, let alone being released from that particular women's open prison fifteen years back.'

'Then she must have changed her name when she got out; started a new life.'

'Do you think I haven't thought of that? I asked them to get me a list of all the women released from prison around that time. They said they'd get back to me,' Heffernan growled, impatient to be fed the information. 'They said it might take some time.'

'Has it occurred to you that if she'd changed her name then it must have been quite well known? A notorious, well-reported murder case, perhaps?'

'Not some poor woman who hit her husband over the head with a rolling pin too hard when she caught him having it off with his secretary?'

'It was only a suggestion.'

'You could have a point, though.' Heffernan sighed. 'We'll just have to wait, I suppose. How did you get on at the Manor last night? Did you see Mr Thewlis?'

'No. We were strictly tradesman's entrance. We didn't go into the main house.'

'Pity. I would have liked to have known how he reacted when a member of the local constabulary turned up unannounced. Did you find anything interesting?'

'There was too much stuff to take in all at once. There's bundles of documents . . . piles of court records. And most of it's in Latin. I thought I'd leave Neil to it.'

'Very wise. I've been thinking, Wes. Do you fancy nipping up to Plymouth to have a word with this ex-wife of Stoke-Brown's? I'm not happy about this boyfriend of Pauline Brent's . . . not happy at all.'

'I've been thinking the same myself. A friend of Pam's who works in Tradmouth library told me that Stoke-Brown came in asking questions about the Manor. He claimed to be related to the family that used to own it, the de Stokes. It's probably got nothing to do with the investigation but . . .'

Gerry Heffernan scratched his head. 'I don't care if he claims to have a great-aunt who fought at the Battle of Hastings, if someone lies to us about his whereabouts in the course of a murder investigation then I want to know why.' He looked at his watch. 'Get on to Stoke-Brown's ex-wife's local nick, will you. Tell them we're on our way.'

Wesley made no reply. He looked at the telephone. He would ring Pam later with the unwelcome news that it was going to be yet another long day. 'What about D'estry?' he said, sorting through his mind for unfinished tasks.

'He'll wait. We can have a word later.'

Heffernan disappeared from view behind his partition as Rachel Tracey, looking offensively alert, marched into the incident room. She wore a crisp navy blue suit and her fair hair hung loose around her shoulders. Wesley looked up and smiled. She rewarded him with a wink. 'Message for the inspector,' she whispered as she passed by. 'Mrs Green wants to see him.'

Wesley raised his eyebrows and nodded.

A telephone rang on a nearby desk and was answered by WPC Trish Walton. 'Sarge,' she called over to Wesley. 'It's Steve. He says to get down to the creek right away. He thinks he's found the murder weapon.'

'He . . .?' mumbled Heffernan emerging from his den. 'Him and half a dozen SOCOs more like. Whereabouts on the creek?'

'At the end of the path leading from the Manor grounds, he said.'

'Okay. Come on, Wes. Let's get down there and see what he's come up with.'

'Aren't you going to see Mrs Green, sir?'

Wesley could have sworn he saw the inspector blush. 'Er, it'll have to wait, Wes. I'll pop along later.' He fixed his eyes ahead, inviting no more questions.

As they walked down the public footpath that forked off the Manor drive, Heffernan began to relax. 'So what have we got, Wes? Pauline Brent was a murderer. But who did she murder and why? We'll have to wait for the bureaucrats to come up with the answer to that one.'

'Perhaps there's someone still alive – a relative of her victim, maybe – who doesn't think she paid for what she did.'

'The bring-back-hanging lobby?'

'That'd fit with the fact that she was hanged, wouldn't it?'

'But who?'

'Her lover's alibi's dodgy . . . I'd say he's our main man at the moment. D'estry could be in the frame but he says he was with Monica, and unless we get a witness who saw him we can't prove otherwise. I'd be interested to know what he was up to on Saturday night when Lee disappeared.'

'Are we still assuming it's a man?'

'I think so. A woman wouldn't have had the strength to haul her up into that tree . . . unless she was very athletic. Any other suspects? Philip Thewlis?'

'Again, it's a matter of finding a link. He seemed quite happy for us to talk to Gemma and his wife, so we've no reason to suspect he's lying, have we?' Wesley shook his head. The inspector had a point. 'And let's not forget Lee Telford,' Heffernan continued. 'If my theory is right, the murderer was out and about at around ten o'clock on Saturday looking for the only witness with a view to getting rid of him. And according to Squirrel's friend, Earth, the killer was a man wearing a coat with the hood up . . . on a warm night,' he added significantly. 'And Lee trusted him . . . followed him. A weatherproof coat . . . we're looking for someone who owns a boat. That just about covers most of the weekenders round this area.'

'Or he goes sailing on someone else's . . . or he just buys expensive sportswear because it looks good. I bet most owners of training shoes don't take regular exercise,' Wesley said philosophically.

'I can see Julian D'estry coming into that category, can't you?'

'Mmm.' Wesley walked on for a few minutes, deep in thought. After a while he spoke. 'I don't think this is a revenge killing. He's not righting a wrong . . . he's willing to kill an innocent witness himself to cover his tracks. He's not consumed with a righteous passion for justice . . . he's clever, ruthless.'

'D'estry again. He's an arrogant sod . . . shouldn't think he's well endowed in the conscience department.'

'That's if Lee was killed by the same man,' Wesley mused. 'He was into drugs, remember. If he got on the wrong side of a dealer

. . . But then, according to Gaz, he got his drugs in Morbay. And he's small fry, so I can't see the dealer coming all this way . . .'

'Fair enough, Wes. You're probably right. I wish these civil servants'd hurry themselves up. I can't wait to hear what Pauline was supposed to have done. I would have guessed at something domestic myself . . . killing an abusive boyfriend or father.'

'I'm not even going to speculate, sir. Appearances can be deceptive,' said Wesley thoughtfully.

They reached the creek. White-overalled scenes-of-crime officers were going about their work on the muddy sand, oblivious to the new arrivals. Steve Carstairs was standing watching them, his hands in the pockets of his Armani trousers. He looked pleased with himself. When he saw the inspector he straightened himself up and tried to look as though he was doing some work. He nodded coolly to Wesley.

'We've found what looks like the murder weapon, sir. Someone had tried to clean it up by dipping it in the water but it still had some blood and hair on it. I spotted it,' he crowed. 'I remembered the shape of the thing that had made the head wound and put two and two together.'

Steve's efforts at addition weren't often successful, but this time he had surpassed himself. Lying in a large plastic bag was an oar. When Wesley looked at it, Steve's reasoning became obvious. The killer had held it and taken a swing at Lee. The triangular section at the business end of the oar had met his head with full force. It would have taken little effort then to haul the unconscious boy into the water. By Heffernan's calculations the tide was high when Lee had taken his last walk: easy to dispose of a body in the creek when the currents would obligingly carry away the evidence. Had the murderer known this? he wondered.

'Who owns this rowing boat, Steve?' Heffernan asked.

'It belongs to the Manor, sir. But anyone can get to this part of the creek.'

The inspector turned away, disgruntled.

Wesley caught Steve's resentful eye. He tried a smile. 'Well done, Steve.' He thought a little fence-mending wouldn't go amiss. Steve nodded curtly and began to study his feet.

'Pity the tide's been in and out a few times . . . no footprints,' said Heffernan, surveying the ground. It was a dull day but the grey sky was still bright. He shielded his eyes and looked out across the water. 'Nice boat,' he said, pointing to a small, sleek cabin cruiser anchored in the deep channel running down the middle of the creek. 'Wonder who she belongs to.'

'Has Philip Thewlis got a boat?' asked Wesley.

'Oh, aye. He's got a boat, all right ... a whacking great gin palace which I know for a fact is berthed in Tradmouth harbour – nowhere near the *Rosie May*, I'm glad to say. It's too big to get down here. That doesn't mean he doesn't have another one, though ... a little runabout.'

'You think that could be his?'

'Well, he's got a rowing boat ... why not a cabin cruiser on the creek? We could always ask.'

'We could ...' Wesley said, tentative. Philip Thewlis, acquaintance of the Chief Constable, was hardly a man who would take kindly to too many unannounced visits. 'Are you going to ring Mrs Green, find out what she wants to talk about?'

Heffernan's expression changed. 'I'll do it later, Wes. No rush. Come on, let's go and see if your mate Neil's up at the Manor.'

He nodded to Steve and marched off down the path. Wesley followed. Steve was more than capable of seeing to things at the creek. Besides, he had to stop his boss doing anything that might cause questions to be asked in places higher than Gerry Heffernan was used to.

Wesley led the way round to the muniment room but they found it locked. Neil would be at the dig. Then Heffernan said the words he was dreading. 'We're in no hurry to get off to Plymouth, are we? Why don't we pay Mr Thewlis a little visit while we're here?'

'Is that wise, sir?'

'Don't let yourself be intimidated by wealth and power, Wesley. My old mum always used to say that if you were scared of anyone the thing to do was to imagine them on the toilet.'

'I'll bear that in mind, sir.' Wesley tried his best not to laugh. Heffernan's words had conjured up all sorts of inappropriate mental images. He lifted the huge iron knocker on the Manor's great oak door and let it fall. He looked up and noticed the carved coat of arms above the door ... the eagle and the ship. He had seen it in Stoke-Brown's studio: the arms of the de Stokes.

It was a full minute before the door was opened by Caroline Thewlis. She smiled, a practised smile to charm those of whom she was unsure. 'Please come in, Inspector. My husband's not in, I'm afraid, but if I can help in any way . . .'

'That's very good of you, madam, but we won't bother you. If you could just confirm that you own that rowing boat that's tied up on the bank at the end of the public footpath . . .'

'I believe we do,' she said with tolerant amusement. 'Why?'

'It's just that one of your oars was used as a murder weapon.'

'I thought that poor woman was hanged or something . . .'

'There's been another murder since then, madam. A young man was knocked unconscious with the oar and then drowned. He was found downstream but our forensic experts are sure that . . .'

'Oh dear, Inspector. This is really most distressing,' Mrs Thewlis said conventionally.

'Did you happen to see a young man walking with another man, possibly wearing a dark weatherproof coat, on Saturday night, about ten o'clock? The light would be fading by then, of course, but . . .'

'No. I'm sorry. I was here all night but I saw nothing.'

'Who else was in the house?'

'My husband. The children. The nanny. We were having a quiet weekend. With the life my husband leads, quiet family weekends are precious, believe me.'

'Do you own the cabin cruiser anchored in the creek? *The Pride of de Stoke*?'

'Yes.'

'Strange name.'

'My husband's idea. The de Stokes owned this house in the Middle Ages, I believe. There's some long-haired archaeologist delving in our archives at the moment. I don't know if he'll come up with anything interesting.'

Heffernan looked at Wesley. 'I'm sure he will, madam. Thank you for your time.'

The two policemen turned to go, walking slowly down the gravel drive towards the village. Caroline Thewlis watched them, then shut the door slowly.

She leaned on the door for a few moments, thinking. The children were out at friends and their nanny was upstairs. Caroline climbed the stairs to Gemma's room and pushed the door. It opened slowly. The young woman inside was lying on the bed reading a magazine, the headphones of a Walkman obliterating all sound. The movement of the door made her look up. She took off the headphones, watching her employer nervously.

Caroline strolled casually into the room, looking around. Gemma Matherley's eyes followed her, wary. 'What do you want?' she asked. 'I'm going for the kids at three . . . that's what was arranged,' she added warily.

Caroline gave a slow smile. 'Don't play the innocent.' She sat down by Gemma and touched her shoulder. 'I know all about you and him. I even know what you two get up to in my bed. When Philip first introduced me to him I thought he was such a gentleman . . . just shows how wrong you can be.'

Gemma looked up, alarmed, then, having no more weapons in her armoury, burst into tears.

Linda Stoke-Brown lived on an unprepossessing modern estate on the outskirts of Plymouth. Gabled porches had been added by the builders to create a cottagey look to the tiny houses, each huddled up to its neighbour to maximise the profit to be gleaned from the available land. The newness of the bricks and the shrivelled sparseness of the small front gardens, their fertility strangled by building rubble, gave the estate a bleak look. Maybe things would improve with time as the vegetation grew. Wesley Peterson parked carefully outside the address they had been given and got out, leaving his boss in the car.

Linda Stoke-Brown was out, but it didn't take Wesley long to establish from the young woman next door, with toddlers clinging to her legs and longing for a bit of excitement to lighten the domestic routine, that Linda worked in the local tax office, just half a mile down the road.

Wesley broke the news to the inspector. 'She's taken the car,' Heffernan commented. 'Not very environmentally conscious, our Mrs Stoke-Brown. If it's only half a mile she could have walked.'

Wesley, mildly surprised by Heffernan's new ecological awareness, made no reply. He was sure he could detect Squirrel's influence.

Undaunted, Wesley drove to the tax office: the fact that they were on police business justified a spot of environmental pollution. It was a modern building, functional and brutal. Wesley wondered if the government always housed its tax gatherers in its most unlovely buildings. The ex-wife, he thought, must envy her former husband's ability to seek solace in art and the beauties of the Devon countryside. She had to exist between the aesthetic wasteland of her box-like home and her soulless place of work.

They were shown into an empty office, where they waited in expectant silence. After a few minutes the office door opened. A woman stood in the doorway. She was slim and against the light she looked youthful. It wasn't until she stepped into the room that the lines on her face and the coarseness of her dyed blond hair destroyed the illusion. Tiny lines radiated from her thin lips. She looked at the two policemen with disdain.

She sat down, saying nothing, and lit a cigarette. Wesley watched her exhale a slow stream of smoke and waited for her to speak.

'I'm glad you're on to him,' she said, the bitterness almost palpable. 'You want to lock him up and throw away the bloody key.'

Chapter Twelve

2 May 1475

Thomas de Monte, the stonecarver, accuses Christina Tandy of withholding a debt. Fined 2d.

An enquiry by jurors who state, regarding certain malefactors in the lord's woodland, that Matilda Tandy and her son Richard are in the habit of carting off the lord's wood and of burning down hedges belonging to the lord or to their neighbour, William de Monte, Each fined 12d.

Alice de Neston and Thomas de Monte, by special favour, have the lord's permission to marry before Michaelmas.

From the Court Rolls of Stokeworthy Manor

'Mrs Stoke-Brown . . .'

'Brown. It's just Brown. He calls himself Stoke-Brown, but it's just a bloody affectation if you ask me.'

'You don't get on with your ex-husband?' said Gerry Heffernan, stating the obvious.

'He walked out on me two years ago. He said he was going to "find himself".' She said this with heavy irony. 'He used to have a good job teaching art at the comprehensive and a lovely house, but it had to be sold when he left. He went to live out in the country . . . to paint. He'd become obsessed.'

'Obsessed?' Wesley was trying hard to follow her train of thought.

'His mother's maiden name was Stoke, and before she died she did all this research into her family tree. She found that her ancestors had owned this village called Stokeworthy . . . the de Stokes, they were called. After she died Charlie kept disappearing

152

off to this village and going off to libraries to look up his ancestors. Then he started on about living in the country . . . how it was a better life.' She rolled her eyes. 'He talked as if the country was some paradise where the manure didn't stink and the yokels danced round the bloody maypole all day.'

'And there was no crime and no EU regulations for the farmers to worry about,' said Heffernan, warming to the theme.

'*Et in arcadia ego*,' added Wesley philosophically.

'That and all.' The inspector gave him a curious glance. 'He must have got a shock when he started living there. He was even burgled the other night.'

'I can't say what goes on in his mind, Inspector. But in the end these dreams – of living in this village and being an artist – took him over completely. He lost a grip on reality and everything went – his job, our marriage . . . everything.' She shrugged as if the whole thing was beyond her comprehension.

'When did you last see him?'

'Like I told the policeman who came to the house, it was about three months ago.'

'Did your ex-husband ever mention a woman called Pauline Brent?' Heffernan sat forward in the plastic office chair, watching his prey.

'That's the woman who was found hanged in that churchyard . . . I heard it on the news,' said Linda, suddenly animated.

'According to your husband, they had a relationship: there were even hints of marriage,' said Heffernan, omitting to mention that the hinting had all been on Pauline's side. He sat back and waited for a reaction.

This was news to Linda. She stubbed her cigarette out violently and stood up. 'He never mentioned her . . . but then he wouldn't. He knew I wouldn't make trouble so long as I thought it was this bloody mid-life crisis thing, but another woman . . .' She drew herself up to her full height, furious and ferocious. 'No. I couldn't deal with losing everything . . . not for another woman.'

Wesley saw it all. She still had some residue of love for the wayward husband, but for him to replace her with another was the ultimate betrayal. If Linda had found out about her rival, mightn't she deny Charles an alibi when he most needed it, as a satisfying act of vengeance.

Linda sat back down in silence, her face set like stone. There was nothing more to discover that day. They told her she was free to return to work.

Instead of returning to her flickering VDU screen, Linda Brown made straight for the ladies', where she locked herself in a cubicle before being sick. Afterwards, she rinsed her face and looked into the brightly lit mirror, which showed up every line and imperfection. Her heart was still thumping inside her like a caged animal trying to escape.

Neil Watson's Latin was good, but the court rolls of Stokeworthy Manor had defeated him. He sat in the gloomy muniment room, gazing at the obscure legal Latin in some medieval clerk's appalling handwriting, and wondered why he wasn't outside enjoying the dig and the sunshine with his colleagues. He was no nearer discovering the identity of the hanged skeleton. The rolled-up membranes of vellum lay on the shelf inside the dusty cupboard, challenging him: they were bulky, about twelve inches wide, and made up of strips of vellum stitched together. Now yellowed and faded after more than five centuries, they held the secret. But the very quantity of the information they contained ruled out any quick discovery. Transcribing the things into legible English could be a few years' work for some dedicated historian.

With a sigh of resignation, Neil turned his attentions to the account books from the late fifteenth century which lay on a lower shelf. Whoever had kept these had at least possessed decent handwriting and had written in clear and concise English.

Being one who had always dismissed any form of accountancy as being strictly for the unimaginative, Neil was surprised to find himself fascinated by the entries and what they told him about the inhabitants of Stokeworthy Manor at the time. My lady, he discovered, had purchased a goodly length of blue ribbon for the son born to her on the night of the Feast of the Annunciation, 1475. A few days later the lord had bought a small pony for my lord his son. Surely not for the newborn baby, Neil thought: perhaps a gift for an older child displaced by the attention given to the new addition to the family. He found payments to Felicia de Monte, a wet nurse, and Alice de Neston, a nursemaid: payments for gifts given to visitors; a considerable sum spent during a visit by My Lord Courtenay, a local bigwig who landed on the de Stokes for dinner; payment to Robert the Minstrel, who provided the entertainment. The account books told the story of the de Stokes's daily affairs as vividly as any chronicle.

Neil flicked through the ancient books, fascinated, resolving to ask Philip Thewlis if he could take them away and study them further. But now he only had time for a tantalising taste, a brief flavour of life in a Devonshire manor house in the late fifteenth century. He picked up another of the volumes and opened it. This one was from later, 1492. My lady's baby son would have been seventeen. He turned the delicate pages slowly and carefully until a long entry caught his eye.

'For payment to Thomas de Monte, master stonecarver, forty pounds. Being for the carving of a great Tree of Jesse in the church of Saint Peter in the village of Stokeworthy to be set upon the south wall there.' The entry went on to describe in detail each of the Jesse figures and their sturdy stone frame. It ended with 'In addition a further carving to be set at the base of the great tree, this to be privy twixt my lord and Master de Monte'. Neil reread the last sentence and scratched his head. What could be 'privy' about a sculpture displayed in a parish church, that most public of places in the Middle Ages?

A loud knock on the muniment-room door brought Neil back to the present. 'Neil,' Matt's voice called. 'We've found another statue. Hezekiah . . . Are you coming to have a look?' Neil sighed and put the account book back on its shelf.

'It's about time we visited Mrs Green,' Heffernan said as they passed the sign proclaiming that Stokeworthy welcomed careful drivers.

Wesley smiled. 'Wonder why she wants to see you.'

As Wesley parked outside Susan Green's cottage, a large BMW pulled slowly out of Worthy Court opposite. The beautiful Mrs Wills was in the driving seat, her aspiring politician husband by her side. In the back sat an elderly couple, the man large and powerfully built, distinguished and still handsome for his years, and a small, bird-like woman, elegantly coiffeured, who stared blankly out of the car window at Wesley. The car disappeared down the road towards the Manor as Gerry Heffernan knocked on Susan Green's front door.

They waited, Heffernan smoothing down his unruly hair and shifting from foot to foot. When the door opened, Mrs Green greeted them with a calm smile and asked them in. Heffernan took a seat on the sofa, his eyes downcast, looking like a nervous and oversized schoolboy. Wesley knew it would be up to him to ask the questions.

Susan Green took a deep breath. 'I've been thinking about a question you asked last time you were here,' she began. 'That's why I called you, Inspector. I guess there's something you should know. I did see Pauline before she came here . . . at least I'm sure it was her. But under the circumstances I thought it best not to mention it. After all, I wasn't one hundred per cent certain and she might have been there for a completely different reason and . . .'

'Please, Mrs Green,' said Wesley gently. 'Just tell us about it and we'll judge whether or not it's relevant.'

'I was a social worker in Birmingham,' she said. 'About fifteen years back we shared a building with the local Probation Service. Ex-prisoners used to visit their probation officer and . . . well, I saw Pauline at the Probation Office. I'd been here a few months before I realised where I'd seen her before. I've a good memory for faces but . . .'

'Could she have been working there . . . voluntary work, something like that?'

'No. She would wait in the waiting room. I had to pass it on the way to my office. I guess she never noticed me.'

'You never mentioned this to her?'

'I believe people should have the chance to make a fresh start without their past being brought up again and again. I never mentioned it because it was likely to have been part of her life she'd rather forget.'

'Is that why you never became friendly with her? Why you were a good neighbour but you kept your distance?'

She looked at Wesley, impressed by his perception. 'It's not something I'm proud of but . . . yeah, I must admit I was a little wary. There is something else I've remembered.' Wesley nodded and sat forward. 'I was in Morbay a few weeks back visiting my osteopath – I've had problems with my back – and I saw Pauline on the far side of the street; I don't think she saw me. She was going into a house. It was divided into apartments and she'd rung the top bell. A red-haired woman let her in.'

The two detectives exchanged looks. Now they were getting somewhere.

'Would you know the address?'

'It's Jubilee Road. My osteopath's at number seventeen and it was directly opposite. The front door was painted lime green ... quite distinctive.'

'Thank you very much, Mrs Green,' said Gerry Heffernan, standing up. 'You've been a great help. Would it surprise you to know that Pauline Brent wasn't the lady's real name?'

She gave a shy smile. 'No, Inspector, it wouldn't. Don't get me wrong, I liked Pauline. But there was always ... something. Would you like a cup of tea?'

Wesley hastily assessed the situation. 'I'll get back to the incident room, sir, to see if there's any word from the Home Office.'

'Right, then. Pick me up here in half an hour and we'll take a little trip to Morbay.'

'Shouldn't we have a word with Mr Stoke-Brown, sir?' Wesley whispered confidentially.

'Okay. We'll call in there before we go.' Heffernan turned to Susan Green, who was standing there expectantly. 'Did you know Pauline was friendly with an artist who lives at the old mill ... a Charles Stoke-Brown?'

Susan shook her head. 'She sure as hell kept that quiet. I'd no idea. Would you like that cup of tea?'

'That'd be great, love,' Heffernan answered with a grin. 'We've just been over to Plymouth and I'm spitting feathers.'

Wesley tried hard to suppress a smile and made a tactful exit.

There was no word from the Home Office. Rachel said she'd get on to them again but Wesley wasn't holding his breath. There was always the Birmingham Probation Office if all else failed, but Wesley had a feeling, purely instinctive, that the address in Morbay might lead them to the truth.

He encountered Steve Carstairs on his way down the village hall steps. Steve nodded curtly. Wesley noticed the two girls, Leanne and Jo, sitting on the wall in front of the village shop with a lost-looking Gaz Sweeting and saw the look that Leanne was directing at Steve. She whispered something to Jo and the two girls giggled. There was a story here, Wesley thought, which would no doubt come out in time, station gossip being what it was.

'Any progress with the Lee Telford inquiry, Steve?' he asked conversationally.

'No, Sarge. There were no prints to speak of on that oar . . . but Dr Bowman rang and said he's had a look at it and matched it to the wound. It was definitely what knocked him out before he went into the water. We're asking everyone who has boats moored in the creek if they saw anything. But no joy yet.'

Wesley was pleasantly surprised. This was the most communicative Steve had ever been without some resentful look or comment. Maybe his experience with Leanne Matherley – whatever it was – had done him good.

As he reached the bottom of the steps, Wesley saw that the group in front of the village shop had been joined by a familiar face. Gemma Matherley, the nanny at the Manor, looked older than her sister, Leanne, not only in years but in her manner. She had a grown-up polish, probably acquired through exposure to a more sophisticated way of life. Some of her mannerisms, the way she held herself, had been directly copied from Caroline Thewlis. Gemma had made good use of her time among the gentry. Standing a little apart from the teenage group, as if she didn't wish to be associated with them, she had a brief discussion with Leanne, then she turned and headed back towards the Manor. Wesley was struck by a sudden thought. Had Leanne revealed anything about her sister's mysterious love life to Steve in the course of their probable liaison? He would ask when he next got the chance . . . tactfully.

He picked the inspector up from Susan Green's cottage and Heffernan took his place in the passenger seat with a contented smile hovering about his lips.

'Good cup of tea, sir?'

'Excellent, thanks, Wes. Nice woman . . . great Beatles fan. When I said I came from near Penny Lane she was most impressed.' He grinned. Then he paused, awkward. 'Er . . . I've asked her for a drink tonight.' He suddenly looked worried. 'Do you think it's all right . . . asking her for a drink, I mean? She wouldn't rather have a meal or something . . .'

'I'm sure if she hadn't wanted to go she would have made some excuse.' Gerry Heffernan might have been twenty years older than him but Wesley felt like a mature man of the world advising his coy teenage brother. 'Where are you going?'

'The Ring o' Bells. Is that all right, do you think?'

'I'd say a country pub's just fine. Just go and enjoy yourself.'

Wesley looked at his watch. 'Do you think artists keep normal working hours?'

'I've no idea. Let's get up there and see, shall we? I don't like it when people lie to us.'

'You reckon it was him who was lying and not his wife out of spite?'

'Didn't you believe her?'

'I don't know. If she'd found out about Pauline and her husband . . .'

They reached Charles Stoke-Brown's studio and hammered on the door, listening carefully for any telltale sound within. There was nothing. The artist and errant husband was out. They would have to come back another time. Wesley turned the car round and set off for Morbay.

Nothing more was said until they reached their destination. Jubilee Road was near the centre of the town. The once swanky stuccoed houses had been built in late Victorian times with the rich in mind. In those days Morbay, just ten miles from Tradmouth round the coast, had been the epitome of the fashionable seaside resort. The genteel had come there for their health and had built the white-painted villas and town houses that gave the town its character. Although half the town retained its relative affluence, the other half, the part given over to caravan parks and the trappings of the cheap seaside holiday, had begun to attract the unemployed, the drifters. Many cheap family hotels had been forced to take in DSS claimants. The place had changed.

Jubilee Road was in the no-man's-land between the two worlds. Fairly respectable but with an increasing number of flats and bed-sitters. The lime-green door opposite number seventeen was easy to locate.

There were four plastic doorbells and Wesley rang the top one. They waited on the doorstep, listening for footsteps on the stairs. Wesley rang the bell again and this time their patience was rewarded. Someone was hurrying down the staircase, and they could see a shape approaching through the frosted glass of the door.

The woman who opened the door wasn't old, probably in her early forties, but she had the look of an elderly pixie, crafty and all-knowing. This woman had experienced a lot in her time . . .

and had seen more. She pushed her dyed red hair back from her face and gave the two officers a look of sheer hatred. 'Look, I don't want no trouble. I had two of your lot here last week and I told them I never solicit. You can have a drink in a bar, can't you? It's a free country,' she added indignantly. Her accent was London, south of the river. She was a long way from home.

'We're not interested in what you get up to in your spare time, love,' said Gerry Heffernan, showing his warrant card. 'We're CID from Tradmouth ... we want to ask you a few questions about one of your visitors. Can we come in?'

She shrugged, and led the way upstairs. Her skirt was short, displaying shapely stockinged legs. She introduced herself as Gloria Bilford, a personal services consultant, and the flat she led them to was on the first floor, large and fashionably furnished. Business was good.

She sat down on the cream leather sofa, her legs on full display, looking Wesley up and down. He turned away, embarrassed. Heffernan nudged him.

'A couple of weeks ago a lady was seen to enter this house after ringing the top doorbell,' Wesley began. 'She was middle-aged, medium height, blonde bobbed hair. She called herself Pauline Brent.'

Gloria Bilford smiled and nodded. 'I didn't know she'd changed her name. Though I can't say I'm particularly surprised ... considering.'

'Considering what, love?' asked Heffernan. 'She's been murdered ... and a lad who probably witnessed it's been done in and all. So if you know anything about this woman ...'

'Oh my God ...' Gloria's hands went to her mouth. 'I didn't know ... honest. I'd no idea she was dead ... oh, that's awful ...' she gasped.

'So you see why we're so interested in finding out her real identity ...'

'You mean you don't know?' Gloria looked up at Wesley with disbelief.

'No. We've been trying to find out. There was nothing from her past among her possessions. She covered her tracks well.'

'Yeah, she would. She said she'd started a new life ... got a nice job ...'

'You knew her from prison?' said Gerry Heffernan, guessing.

160

'That's right. Open prison up near Birmingham. I was in for the usual and she was near the end of her sentence.'

'What was she in for?'

'You mean you really don't know?' They shook their heads. 'She was Pauline Quillon . . . the child killer.'

Chapter Thirteen

14 May 1475
The jury state there is a certain vagrant going about the village
of Stokeworthy. He came to the manor and Alice de Neston,
fearing for the safety of my lady's baby, did chase him off but
does not know where the man went to and did not see his face.

Elizabeth Webster is indicted for using charms and sorceries
contrary to good faith to cause Felicia de Monte's milk to sour
and my lady's baby to sicken. Fined 6d.

Christina Tandy states that John Fleccer be newly returned
to the village and that he did affright my lord Simon and did
take a coin from him.

From the Court Rolls of Stokeworthy Manor

The policemen both looked blank. 'Say that again, love,' was
Gerry Heffernan's only comment.

'Pauline Quillon. She was looking after this baby for some rich
family and it died. She was only eighteen when it happened. Got
twenty-five years . . . served fifteen.'

'So this happened thirty years ago?' Gloria nodded. 'So how
come she was visiting you?'

'I met her in the middle of Morbay a few months ago. She was
shopping. She was a bit embarrassed at first but we got talking . . .
went for a coffee. Then she came to visit me here.'

'For any particular reason?'

'Just social. We always got on well inside, you see. She was a
nice girl.'

Heffernan looked puzzled. 'I always thought child killers were
given a hard time inside . . . bottom of the heap.'

Gloria shook her head vigorously. 'Not Pauline. You see, she always said she never done it . . . that she was innocent.'

'And you believed her?'

Gloria Bilford looked Heffernan straight in the eye. 'Everyone did . . . all the girls inside. It wasn't like it is today . . . you didn't have all these retrials and telly programmes about miscarriages of justice. Once you were in, you were in. But last time I saw her I asked her if she'd thought about reopening the case . . . clearing her name. I told her that if she proved she was innocent she could be in for some compensation . . . you never know your luck. She looked at me a bit strange and said she was thinking of doing something but she didn't want to say anything yet in case it didn't work out. I don't know what she meant but . . .'

'So you think she was innocent?'

'Oh yes. Pauline loved kids . . . wouldn't harm a hair on their heads. She was innocent all right.'

For once Gerry Heffernan seemed lost for words. They were halfway back to Stokeworthy before he spoke. 'What do you make of it, Wes?'

'Certainly gives us a whole new angle to the case. If she killed a child, the parents or relatives could be out for revenge.'

'It explains the hanging in a way. Maybe the killer thought she should have been hanged at the time. But it doesn't explain Lee Telford, does it? The sort of person who'd take justice into their own hands would be focused on that one thing, surely. They wouldn't go committing another murder . . .'

'They might have got cold feet at the prospect of what they'd done coming to light and got rid of the witness.'

'So much hate, Wes.'

'If someone killed your child it's natural to feel like that, isn't it?'

'I suppose so. But it's not nice, is it? . . . reminds me of a lynching. And it's not just hate, there's something else . . . something calculating. Why was everyone in that prison so sure she was innocent?'

'Perhaps they wanted to believe it. We've all heard that Pauline was seen as a nice woman. Perhaps they couldn't bring themselves to acknowledge what she'd done. It was easier to believe she was innocent.'

163

'Now we've got a name we can find out the details ... see where the evidence pointed. I think our priority is to find the dead child's family.' Heffernan looked at his watch. 'We'll see if Charles Stoke-Brown's at home, then we'll call in at the village hall and rustle up as much information as we can about Pauline Quillon. Then we can get off home ... start again in earnest tomorrow.'

'Don't forget about your date, sir,' said Wesley with a smile as they parked outside the incident room.

'Oh, there's no danger of that.'

They found Charles Stoke-Brown in his studio cleaning his paint-brushes. But there was an automatic nature to his movements which suggested that his mind was on other things. A glass of whisky, newly poured from a half-empty bottle, stood awaiting his attention.

He didn't invite the policemen to sit down but leaned against the windowsill waiting, staring at the painting that stood on an easel in the corner of the room: a painting of Pauline Brent, naked, lying on a scarlet chaise-longue. Although the pose was abandoned, the face of the subject was strangely innocent; Madonna-like eyes stared into the distance as if contemplating eternity.

Wesley found his own eyes drawn to the painting as if this, rather than any snapshot, caught the essence of the woman who had been Pauline Quillon. Charles took a long drink of whisky, emptying the glass, and poured himself another.

Heffernan began, blunt. 'Your ex-wife won't give you an alibi. She says she hasn't seen you for three months.'

Charles shuffled his feet. 'I told a stupid lie. I thought Linda would cover for me once I'd explained to her but her bloody phone's been on the blink ... I couldn't get through.'

Wesley thought the man was an optimist. Linda Brown hadn't seemed the type to lie for a man who'd let her down so badly. 'So where were you last Friday night?'

Charles hesitated. 'It was a nice night so when Pauline said she wasn't coming round I went for a drive. I stopped for a drink in Whitely ... pub called the Wheatsheaf. I don't know whether anyone saw me.'

'Were you on your own?'

'Yes, of course. I'd have a witness otherwise.' It might have been Wesley's imagination but he thought the artist was lying.

'Have you a photograph of yourself we could show to the staff at the Wheatsheaf to confirm your story?'

Charles Stoke-Brown reddened. 'Can't you just take my word for it? They won't remember. They were busy.'

'It's surprising what people remember, sir,' said Heffernan pointedly.

Charles rooted through the chaotic interior of a paint-stained cupboard and produced a tattered photograph of himself with his wife in happier days.

'Thank you, sir,' said Wesley as he took it. 'We'll let you have it back, of course.'

Charles drained his glass and poured another drink, waving the bottle vaguely at Wesley, who shook his head. He raised the glass to his lips then, as an afterthought, held it towards Pauline's picture, as if toasting it. 'Here's to the family curse,' he said obscurely.

'You're a descendant of the de Stokes, I believe?'

The artist looked up. 'How do you know that?' Realisation dawned. 'I suppose Linda told you. She called it my obsession. At the time my research into the family offered a diversion from my life as a suburban schoolteacher. Lord of the manor.' He spoke the words with heavy irony. 'The past provided an escape from my dull little existence. Can you understand that?'

Wesley nodded. 'Is that your family's coat of arms?' he asked, pointing at the shield on the wall, the eagle and the ship.

'That's right. How did you know?'

'I recognised it from the Manor. There's one carved over the door. So you know about the family's history?'

'A fair amount.'

At that point Gerry Heffernan decided to drop his bombshell. 'Did you know Pauline Brent wasn't who she said she was? She'd been in prison for murdering a baby.'

Charles stared at Pauline's picture, shaking his head. 'No. That's not true. She was one of the gentlest people I've known. It can't be true.' He took a desperate gulp of whisky.

'I'm afraid it is. Her real name was Pauline Quillon.'

Charles sat in silence for a few moments, taking it in. When he spoke he sounded calm, thoughtful. 'She asked me once if you

165

had to produce a birth certificate when you got married. I didn't take much notice . . . I thought she was pushing things so I avoided the subject. I never thought anything of it at the time but she seemed worried about it. And she'd been acting a bit strangely just before she died . . . said there was something she had to sort out. But it's rubbish.' He waved his glass at them. 'I can't believe Pauline would kill anyone . . . especially not a baby. If you'd known her . . .'

'So you knew nothing about this?'

'No. She said the past wasn't important and I agreed with her. She never spoke about it and I never asked.' He looked up hopefully. 'Maybe she was wrongly convicted . . .'

'That remains to be seen, sir.' Heffernan nodded to his sergeant. It was time to go. 'Thank you, sir,' he said with finality. 'We'll be in touch.' They began to walk towards the door.

'Just one thing before you go, Sergeant.' Wesley turned. 'There's a policewoman, a DC, er . . . Tracey, is it? If you see her would you ask her if she's thought about my proposition? I asked her to model for me you see, and . . .'

'I'll mention it if I see her, sir,' Wesley said, suppressing a grin.

'What was all that about?' asked Gerry Heffernan as they left the mill.

'Just Rachel being offered a career move. Stoke-Brown looking for a new model. Off with the old and on with the new,' said Wesley, cryptic.

'The randy old goat,' was Heffernan's only reply.

Wesley sat down to a meal of sausage and chips. Pam, who had already eaten, sat watching him. She looked drawn and worried.

'How's the case going?' she asked.

'We've just found out that our murder victim was a convicted child killer . . . released from prison fifteen years ago and changed her name. She started a completely new life under a new identity: that's why she's been so hard to pin down.'

Pam leaned forward, interested. 'So you'll interview the people involved in her case . . . the child's family?'

'That's the first thing. We've had those details from the Home Office. The crime was committed in the next county. Dorset – Lyme Regis. The local police there are sending someone over with the file first thing tomorrow.'

'It's bound to be the parents or some other relative . . . just think how we'd feel if anything happened to Michael. I'd happily string up anyone who harmed him, wouldn't you?'

'Maybe.' He looked at his son, who was kicking happily on his play-mat, directing his wide, toothless smiles at his adoring parents. 'But whoever killed Pauline also killed a teenage lad from the village . . . would a grief-stricken parent do that, do you think?'

Pam shrugged and shook her head, preoccupied. Wesley thought it was time he tackled her. Something was wrong and he needed to find out what it was. 'What's the matter, Pam?' he asked gently. 'You've been worried about something. Look, I know I've not been here much because of this case, but . . .'

'It's nothing.' She paused, considering her next words. 'I went to see a childminder today, from that list they gave me. She . . .'

The doorbell rang. The moment was lost. Pam hurried away to answer it. Wesley heard voices in the hall and strained to hear what was said. He heard the words 'any news yet?' and the newcomer reply that she had asked but was still waiting to hear. Pam came back into the room with Anne, the librarian.

'Hello, Wesley. Nice to see you again.'

'Had any luck with the de Stokes?'

'Oh, them. As a matter of fact . . .'

The doorbell interrupted her. Pam made no move so it was left to Wesley to answer the door. Neil stood on the doorstep grinning, a carrier bag in his hand. 'Hi. Just thought I'd bring you up to date with things. Can I come in?'

Wesley stood to one side and Neil found his way to the living room. He stopped when he saw Anne. Wesley introduced them and could tell that Neil was looking at the librarian appreciatively. Anne was widowed, he remembered . . . and Neil had been in need of the love of a good woman for years. There could be something in the air . . . even Gerry Heffernan was escorting Mrs Green to the Ring o' Bells.

Neil turned to Wesley. 'I came to show you this. It's about our Jesse tree.' He handed the ancient account book over to Wesley very carefully. Wesley carried it over to the table and read the entry while Neil explained it to Pam and Anne.

'I wonder what this mysterious carving was. And would you know if you found it?'

'I think so. All the statues we've found so far have been descendants of Jesse . . . just what you'd expect. There's usually Christ in glory at the top. We've still to find that so there's more digging to do yet. We hope to find the whole lot eventually and maybe restore them to the church . . . just temporarily so the whole thing can be photographed *in situ.*'

'Why not leave them in the church?' said Anne. 'After all, that's what they were made for.'

'I think the powers that be would like them safe and sound in a museum.'

'That's a shame,' said Anne with sincerity. 'I'd love to see the statues you've found.'

Neil rose to the bait. 'They're in Exeter for conservation. I'll take you over there one day if you like.'

'Thanks. I work in the library part time at the moment but I'm free on Mondays, Wednesdays and Fridays.' Anne stopped herself, hoping she wasn't sounding too keen. Pam and Wesley exchanged looks.

'Right, then. I'll arrange something.' Neil changed the subject. If he had a captive librarian, he might as well make use of her knowledge. 'I've been going through some old documents at Stokeworthy Manor. Do you know if there are any translations of the medieval manorial court rolls for Stokeworthy? They all seem to be there but they're impossible to read.' It was a long shot, but it was worth a try.

Anne smiled with satisfaction. 'That Charles Stoke-Brown was asking for a translation. He said he was researching the de Stoke family. We don't have a copy in Tradmouth but there's one in Exeter, written by a local antiquary last century. There could be more copies in private hands, of course.'

'Maybe Thewlis has got one,' Neil suggested.

'You can always ask him,' said Wesley with a wry smile.

'I might wait till he's out and ask his wife. She might be a bit more sympathetic to the cause. If I don't get any joy, I'll dig out the Exeter copy. Fancy a drink, Wes?' Neil remembered his manners. 'Or anyone else?' he added, looking at Anne.

'I've got to get back,' Anne explained. 'I've left the kids at my mum's.'

Neil found it hard to hide his disappointment: he assumed he had misread the situation. 'I'd better be off, then. I said I'd meet Matt and Jane at the Tradmouth Arms. Can I tempt you, Wes?'

'Not tonight, thanks,' Wesley said, sensitive to Pam's frosty stare. 'I'd better get an early night. Tomorrow's going to be a long day.'

The constable from Dorset arrived at the incident room first thing bearing two bulky box files. He apologised for their dusty appearance but explained that they had been lying in the station cellars for thirty years. Refreshed by a cup of freshly brewed constabulary tea, he wished everyone luck and departed for home.

Gerry Heffernan bore down on the files like a ravenous lion. Wesley and Rachel stood behind him, trying to glimpse the papers over his shoulder. There was a lot of material: pathology reports, witness statements. Heffernan turned the pages slowly, taking in the information, pointing out the salient details to his sergeant. A six-month-old baby boy had died while in the care of his young nanny, Pauline Quillon. The family's housekeeper, a Mrs Piert, had provided the bulk of the prosecution evidence. It had been a warm summer day and Pauline Quillon had had sole charge of the two children, the baby and his elder brother, aged seven. They had been in the garden for a while when Pauline came rushing back to the house in a panic. The baby was unconscious and wouldn't wake up. Mrs Piert ran back with Pauline to see to the baby, but by the time they reached him he was obviously dead. An ambulance was called and the parents told. The next day a post-mortem was held and the police became involved. It seemed that the baby's head had been banged hard against a tree. There was even bark embedded in its skull. Pauline, the only person present, was arrested, tried and found guilty of murder.

'An open-and-shut case,' Heffernan concluded.

'Except that Pauline denied it . . . and kept denying it. Perhaps she couldn't face what she'd done.'

'Or she was telling the truth. Where were the parents while all this was going on?' The inspector searched through the files. 'Here we are. The father was in the garden dead-heading the roses and the mother was lying down upstairs with a headache.'

'So they were both about. Did Pauline leave the baby unsupervised at any time?'

'Looks like it. Here. She went back to the house to get a drink for the baby, she said. Then she found the child unconscious when she returned. Mrs Piert says in her statement that she was in the kitchen all the time and Pauline didn't return to the house. No drink was found near the baby, which indicates that Pauline must have been lying.'

'Where was the elder child?'

'I can't see any mention of him.' Heffernan flicked through the statements. 'But then I haven't had a proper look yet. Here, Rach, you have a look through these. See if you can pinpoint where everyone was at the time of the baby's death.' He handed the papers to Rachel.

'So you think this Pauline might have been innocent?' said Rachel, sceptical.

'Probably not but it's worth considering.' Gerry Heffernan sat back and patted his belly. 'Get us a coffee, will you, Rach. I need something to wake me up.'

Rachel put the papers back on the desk with controlled resentment. She had not joined the force to make coffee for men. Wesley gave her a sympathetic look.

'How did your date with Mrs Green go?' he asked when Rachel was out of earshot.

Gerry Heffernan did not look the type of man to blush, but Wesley noticed a definite reddening of his chubby cheeks. 'Er, it was just a drink, Wes . . .'

'Have you arranged any more, er . . . drinks?'

'Not yet.' Rachel returned with a cracked village hall cup full of cheap instant coffee and placed it firmly on her boss's desk, spilling the muddy liquid over some files. Heffernan looked up at her nervously and said nothing. Rachel took the statements about the baby's death over to her desk and sat down. 'What's up with Rach today?'

Wesley smiled and shrugged. One day, perhaps, he'd explain the world of gender politics to his hapless boss, but now probably wasn't the time. After a few minutes Wesley returned to his own desk to make a start on his mountainous paperwork, only to be joined by Rachel. She sat on the edge of the desk and leaned forward, excited.

'The brother was there. He was playing in the garden with a neighbour's son.' She thrust the badly typed statement in front of Wesley's nose. 'Look at the name.'

170

Wesley took the statement from her and began to read. 'Well, well. I presume it's the same one.'

'Aged twelve. That would be about right. And look at the family's name ... and the brother.' Rachel's eyes gleamed. 'So the dead baby's family was called Wills ... the elder brother was a Timothy. It would be too much of a coincidence if ...'

'And the neighbour's son was a Philip Thewlis.'

'Are you going to tell the boss or shall I?' Their eyes met and Rachel's already pretty face was illuminated by a wide smile of triumph, all resentment forgotten.

Chapter Fourteen

21 May 1475
For the supper given by my lord for Lord Courtenay:
2 peacocks;
3 sheep, 5 geese; 2 pigs; sundry pies and pastries......£4. 3.6
1 June 1475
Boots for my lord Simon..12.6
Gown for my lady...15.6
6 June 1475
To the priest for burial of my lord's babe........................14.0
For coffin and tomb...£3. 4.6
For masses to be said...£5. 3.4
For mourning clothes...£2.11.8
For candles to be carried...5.6
From the household accounts of Stokeworthy Manor

Neil left his colleagues and students digging busily in the trenches. The site looked like a battle zone. No sooner had one statue been unearthed than another one was being gently uncovered with trowels and brushes. He had never seen such industry at a dig before. Egged on by the quality of the art they were bringing back into the light, and the knowledge that they were making a discovery of national importance, each digger worked swiftly and with calm enthusiasm to reunite the Jesse tree's ancient worthies with the human race.

Neil yawned as he walked towards the Manor. He had spent the previous evening reading the three volumes of the manor accounts that he had taken out of the muniment room and, unable to put them down, had eventually finished them at two in the morning.

The life of the Manor between 1475 and 1500 had unfolded before him as he had relived the visits of the local gentry and gasped at the amount of food they had managed to get through. He had mourned with Lord and Lady de Stoke at the death of their infant son in 1475 and noted with interest the payments for the burial, the mourning clothes and the prayers for his tiny soul. The baby's death had also had economic repercussions for two village families. Not only were the wet nurse Felicia de Monte's services no longer required but Alice de Neston, the baby's nursemaid, no longer appeared on the payroll. There were several mentions of a Lord Simon, presumably the baby's elder brother, the lucky recipient of the pony. As Neil had read through the accounts he had come to the point when the old lord of the manor died – his funeral being a lavish affair with many tapers burning in the church and Masses said for his soul – and his son took over the running of the estates. It was this son, Simon, who had commissioned Thomas de Monte, the local stonecarver, to create the Jesse tree for the church.

Neil found himself thinking about the skeleton, the unknown woman who had lain near the cross roads in the unmarked, unhallowed grave, so close to the Jesse tree's beautifully carved figures. Who had she been . . . and why had she been hanged by the neck in this quiet Devon village at such a tender age? But unless there was something in the Manor court rolls about the girl's death, her fate and identity would remain a mystery.

He neared the Manor, struck once more by its beauty. This was one house he would never tire of seeing. The de Stokes had built it. In 1542, on the death of Lord Simon, who had left no heir, it had passed to a distant cousin. *Sic transit gloria mundi*, thought Neil in a rare fit of philosophising.

He walked quickly round to the back of the Manor to replace the account books before calling on Philip Thewlis. Squirrel hadn't seen him go out that morning so, presumably, he'd be working in his fully equipped office in what used to be the Manor's courtroom. It was a fair bet that the Manor library would contain a translation of the court rolls. It was the obvious place to look. He knocked on the front door, knowing that the tradesman's entrance would be more fitting for one of his mud-stained appearance, but there was no way he was going to play the importunate peasant to Philip Thewlis's lord of the manor. Neil

Watson, field archaeologist heading the Stokeworthy excavations, would use the main entrance.

Caroline Thewlis answered the door, elegant in flowing black trousers and an expensive grey jersey tunic. She smiled and asked how the dig was progressing. Neil, sensing he was on a winning streak, lost no time in making his request.

'No problem. Of course you can look in the library. Borrow what you like. Feel free.'

This was what Neil wanted to hear. 'Are you sure your husband won't mind?' he asked, thinking this was too easy.

'He doesn't have to know,' she whispered conspiratorially.

'Where is he?' As soon as Neil had asked the question he knew he'd gone too far. It was really none of his business.

Caroline didn't take offence. Quite the reverse. 'I've really no idea. He disappeared without a word about an hour ago. He could be somewhere around the house, but ...' She looked at Neil appraisingly and touched his T-shirt. 'It's a big house. You can get up to anything in this house and nobody's any the wiser.' There was a hint of suggestion in her voice. She looked him straight in the eye.

Neil swallowed hard. 'I mustn't be long away from the dig. Er, if I could just have a look in the library ...'

'Then perhaps you could have a little look at my bedroom. There're some rather interesting carvings on the fireplace. I'm sure you'd find them ...'

Neil had thought he was imagining things at first. Now he knew he wasn't. Caroline Thewlis was an attractive woman. He didn't know whether it was the thought of her husband lurking behind the oak panelling which was putting him off or the fact that he felt like the pursued rather than the pursuer, but the library suddenly acquired a new allure. 'I'm sorry, but I really do have work to do.'

She gave a meaningful half-smile. 'That's fine, but the offer still stands ... any time.'

She watched Neil as he made his escape. He could feel her eyes on his back, and it was with some relief that he entered the low-beamed library and shut the door behind him. He looked around. The book-lined room was cosy. A fine Elizabethan fireplace graced one wall and the leaded windows, curtained in warm red velvet, let in shafts of dappled sunlight. The armchairs and sofa near the fireplace were worn and comfortably faded.

174

Neil approved: if he could ever afford a library of his own, it would be exactly like this. He looked around the walls; row upon row of books, the sort of venerable volumes always found in the libraries of great houses. No cheap paperbacks here: if the Thewlises went in for thrillers or bonkbusters they kept them strictly out of sight.

Neil's eyes began to ache as he examined the titles on the wall opposite the fireplace. This was harder than he'd anticipated. Each tooled leather spine seemed to merge into the next. But he had to carry on; be systematic. He rubbed his eyes and continued. There were some interesting titles: county histories, works of local anti-quaries. He was tempted to take them down and see what juicy snippets of historical information they contained, but he controlled his scholarly urges. He was looking for one thing and one thing only.

It was half an hour before he found it. 'Proceedings of the Manor Court of Stokeworthy. Volume 1:1450–1500' was an unimpressive volume but he took it down off from the shelf with glee and opened it carefully. The Victorian scholar who had translated it from the obscure legal Latin had done a good job, he thought. Caroline Thewlis had said he could borrow what he liked, so he tucked the bulky volume under his arm and marched from the library, feigning a confidence he didn't feel. He would let himself out quietly, as he had no desire to encounter Philip Thewlis . . . or his wife, for that matter.

Tiptoeing down the corridor that led from the library to the front door, he passed a door, half open. An urgent whisper from within caused him to stop and stand, breath held, trying not to betray his presence. There were two people in the room, a man and a woman. He could see the woman but the man was out of view. He recognised the woman as the nanny he had rather liked the look of – Gemma Matherley. The desperation in her voice told him that this was no cosy chat. He could make out the odd sentence.

'The police have been here . . . I could tell them I saw you. Why shouldn't I?'

The man's replies were inaudible, deep and muffled. Although Neil had thought at first that it was Thewlis, he now began to have his doubts. The voice was unfamiliar. Gemma moved out of sight and Neil took the opportunity to move off quietly towards the front door. When he was outside he took a deep breath, looked at the dusty volume in his hand and smiled.

'So,' said Gerry Heffernan, leaning back precariously in his chair, 'Philip Thewlis is an old friend of this MP fellow.'

'He's not an MP yet,' corrected Wesley. 'Just a candidate. And his parents, the parents of this dead baby, have got a place next door to Timothy and Jane Wills at Worthy Court.'

'Has anyone been to the Wheatsheaf to check Stoke-Brown's alibi?'

'Yes. It seems the landlady remembers him quite well ... not one of her regulars, she said, but he did chat her up. I think, reading between the lines, she rather fancied him. She said he was with another man. They did a lot of talking, she said, and Stoke-Brown handed the other man a carrier bag.'

'Curiouser and curiouser. At least it gives him an alibi for Friday night. Wonder why he didn't mention he was with someone.' Heffernan's mind returned to the Wills family. 'Who spoke to these Willses, then?'

Wesley had the report to hand. 'PC Johnson and WPC Walton took a statement. The Willses had arrived at Worthy Court from London around six thirty on the night Pauline died and were with their daughter-in-law all evening ... until after midnight when Mr Wills senior and Jane Wills went over to the pool with Mr and Mrs Bentley to complain about D'estry's noise. Timothy Wills was at some do in Bloxham all evening.'

'So the whole family have alibis?'

'It seems that way. Shall we have a word?'

'Hang on, Wes, first things first. What have you found out about this dead baby case?'

'Pauline claimed that she left the baby to get a drink from the kitchen, then when she returned he was unconscious. The housekeeper said that she hadn't been near the kitchen and there was no drink there when she was called to the scene. The police reports confirm this. The father was dead-heading roses ... no witnesses. The mother was lying down in a darkened room with a headache ... again no witnesses. The elder boy, aged seven – Timothy, prospective MP for Bloxham – was playing with a boy from the village – Philip Thewlis, aged twelve, now lord of the manor of Stokeworthy.'

'Where were they playing?'

'In the garden.'

'Then surely . . .'

'It's not what we would call a garden.' Wesley grinned. 'Eight acres, apparently. More like the grounds of a big house. There was a separate rose garden: that's where the father claimed to be. Then there was a wilder bit where the two boys were playing. Pauline and the baby were in a section closer to the house. I've got a plan of the garden here if you want to see it.' He spread a large yellowed sheet on the desk in front of them.

'Some garden. I see what you mean. This Wills family have never been short of a bob or two, have they? Right, Wes. I think I'd like to see this lot myself. I'll take Rach . . . she's good with old ladies. I'd like you to go and see Thewlis up at the Manor. I can trust you not to frighten the horses. Take Steve . . . but make sure he keeps his mouth shut.'

'I think I can handle Thewlis, sir . . . and Steve seems to have been rather quiet recently.'

Heffernan grinned wickedly. 'I think we've got a Miss Leanne Matherley to thank for that, Wes . . . if my informants are reliable, which I'm sure they are. Meet me for lunch at the Ring o' Bells at one. We'll compare notes.'

Wesley nodded. He would have liked to have tackled the Wills family himself, but he saw the wisdom of his boss's reasoning. He looked around the incident room for Steve, fearing that the journey to the Manor would be hard going.

Timothy Wills wasn't at home, nor were his wife and children. He was at a constituency meeting, his father informed the untidy Liverpudlian police inspector who stood on his doorstep, and Jane was out with the children shopping in Morbay. Mr Wills senior was a tall, well-built man in his sixties. In his youth he had been strong and good-looking . . . still was, thought Rachel, who stood behind her boss. Robert Wills had an air of authority, almost of arrogance. He was not a man who was used to being crossed . . . or having his word questioned. He was several inches taller than Gerry Heffernan and stood looking down on him, straight-backed and almost defiant. When the inspector outlined the reason for their visit, Robert Wills's expression didn't change.

'I suppose you'd better come in, Inspector,' he said resentfully,

177

standing to one side. 'I would ask you not to discuss what happened in Lyme in detail in front of my wife. Even after all these years she finds the subject painful. You can understand that, can't you?'

'We'll try our best not to upset her,' said Rachel gently. Heffernan looked at her gratefully.

Robert Wills led them into the sitting room, where his wife was perched on the edge of a chintz sofa, twisting a handkerchief in her fingers. Rachel sat by her.

'I'm sorry to bring this all up again, madam,' Heffernan began. 'But the woman who was found hanging from a tree in the churchyard last Friday was Pauline Quillon, the nanny you employed thirty years ago who was convicted of murdering your baby.'

There was a sharp intake of breath from Mrs Wills. 'No . . . it's not possible . . .' She turned on her husband. 'How could you have bought this place . . . knowing that woman was here . . . how could you?'

'I didn't know, my dear . . . honestly. How could I have known?' her husband crooned, taking hold of her hand.

'To be fair, madam,' the inspector interjected, 'she had changed her identity. We had a hard job finding out her real name ourselves.'

Mrs Wills wasn't listening. She ran from the room, clearly distressed. Rachel looked at her boss, wondering whether to follow, but Heffernan gave an almost imperceptible shake of his tousled head and Rachel stayed where she was.

'Had you any idea that Pauline Quillon was living across the road, sir?'

'No, Inspector. If I had I certainly wouldn't have brought my family here.'

'Why did you bring your family here?'

'It was Timothy's decision to buy these two weekend places. He has known the developer, Philip Thewlis, for many years, and when he was offered these properties at a discount price . . . and of course, it's near his prospective constituency. He wants to spend as much time as possible down here to . . .'

'Quite. So nobody in your family had any idea that Quillon was living close by?'

'Certainly not, Inspector.'

'How would you have felt if you'd known?'

Robert Wills shook his steel-grey head, an expression of bewilderment on his face. 'I really don't know.'

'But she killed your child.'

'That was a long time ago.'

'Do you think she should have hanged at the time for what she did?'

'I really don't believe in capital punishment, Inspector. It wouldn't have brought Peter back, would it?'

'But surely you wanted revenge. The woman was living here quite happily ... and your son was dead.' Heffernan looked at Robert Wills intently. The man put his hand to his face, a nervous action. The sleeve of his shirt fell back a little to reveal the edge of a bandage. 'Did you ever visit the doctor here in the village, sir ... Dr Jenkins?'

Rachel looked at her boss. She knew what he was after.

'No, Inspector. I have a man in London ...'

Heffernan stood up. 'We might want another word, sir ... and we'd like to talk to your wife when she's feeling better.' He turned to go and was halfway to the door before he asked his final question. 'Just remind me, sir. Where were you last Saturday night?'

'I thought it was Friday when she ...'

'Just answer the question, please, sir.'

'I was here ... with my wife, and my son and daughter-in-law and the children. We had a meal.'

'Do you possess a dark-coloured weatherproof coat, sir?'

'Yes. Why?'

'No reason. Thanks for your help. You'll be here when we want another word, won't you?'

Robert Wills, so used to giving orders, knew when he was receiving one. Rachel was sure she could see fear in his eyes as he shut the front door of 6 Worthy Court.

'What did you make of that, sir? I think it came as a real shock to Mrs Wills that Pauline lived here. I'd say she had no idea.'

Heffernan smiled, a secret smile. 'I agree. But it's her husband I'm interested in. I reckon he was lying through his teeth.'

'I understand our pet archaeologist in the woods is a friend of yours, Sergeant.' Philip Thewlis looked Wesley up and down with amused distaste. Steve Carstairs had the good manners to study his notebook.

'We were at university together, sir.'

'Ah.' Thewlis sat back on the sofa, completely at ease. 'You're the new breed of graduate copper, are you?' His eyes twinkled, almost as if he was relishing the prospect of an intellectual challenge.

Wesley wasn't going to let himself be sidetracked. He came straight to the point. 'I believe you're a friend of Timothy Wills, who's standing in the Bloxham by-election.'

Thewlis showed no sign of nerves. 'I've known Tim for years. It's no great secret.'

'Is your acquaintance the reason for him having a weekend home down here?'

'I suppose you could say that. My company built Worthy Court and I gave him first pick of the properties there. As I said, we're old friends.'

'You were there on the day his baby brother died, weren't you?' Wesley said casually.

Thewlis looked up sharply. This had touched a nerve. His answer, when it came, was well considered. 'It was a great tragedy for the Wills family . . . terrible.'

'Has Timothy ever talked to you about his brother's death?'

'Not at all.'

'Did you know the nanny who was convicted of the baby's murder?'

'I must have seen her, of course. We lived virtually next door . . . Tim in the big house and me in, er . . . rather humbler surroundings. But I can't say I remember her.'

'Would it surprise you to learn that the lady who was murdered – the one who visited you to complain about your behaviour with your children's nanny – was Pauline Quillon, the nanny who was convicted of killing the Wills baby?'

Thewlis looked down, deep in thought. He said nothing.

'She changed her name . . . and her identity. When she was released from prison she started a new life here. When she visited you did she mention the Wills family?'

Thewlis looked up. His words, when they came, were carefully considered. 'As a matter of fact she did reveal her identity. I was shocked, of course . . . didn't believe her at first. She began as I've already told you – discussing my supposed affair with Gemma. Then she asked me if I recognised her. I said no.' He paused. 'Then she said who she was. I was horrified, as you can imagine. I told her to get out.'

'Did she say anything else?'

'Before she left she said I was making a mistake – that she was innocent, that I could help. I really don't know what she meant. As far as I'm concerned, Sergeant, the whole affair is finished. There's no point in bringing up such painful memories for Tim's family. They've had enough tragedy in their lives.'

'How long have you lived here, Mr Thewlis?'

'Well, I've owned the Manor for about seventeen years ... one of my first acquisitions. We used to spend the odd weekend here but we've only lived here for the past year. We got so sick of London and moving around. The children needed some stability. And, after all' – he smiled benignly – 'they come first.'

'Tell us about Timothy Wills.' Wesley leaned forward. 'Is he an ambitious man?'

'He was a QC by the time he was thirty-five and now he's aiming for Parliament. I'd describe that as ambitious, wouldn't you?'

'And his parents, what sort of people are they?'

Thewlis looked uneasy. 'I really couldn't tell you, Sergeant. I have little to do with them.'

'But you must have some sort of impression . . .'

'I'm sorry. I can't help you.'

Thewlis looked at his Rolex watch ostentatiously. 'You'll have to excuse me. The helicopter's due in fifteen minutes to take me to a meeting in London. If that's all . . .'

Wesley stood up and Steve, somewhat confused, shuffled to his feet, dropping his notebook in the process.

'We'll see ourselves out,' said Wesley.

Remaining seated, Thewlis nodded curtly, and Wesley led the way back into the hall. 'The tradesman's entrance is down this way,' he whispered to Steve. They tiptoed towards the kitchens. The house was quiet and Wesley wondered where everybody was. At last they reached the lobby near the kitchen entrance, and to Steve's surprise Wesley began to search through the coats that hung from hooks on the wall.

'You can't do that ... the boss said he's a mate of the Chief Constable.'

'Nobody's above the law, Steve.' Wesley pulled an expensive-looking navy weatherproof jacket down from the hook and began to examine it carefully. He turned to Steve, holding out the anorak's right sleeve. 'Does that look like blood to you?'

Steve just stood there, opening and closing his mouth like a goldfish as the distinctive sound of the helicopter rotor blades drew nearer.

'That's it. The last one,' said Matt with considerable satisfaction as the delicately carved statue was removed from its earthy bed and placed carefully on a clean sheet of plastic. 'Christ in glory. Look at the carving ... look at that face.'

The students crowded round to stare at the thing that was re-encountering the daylight after almost five centuries. The sculptor, Thomas de Monte, had possessed a rare gift. The face of Christ, so benign yet so powerful, would have made more impression on the medieval peasants of Stokeworthy than a thousand scholarly words. This statue was up there with the masterpieces of the Italian Renaissance, and Neil Watson, watching from the sidelines, felt a warm glow of professional and personal pride that he had been involved in its discovery.

'That's the lot,' said Matt with finality, climbing out of the trench. 'Jesse himself, twelve of his descendants and Christ in glory. I think this calls for a drink.'

'Have the geophysics team been over the ground again?' asked Neil, remembering the 'privy' carving mentioned in the accounts and the strange space beneath Jesse on the church wall.

'Yes. They checked again this morning. No more anomalies ... well, nothing that resembles a stone statue. That's everything. Do we start on the deserted section of the village next?'

Neil nodded and grinned. 'Yes, That should keep us busy for another few weeks.'

Squirrel and Earth, watching from the trees, punched the air in triumph as Philip Thewlis's helicopter whirred threateningly overhead.

Wesley bought the drinks and returned to the table where Gerry Heffernan was sitting, his eyes closed in thought. 'What do you make of it all, Wes?' he asked in quiet desperation as his sergeant placed his pint of best bitter on the mat in front of him.

'Well, Thewlis was there when the baby was killed. He's still a close friend of Timothy Wills. He knew Pauline Quillon's identity because she told him who she was. I think he knows more than he's letting on. He also owns a dark blue weatherproof coat with what looks like a few spots of blood on the sleeve.'

'It needs tact this, Wes. He's a mate of the Chief Constable.'

'Just because someone's got money and connections shouldn't mean they're above the law,' said Wesley, indignant.

'I couldn't agree more . . . in principle. But we'll have the Super breathing down our necks if there's a complaint, so we'll just have to be a bit careful . . . and make sure he doesn't get away with anything,' Heffernan added with a grin. 'Not that I think he's got a motive.'

'What did you make of Mr Wills senior?'

'A big man . . . strong. He could easily have done it. He had the motive and, if we can break his alibi, he had the opportunity. He might not be as young as he was, but I could certainly see him strangling Pauline Quillon and stringing her up, no problem . . . and he owns a dark coat.'

'Do you think he did it?'

Heffernan thought for a moment. 'I'd say he's our number one candidate.'

'What about his son . . . our prospective MP?'

'Where's his motive? And by all accounts he was in Bloxham at the time of Pauline's death.'

'Yes, and he hardly strikes me as the brooding, vengeful type. Like most ambitious people I should think he's got a selfish streak . . . it wouldn't be in his nature to risk everything to avenge some long-dead baby brother he probably doesn't even remember. I should think Timothy Wills is only concerned about Timothy Wills, wouldn't you?'

Gerry Heffernan nodded solemnly before imparting his next piece of juicy information. 'Robert Wills told me he'd never seen Dr Jenkins.' He sat back and looked Wesley in the eye. 'I rang the good doctor when I got back to the incident room, and guess what?'

'He'd seen him?'

'Yes. He'd gone into the surgery with a sprained wrist a few days before Pauline was killed.' Heffernan took a triumphant sip of beer.

'So Pauline would have been on reception. They could have recognised each other?'

'Exactly.'

'Shall we pull him in?'

'Patience, Wes. There's someone I want to talk to before we make a move. I rang the station at Lyme Regis, had a chat to a sergeant there. He says Mrs Piert, the housekeeper, still lives in the area ... place called Charmouth.'

'I know it, sir. Famous for its fossils.'

'There's no answer to that, Wes,' said Gerry Heffernan as he drained his glass.

Neil Watson leaned over a pile of fresh computer print-outs laid on the desk in the glorified garden shed at the edge of the clearing that served as a site hut. The geophysics print-outs told him what was likely to be found underground: stone walls, hearths, ditches ... it was all there if you knew what you were looking for. But Neil's mind wasn't on his work. The translation of the Manor court records lay at the side of the desk, inviting. He pushed the computer print-outs aside and picked it up.

He had no idea whether the hanged girl would get a mention in this particular volume. She could be earlier ... or later. A bone had been sent off for radiocarbon dating but the results wouldn't be known for months. But experts assured him that the delicately carved marble crucifix found with the skeleton had most probably been created by the same hand as the Jesse tree ... Thomas de Monte. He began to read, starting at 1470, and was soon engrossed in the cases that came before the lord of the manor. Most entries were neighbourly squabbles or petty offences: trespassing, poaching or pinching neighbours' firewood. He thought of Wesley; as a modern policeman he would find it amusing. There were burglaries, muggings by bands of itinerant footpads ... all human crime was there in the fifteenth century. Retribution usually came in the form of fines, whippings or a day spent in the village stocks. Neil began to turn the pages more quickly but came across no reference to hanging. Violence was common, with neighbour beating up neighbour, as was dishonesty. The blacksmith's son, John

Fleccer, featured prominently – the original wayward son. No doubt he caused his poor father a lot of grief and social embarrassment. Murder, however, had yet to make an appearance. It wasn't until he reached the proceedings for June 1475 that things began to get more serious.

Chapter Fifteen

7 June 1475
Regarding the death of my lord's baby son, the hue and cry was
raised and the malefactor found in the house of Thomas de
Monte and given over to the custody of the constable.

My lady's maidservant, Christina Tandy, stated that she saw
the nursemaid, Alice de Neston, at the door of my lady's
chamber with a bolster in her hand and her look was most
murderous.

There is no doubt in her mind that the said Alice did kill the
innocent babe. Elizabeth Fleccer did see Alice de Neston flee
the house before the hue and cry was raised.

The jury found Alice de Neston guilty and ordered her to be
hanged by the neck, this sentence to be carried out most swiftly
by Adam Derring who is skilled in these matters. Lord have
mercy on her soul.

From the Court Rolls of Stokeworthy Manor

Pam Peterson stood in the doorway in her dressing gown,
resentful. Michael was still asleep after being awake half the
night. Why was it, she wondered, that babies seemed contented
with a nocturnal existence ... did parental example count for
nothing? Wesley, who had slept blissfully through his son's
mistimed misbehaviour, kissed his wife on the cheek.

'So what time will you be home?'

'We've got to go over to Lyme Regis to interview a witness. I
might be late. Sorry.' He shrugged apologetically, hoping that his
refusal to go out for a drink with Neil the night before had earned
him some merit points. He had been tempted – especially when

Neil had phoned to say he had discovered something important about the skeleton at the dig – but he had played the dutiful husband and spent the evening at home. 'Are you all right, love?' he asked. Pam still looked worried and drawn.

'I'll be okay,' she replied coolly. 'Off you go to Lyme. Wish I was coming with you. Lovely day for the seaside.'

He kissed her again. She was right; it certainly had the makings of a lovely day. The sky was clear blue with dribbles of white cloud, and the seagulls circled noisily overhead.

When he'd picked up Gerry Heffernan they took the car ferry that chugged across the River Trad and travelled swiftly down the A roads towards the neighbouring county of Dorset, the car windows open to let in the fresh air. Just before eleven o'clock they arrived at Mrs Piert's local police station to find out what they could from the people with the local knowledge.

The uniformed sergeant who had spoken to Heffernan over the phone was a large, bearded man with the physique of an all-in wrestler. He greeted them with a wide smile and a cup of tea. 'You're not from round these parts, then.' He stared at Wesley with thinly veiled curiosity.

'He's from the Met,' said Heffernan jovially. 'But don't hold that against him.'

'You'll find it a bit different down here to what you're used to, then.'

Before Wesley could reply, his boss got down to business. 'So what have you got for us on this Mrs Piert?'

'Oh, she's a nice old lady . . . my wife's mother knows her from church. She won't give you much trouble.' He winked. 'Actually, I did get something for you. Hang on.' He opened the drawer of his desk and began a search, eventually pulling out a large brown envelope. 'I went down to the local paper and they made me copies of these. They're the reports of the case that were in the paper at the time. Here, have a look.' He pushed the envelope across to Wesley.

Whoever had been writing for the local paper back in 1969 had probably gone on to make a career for themselves working on one of the more lurid tabloids. The headlines were short and to the point. 'Killer nanny.' 'The monster with the face of an angel.' 'The slaughter of the innocent.' 'Nanny bashed baby's head against tree, court told.' The story was one of unspeakable horror,

187

obviously to the editor's delight. A young girl of previous good character, who by all accounts was a quiet, gentle creature, had deliberately and brutally killed a helpless baby for no apparent reason. She had seemed a little nervous and excited before it happened, according to a witness – probably Mrs Piert – but had otherwise behaved completely normally that morning. There was no explanation for her act and she continued to deny it throughout the trial. The lie she had told about fetching a drink seemed to have damned her in the eyes of the jury. But she had offered no explanation. Bloodstains had been found on her dress but she could have acquired them when she tried to revive the baby. She had seemed confused, as if she were hiding something. This had been enough to earn her a life sentence.

Wesley recalled the people who had known her in Stokeworthy. They had all spoken of her quietness, her considerate nature ... and her love for children. What had gone wrong on that summer day in 1969? What had made her kill little Peter Wills?

They finished their tea and thanked the sergeant. Armed with directions, they drove to the nearby village of Charmouth, set high above its fossil-rich cliffs and fine sandy beach. Mrs Piert's cottage was easy to find at the end of a farm track next to a campsite, which was starting to fill up nicely with summer visitors.

The old lady herself was tall, straight-backed and capable-looking. She must have been in her late seventies but nature had been kind to her, her only concession to age being a pair of reading glasses on a silver chain around her neck. She wore a brightly flowered shapeless frock with a duster stuffed in the pocket. They had interrupted her housework.

'I thought that business was all finished with,' she said as she led them through into a small sitting room crammed with photographs of grandchildren and cheap souvenirs. She ordered them to sit down while she made a cup of tea. She returned with the tea and a plate heaped with home-made fruit cake. 'That Pauline,' she began, sitting herself down. 'She seemed such a lovely girl. Didn't have no family and seemed so fond of the kiddies. It certainly taught me something.' She leaned forward and tapped Gerry Heffernan on the knee. 'Never judge a book by its cover.'

'Can you tell us in your own words what happened that day,

Mrs Piert?' said Wesley, politely. 'I'm sorry to put you through it all again but it could be important.'

'You say Pauline was found hanged. Best thing, if you ask me. If they'd had hanging then she might have thought twice before . . .'

'So you think she did it?'

'She was found guilty, wasn't she . . . by twelve good men and true. Anyway, who else would have done it? And she told a lie about fetching that drink. I was in the kitchen and she never came near it.'

'What did you think at the time? Did you suspect anyone else? The father, for instance?'

Mrs Piert sat for a moment, lips pursed in disapproval. 'He was a man capable of many things, was Robert Wills . . . cheating on his wife mainly. But why would he want to go killing his baby? It's ridiculous.'

'Tell us about him,' said Wesley quietly.

'Big man, he was . . . powerful, attractive to women. I saw her looking at him and I thought, aye-aye, my girl, it won't be long before he has you up against a wall when his wife isn't looking . . .'

'Saw who looking at him?'

'Why, Pauline, of course. And it's not like she was the first. The nanny they had before her . . .'

'So you think Pauline Quillon and Robert Wills were having an affair?' Wesley and Heffernan looked at each other. This was something new.

'Oh, I'm sure of it. I wasn't born yesterday. I could tell from the looks they used to give each other . . . the way they'd be talking and stop when I came into the room. You can tell.'

'What about Mrs Wills? Did she know about this?'

Mrs Piert was getting into her stride. Gossip was one of the few pleasures in life she had left. 'I couldn't say whether she knew. She might have done but she didn't let on. I suppose she must have had some idea . . . with it going on under the same roof. She was a neurotic woman, that's the only word for it. Always lying down with headaches . . . yelling at Pauline. And she never had much to do with that boy.'

'Timothy?'

'That's right. Little angel he was . . . considering. His mother never took much notice of him ... she made more fuss of the baby. And his father was away a lot, and when he was home he spent most of his time running after anything in a skirt.'

'What was Timothy's friend like? The boy who lived in the village ... Philip Thewlis?'

'Him! His dad did odd jobs for the Willses. But the lad was bright ... and he liked to be well in with the family at the big house – that's why he palled up with Timothy. Always reminded me of that French general ... what was his name?'

'Napoleon?'

'That's him. Scruffy little thing, he was ... smelt a bit and all. But he was a lively lad, needed an eye keeping on him. I caught him with the baby once ... throwing it up and catching it, making it laugh. I had to tell him to be careful but he said the baby liked it, that he didn't mean any harm ... and I don't think he did. Always setting up little businesses, he was, even as a kid – selling compost from his garden, buying eggs from the local farmers and selling them at a profit outside his house. I've seen him on the telly ... always knew he'd go far. They say he's going to be a lord, soon. When I think of what he was like ...'

'Was he very friendly with Timothy?'

'They were different ages, of course, but they played together in the holidays ... the way kids do when there's no one else. I don't know if the Willses approved I think they thought Philip was a bit ... you know, beneath them.'

'On the day of baby Peter's death, where were the boys?'

'Playing in the garden ... in the trees at the back. The police asked me all this at the time.'

'Where was Mr Wills?'

'He said he was in the rose garden.'

'And Mrs Wills?'

'Upstairs ... lying down. She'd just been speaking to Timothy. He started crying when she told him. Then she had one of her tantrums ... said she couldn't stand children, wished she'd never had any. And this was all in front of the boy,' Mrs Piert added disapprovingly.

'What did she tell Timothy, Mrs Piert?' asked Gerry Heffernan.

'That he was going off to boarding school. I didn't think he'd like the idea at first ... but he seemed to come round after a few tears. He was off playing with young Philip soon after.'

'Where was he when the baby died?'

'With Philip, like I said. The police asked all this at the time.'

'So both Mr and Mrs Wills were alone when it happened?'

'I suppose so, yes. I was busy in the kitchen getting the lunch ready. There wasn't time for me to go spying on people. I had work to do.'

'I'm sure you did, Mrs Piert. Just how unstable was Mrs Wills?'

'She was stark raving mad if you ask me. Mind you, it was all her money, you know ... I reckon that's why he married her. Have another piece of cake.'

Wesley accepted gratefully. 'What did you think of Pauline, Mrs Piert? Forget about her conviction ... what did you think of her at the time?'

Mrs Piert thought for a moment. 'She was a good, sweet-natured girl. Not too bright ... easily led. I must admit I liked her, and if I didn't know what she'd done I'd have said she was a lovely girl.'

'Can you see her covering up for someone ... for the real killer?'

Mrs Piert frowned. This was something she hadn't thought of before. She looked Wesley straight in the eye. 'Do you know, I think I can. That's just the sort of thing she would have done. Yes. You could be right.'

Wesley bit into the rich, moist fruitcake, his mind working overtime.

'Would you spend fifteen years of your life in jail for something you knew someone else had done, Wes?'

'It's a matter of evidence, isn't it. You might know you're innocent but without new evidence how do you set about proving it?'

Gerry Heffernan sat back in the passenger seat, deep in thought.

'Remember what she said to Gloria Bilford. I think she had new evidence ... and threatened to expose whoever really killed Peter Wills.'

'No, Wes. What new evidence could she have had? We didn't find anything in her cottage – no papers, no correspondence from new witnesses. And she hadn't contacted Mrs Piert. No, I reckon it was revenge. The dad did it, 'cause she'd killed his son ... or the mother and the dad helped her deal with the body.'

'Would Timothy, the brother, want revenge?'

Heffernan shrugged. 'Can't see it, can you? He's in the middle of a political campaign. Anyway, Mrs Piert said he didn't take too much interest in his baby brother. No. He hardly strikes me as the type who'd brood about something like that. He'd be more concerned with how the election was going. I think we can count him out.'

'So who killed Lee Telford?'

'Robert Wills again . . . Telford saw him.'

'It doesn't fit, sir. I don't think she killed the baby, in which case . . .'

'She knew who did and tried to blackmail them?'

'Or tried to get them to tell the truth. I don't think blackmail was her style.'

'And what good would that have done her?'

'It would clear her name.'

'She was living quite comfortably under a new identity. Why should she want to change things? Anyway, I reckon if anyone killed that kid it was the neurotic mother. It happens . . . any psychiatrist'll tell you. And Mrs Piert thought she was off her rocker. I can just see her going down and throwing the kid around, especially . . .' The inspector's eyes lit up. He sat forward in his seat. 'Especially if she'd just caught her husband in the rose garden having it off with the nanny. It fits, Wes. Pauline didn't fetch a drink . . . she wasn't with the baby because she was getting up to hanky-panky with its dad. The neurotic wife discovers them and hits out at the baby . . . his son.'

Wesley smiled. He had been thinking along the same lines. 'I think you could be right, sir. But it still doesn't get us much further with Pauline's murder . . . apart from hitting the revenge theory on the head. Unless Pauline threatened to accuse Mrs Wills . . .'

'And they closed ranks and her husband disposed of Pauline. I think we've cracked it, Wes.' Heffernan grinned with satisfaction.

'So do we tackle them when we get back?'

'What do you think?'

Wesley thought for a moment. 'I think I'd like another word with Philip Thewlis. I think he knows more than he's letting on. If we can get more information from him about what actually happened that day . . .'

'Go for it, Wes,' Heffernan said encouragingly. 'I wouldn't trust him an inch.'

Philip Thewlis's expression was one of patient exasperation. He sat, apparently at ease, on the Regency sofa in the low-beamed drawing room. But Wesley could tell that their arrival was as unwelcome as a visit from the taxman; a thing to be resented but politely endured.

After a few innocuous questions, Thewlis looked Wesley in the eye. 'Look, Sergeant,' he began. 'I'm afraid I haven't been quite straight with you about what happened when Tim's brother was killed. The police asked me at the time where I was and I told them I was playing in the woods at the back of the garden with Tim. That was perfectly true but . . . I'd bought these binoculars. I was an entrepreneur even then, Sergeant.' He smiled. 'I saved up money I'd earned from various schemes and bought the best binoculars I could afford. I got them from the house and . . .'

'You saw something?'

'Yes. I was twelve, you understand. Just starting to get interested in . . . you know . . .'

'Sex?' asked Heffernan, straight-faced.

'That's right, Inspector. I told the police that I went to get the binoculars. What I didn't mention was that I used those binoculars to spy on the rose garden. Tim's dad was, er . . . with Pauline, the young nanny. They were . . .'

'I think we've got the picture, sir. I presume you didn't give young Tim a go with these binoculars . . . under the circumstances?'

'Of course not. He was only seven.'

'So you're telling me that when you and Tim were in the woods – when the baby was killed – Pauline was with Robert Wills in the rose garden?' Thewlis nodded. 'Why didn't you say this at the time? You could have saved a young woman from fifteen years in prison.'

'At the time I was embarrassed. I didn't want it to be known I'd spied on them so I kept quiet about it and told myself that Pauline must have killed the baby before . . . or afterwards. I thought that if the police had arrested her she must have done it. Perhaps she did, I don't know. Then she turned up here.'

'So what really happened on Friday night?'

'It was just as I'd said. She told me that one of our cleaners, Mrs Matherley, was concerned about the welfare of her granddaughter, our nanny, Gemma. Mrs Matherley had told her, apparently, that I was having an affair with Gemma. Of course, nothing could be further from the truth. I'm a happily married man,' he said convincingly. 'And even if I weren't, I would hardly conduct a liaison so close to home. But thinking about it I can see why she was so concerned. It obviously bothered Pauline that a young girl might be "taken advantage of", as she put it. I suppose that's what happened to her . . . with Robert Wills – an employer taking sexual advantage of a young employee. But we're not all like that, I assure you.'

'Quite,' said Wesley. 'Is there anything you forgot to tell me last time I was here . . . about when Pauline Quillon came to visit you?'

Heffernan looked at Wesley, impressed by his tact. Thewlis frowned with concentration, as though he was making a decision.

'As a matter of fact there is something, Sergeant. She mentioned that she'd bought the cottage here in Stokeworthy because she'd read in a magazine that I owned the Manor. She said she'd been plucking up courage to come and speak to me ever since I moved in last year. Then she . . . then she asked me to tell the truth about the Wills baby's death.'

'She knew you'd seen her in the rose garden?'

'How could she? No. It must have been something else.'

'What?'

'I've no idea.'

'What did you say?'

'That I couldn't help her. That I thought she should go. I had set her mind at rest about Gemma and I couldn't help her about the other matter. That was it.' He stood up. 'If you'll excuse me, I must get back to work.'

They knew when they were being dismissed. But Wesley had one more question to ask. 'Just routine, sir, but do you own a navy blue weatherproof coat?'

'Er, yes, Sergeant. I keep one for when I'm on my boat. Why?'

'Do you mind if we have a look at it? Just routine, you understand.'

Thewlis gave him an enquiring look but said nothing. He left the room and returned a few minutes later with the coat. He gave it to Wesley.

'What's this on the sleeve, sir? Looks a bit like blood.'

Thewlis took the coat and examined the stain. 'It's rust. It had been raining and I left it next to an old capstan in Tradmouth when I was loading some provisions aboard my yacht. It stained. You're welcome to take it away and examine it if you like,' he added with casual amusement.

'Thank you sir. We'll just take it to check if you don't mind,' said Wesley as he took the coat back. 'Sorry to have bothered you, sir. Thank you for your time.'

Philip Thewlis showed them out. When they were safely away from the house he turned to see his wife waiting in the library doorway.

'If they come again, I'm telling them about him, Philip. I'm sick of all this, I really am.'

Thewlis said nothing but marched to his office, slamming the door behind him.

They had parked on the main road outside the grounds. It gave Wesley an excuse to pass the dig. Heffernan could read him like a book.

'Hurry up, Wes. I want a word with Mr Wills.'

'I won't be long, sir. I'll just see how Neil's getting on . . . and we haven't had lunch yet.'

'I wondered why I felt so weak,' said the inspector, who looked far from starving. 'I'll go and order something at the Ring o' Bells and you have a word with your mate. Okay?'

This sounded like a satisfactory arrangement to Wesley. He found Neil watching the geophysics team as they surveyed the outer edge of the clearing, the possible site of the abandoned part of the medieval village. The team of three walked in straight lines, prodding the ground with their machines. Neil turned and his eyes lit up when he saw his friend. 'Wes. I've been trying to get in touch with you. Guess what?'

'What?'

'I've found the case in the court roll translation. June 1475. Remember that baby I told you about . . . the one mentioned in the account books?' Wesley nodded. He remembered something about it, but not in detail. He had another baby to think about –

Peter Wills. 'Well, it was killed . . . by the nursemaid. Come to the hut and I'll show you.' He led the way to the hut where the translation lay on the desk he used. He found the correct page and thrust it into Wesley's hands.

Wesley read. 'Felicia de Monte did say that Alice de Neston was alone with the son born to my lady. She went to the kitchens and when she did return the babe was dead. She found Alice there by the cradle in great distress, saying she was out of the room and had no knowledge of how the babe did die. Alice did run from the house and the hue and cry was raised by my lord's steward, my lord and my lady being from home. The maid was found in the house of Thomas de Monte, her promised husband, and brought back to the manor to be close confined until her trial.' Wesley read on. Witnesses were brought to testify, mainly people like Christina Tandy, who Alice didn't get on with if some of the court cases over the previous months were anything to judge by . . . it was probably a chance for them to settle old scores. Alice de Neston was accused of smothering the child with a bolster found nearby. Alice vehemently denied it, saying she loved the child and would never harm him. It seemed that Felicia de Monte, who was a relation of Thomas, tipped off the constable that Thomas was hiding her. Alice was brought to trial and the full force of medieval law, without benefit of forensic evidence or full police investigation, bore down upon the unfortunate girl. The fact that it was the lord of the manor's son who had died ensured that the punishment was swift and dreadful. She was taken out of the court to the churchyard, hanged from the yew tree by an Adam Derring – possibly a former hangman, who at least ensured her a swift departure – and buried in unhallowed ground at the crossroads. No searching questions asked . . . and no appeal.

Wesley looked up from the book, feeling uncomfortable. 'Poor girl,' he said. 'There's not much evidence against her . . . and what there is is all circumstantial.'

'Thought you'd be interested . . . as a policeman.'

'I am. It was Thomas who carved that crucifix buried with her, I suppose?'

'Well, they were engaged.'

Then something occurred to Wesley. 'Who else knows about this case?'

'I've shown this translation to Matt and Jane . . . and I've mentioned it to Daphne Parsons on the phone. Why?'

'I wasn't thinking of them. Who else in the village ... or at the Manor?'

Neil shrugged. 'It took me long enough to find it. I suppose Thewlis could know, or his wife – if they actually bothered to read the books in their library – or any of their friends or staff who had access to it. Any local historian could know of its existence. That friend of Pam's said that someone was asking for a translation, but there's only one other, in Exeter.'

'Charles Stoke-Brown,' said Wesley thoughtfully.

'That's right. Why?'

'It's too much of a coincidence. One nursemaid is accused of killing a baby back in the fifteenth century and is hanged from that particular tree ... then another woman accused of killing a baby in her charge dies in the same way on the same tree. Someone's trying to make a point ... someone who knows about Alice de Neston.'

'What are you on about, Wes?'

Wesley turned to go. Gerry Heffernan would be waiting for him in the Ring o' Bells. 'Never mind, Neil. I'll explain when I've got the time.'

He explained all to Heffernan over lunch, keeping his voice low, as though he suspected that the walls in the Ring o' Bells were equipped with very powerful ears.

The inspector didn't share his misgivings. 'So you think whoever hanged her knew about this medieval case? There can't be that many people who go rooting through old books.'

'It is an acquired taste, I admit,' said Wesley. 'But I don't believe in coincidences as dramatic as that. Whoever hanged her up in that tree knew all about Alice de Neston being hanged for the same crime back in 1475. They were making a point.'

'Meaning they didn't think she was innocent. That rules out Thewlis, who knew she was.'

'And Robert Wills, who knew exactly what she was up to when the baby died but still let her go to prison.'

'So that leaves us with Mrs Wills ... and little Timothy, of course – our revered parliamentary candidate.'

'And Charles Stoke-Brown, descendant of the de Stokes, who could easily have found out about Alice in the course of all his research.'

'What's his motive?'

'I've no idea. Lover's quarrel?'

'He didn't know her real identity.'

'That's what he's told us . . . doesn't mean it's true. People have been known to lie to us from time to time,' Wesley added with a wry smile.

'Well, he seems to have an alibi, courtesy of the landlady at the Wheatsheaf and this mysterious man he met there. But anything's possible, Wes. I feel as confused about this case now as I did at the start.' Heffernan sighed. 'Let's pay the Wills family another visit.'

They finished their drinks in silence and walked slowly to Worthy Court. There was a car in the courtyard, a large silver Mercedes. It stood gleaming in the thatched quadrangle like an alien spaceship that had found itself on the wrong film set.

'I see our friend D'estry's back for the weekend. Must have left work early.'

A face peeped from D'estry's window: Monica, minus make-up and looking tired after the long journey from London. Wesley raised a hand in greeting and she disappeared behind the curtain. They reached the door of number seven and knocked.

Jane Wills opened the door. She made no comment as she led the way into the living room.

'I suppose you've found out my father-in-law visited Dr Jenkins?' Jane came straight to the point. 'It was a stupid lie. I don't know why he said it really.' She spoke with quiet confidence, almost exasperated, like a teacher discussing a child who has just done something spectacularly stupid. She continued. 'He told us all about it. He went to the surgery and recognised that nanny. It was a shock for him . . . to see her there. Completely unexpected.'

'Where was your father-in-law the night Pauline Quillon died?'

'He was here . . . like he said. I'm sure he had nothing to do with . . . I know him. He's just not capable of something like that.'

'And he was here all night?'

'Er . . . yes.' She sounded unsure. 'Well, he might have slipped out. I can't really remember.'

To Wesley's surprise, the inspector stood up. 'Well, thank you, Mrs Wills. We'll be in touch.'

Heffernan led the way, hurrying outside out of Jane Wills's earshot. 'That's it, Wes,' he said with satisfaction. 'She's told me all I wanted to know.'

Monica Belman got out of the shower and walked, damp and naked, past Julian, who was lying on the king-sized bed. 'I saw those two policemen ... that scruffy one and the rather dishy black guy.'

'So?' After a hard week on the dealing floor, what Monica had to offer held more interest for Julian than the comings and goings of the local police force. He reached out and touched her bare thigh.

'I think I should tell them what I saw.'

'I've told you, it's none of our business. Don't get involved. Anyway, what did you see? Nothing. You hardly saw someone stringing that old bird up, did you? Now come to bed. I need to unwind.'

Monica pushed his exploring hands away and slipped her dress on.

'It's one of them, I know it is. I can feel it in my water, Wes.'

'Which one?'

'The father. I want to get him in for questioning. Agreed?'

'There's one thing you're forgetting, sir. He was the one person who knew Pauline Quillon didn't kill his son. He was with her at the time it happened, according to Thewlis.'

'Has it occurred to you, Wes, that we only have her word for it that that baby was alive and well when she left it unattended under the trees to get this fictitious drink? She might have killed the baby before her frolic in the rose garden with her employer.'

'Killed a baby then calmly had it off with its father? I suppose if he'd rejected her she might have killed him afterwards. But no ... I can't see Pauline doing that, can you?'

'We never knew her.'

'But we've talked to enough people who did. To do that she would have had to be ... I don't know. Cold, evil.'

'There's a lot of wickedness in this world, Wes. If there wasn't we'd be down the benefit office drawing the dole. I think it's quite feasible that she had a row with the father in the rose garden then killed the baby in a temper ... for revenge.'

Wesley, unconvinced, followed his boss back to the village hall. Rachel greeted them at the door.

'There's someone to see you, sir. Lady called Monica Belman.'

Wesley and the inspector exchanged looks. 'Wonder what she wants,' Heffernan mumbled as he shambled towards his desk, where Monica was waiting. Her split skirt had fallen open to reveal a length of tanned leg. Steve Carstairs and PC Johnson, sorting through paperwork on their desks opposite, couldn't take their eyes off her.

'I believe you want to see me, Miss Belman.'

She nodded. 'I saw someone on the night that woman was murdered – the one Julian had words with.'

Heffernan sat down, trying not to sound too enthusiastic. 'Who did you see?'

Wesley stood quietly at the side of the desk. Monica looked at him and gave him a nervous half-smile.

'I was getting something out of the Merc, about half eight. He came out of his place and I watched him go over and knock on that woman's door. I don't think he saw me.'

'Who was it you saw?'

'The old bloke . . . grey hair. Wills, I think he's called.'

Neil followed Caroline Thewlis into the drawing room. He thanked her and handed her the book, saying he had made copies of the relevant pages.

'You can keep it for longer if you like.' She handed the book back and he took it gratefully. 'Aren't you going to tell me what you found out?'

Caroline poured him a cup of coffee from the cafetière that stood on a polished oak chest as he told her, in simple, tabloid terms, about Alice de Neston and her unfortunate end.

Caroline shook her head, horrified. 'So they just took a girl out and hanged her from the highest tree . . . like something out of the Wild West?'

'It wasn't usual, I assure you. Normally such a serious case would have been tried at the assizes in Exeter. Manor courts usually dealt with trivial things – squabbles between neighbours, that sort of thing. But I suppose with it being the lord's son, the steward and the villagers just took the law into their own hands.'

'I suppose so.' Caroline put down her empty coffee cup and turned to Neil, invitation in her eyes. 'I'm sure you'd be interested in the carving in the bedroom. It's set into the fireplace ... and there's some Latin writing on it. Can you read Latin?'

'A little,' said Neil modestly. His tutor had once said he read it like a native. He had hoped she meant a native of ancient Rome, but he hadn't been sure at the time.

'Come on, then. What are we waiting for?' She held out her hand, inviting. Neil wondered whether he was misreading the message that flashed from her eyes. Her husband was out. Squirrel had reported seeing him go off in the Rolls that morning, which meant he wasn't going very far. So when was he due back? He hardly liked to ask.

He allowed himself to be led up the fine oak staircase, feeling somewhat nervous. Things were moving too fast ... and he wasn't used to dodging irate husbands. Caroline flung open the ancient oak door that led into what had been the great hall's solar, the lord's private apartments, a refuge from the sounds and smells of his household retainers. It was now a large and handsome oak-panelled master bedroom, brightly lit by the jewelled lead lights of a large oriel window, a pillar of brilliance in the corner of the room. A fine Elizabethan tester bed, which would have dominated a smaller room, stood comfortably against one wall, its yellow silk hangings reflecting the sunlight. The fireplace opposite the bed was magnificent: early Tudor, Neil thought. An ancient cradle stood in a corner of the room, filled with fresh flowers.

'Wow,' was Neil's only comment. 'Where did you say this carving was?'

'It's over there above the fireplace.' Caroline sounded slightly disappointed. Then a thought struck her. 'Do you think this is where it happened? Where that baby was murdered?'

'Probably.'

'Oh, that's awful, Neil. I'll never be able to be in here alone again without thinking ...'

'When you get a house like this you get the ghosts that go with it.'

'Do you believe in ghosts?'

'No,' replied Neil, matter-of-factly. He strolled over to the fireplace and looked up, his heart beating faster.

He recognised the style, masterly and powerful. This was a block of stone carved with a scene . . . a scene of murder: one man striking another. Beneath it was a Latin inscription. He thought of the vacant space below the figure of Jesse on the church wall. This block would have fitted perfectly. He stared at the Latin, translating in his head. Then he turned to Caroline, who was sitting on the bed watching. 'Have you got a piece of paper? I'd like to write this down for a friend of mine.'

She left the room without a word, as Neil stared at the carving. What a thing, he thought, to wake up to . . . but if the inscription was to be believed, it was put there for a purpose. *Misere mei, Deus*, it said. Have mercy upon me, oh God.

His thoughts were interrupted by the sound of voices, probably coming from the ground floor. He crept out onto the landing passage and stood at the top of the stairs, shamelessly eavesdropping. The first voice he heard was Caroline's. 'You've abused my house, abused my hospitality, creeping around with this little . . . slut. Her grandmother thought she was having an affair with Philip. That woman actually accused him . . .'

Neil couldn't make out the reply but it was a man's voice, low and appeasing.

Then a sobbing female voice, young, local. Gemma Matherley. 'But he loves me . . . he's going to leave his wife. Anyway . . .' Gemma was gaining in confidence. 'You said for me to treat this house as if it was my home . . . you said that when I first came.'

'It's the deceit I can't stand, Gemma.'

At this point Neil heard the front door open. 'What the hell's going on?' Philip Thewlis didn't sound pleased to come home to domestic discord.

'I've caught this so-called friend of yours *in flagrante delicto* with our nanny . . . our nineteen-year-old nanny. She says he often comes here for a bit of . . . extracurricular activity. How much do you know about this, Philip?'

Nepoleon had met his Waterloo. 'Well, actually, dear, I said he could visit the house whenever he wished . . . and Gemma's over sixteen. She can make her own decisions.'

'Not in my house, she can't.' Caroline turned on her heels.

The man's voice was heard now, clearer, more confident.

'Well, actually, I've not told Gemma this yet but I feel that for the sake of my family – and with the by-election coming up – I think perhaps we should end things now. I assure you, Caroline, I shan't abuse your husband's hospitality again.'

'You bastard, you rotten bastard. You hypocritical ... You think you can screw me then just end it when it suits you. If your precious wife ...' Gemma's voice trailed off.

'It's no use telling her. She knows already. I've assured her it's over. She's been very understanding. Please, Gemma, let's be grown up about this ...'

'If you'll excuse me, gentlemen, you'll have to spare me the clichés,' said Caroline, coolly. 'I've got an archaeologist in the bedroom.'

Philip Thewlis watched, open-mouthed, as his wife glided elegantly up the stairs.

Robert Wills was taken to Tradmouth police station for questioning. As he sat on the cheap plastic chair in the interview room, Wesley Peterson switched on the tape recorder and said the required words.

'Pauline didn't kill your son, did she?' he then asked quietly.

Robert Wills shook his head. 'No, she was with me. We were ... we were making love.'

'And you didn't tell the police this at the time? You let an innocent woman go to prison?' Gerry Heffernan could hardly control his indignation. 'She did fifteen years. You could have ...'

'If they had had the death sentence, Inspector, I'd have thought twice about what I did, but sometimes there's a hard choice ... between one evil and another. I did it to protect someone ... someone I knew couldn't cope with ...'

'Your wife? She killed the baby?'

Robert Wills nodded sadly. 'I suppose they'd be more understanding today with all their psychiatrists and ...'

'So you let Pauline go to prison to protect your wife?'

'I suppose it was partly the guilt ... that my affair with Pauline could have tipped my wife over the edge.' The man's eyes were filling with tears. 'That she was driven to do such a terrible thing ... that I was responsible. And now ...'

'Did your wife confess to what she'd done?'

'We never talked about it. There are some things you don't put into words.'

'Do you know who killed Pauline, Mr Wills?'

'I swear I've no idea.'

'Did you tell the truth about you all being together on the night she died?'

Robert Wills looked uneasy. 'Yes ... of course. We were together that night.'

'You were seen calling at Pauline's cottage.'

Wills looked at Wesley with horror, then his expression changed to one of resignation. He'd been found out.

'Yes. Yes, I did,' he said nervously. 'I called because she'd said she wanted to talk to me. I was horrified when I saw her in the surgery, as you can imagine. And I think she was shocked at first. I shouldn't have gone. I should have left well alone ...'

'What did she want?'

'She wanted me to tell the truth ... about what had happened that day. She wanted to clear her name, she said. She wanted the case reopened.'

'Why now?'

'She said that she was innocent and it was time she cleared her name and stopped paying for something she hadn't done. She also said she was thinking of getting married – some artist she'd met – and when she had to produce her birth certificate everyone would know her true identity and ...'

'So you thought about your wife?'

'Of course ... although Pauline didn't mention her by name, she must have guessed what really happened. I told Pauline it was better to leave things as they were. It would do more harm than good to bring up the past again ... and besides, it was Pauline who left Peter alone when she should have been looking after him. She must bear some blame.'

'How did Pauline take that?'

'She said she wasn't going to give up. She would clear her name. She'd seen all these cases on television, she said ... the Birmingham Six and all the rest. She said she was innocent too and why shouldn't she prove it. But my wife's not well, she hasn't been for a long time. I told Pauline there was no question of it all being raked through again. Then I left her. I didn't want to be long. I didn't want my family wondering where I was.'

'Did you see her alive again after that?'

'No. And before you ask, my wife was in all evening.'

'And your son?'

'He was over in Bloxham at a dinner. He got back after midnight. Why? Tim doesn't know anything about this.'

'Are you sure?'

'He was just a child when it happened. We've never discussed it. I don't suppose he even remembers.'

Gerry Heffernan leaned forward, looking Wills in the eye. 'If it came out that your wife killed the baby and that you conspired to let an innocent girl spend fifteen years in jail, it wouldn't look too good for your family, would it? And don't give me that hypocritical rubbish about her being to blame. Think about why she left the baby alone in the first place – so you could get your leg over. I bet it wasn't her idea. I'd say you'd have been prepared to do anything to prevent the truth coming out, Mr Wills. And making it look as if she'd hanged herself . . . that was a stroke of genius. That would have wrapped the case up nicely. The nanny hangs herself in a fit of remorse and nobody ever finds out the truth. You were the only person who knew the truth, weren't you, Mr Wills?'

Robert Wills swallowed hard and asked for his solicitor.

Neil got his piece of paper; an expensive sheet of deckle-edged notepaper from Caroline's personal supply. She sat on the bed watching as he copied the Latin inscription.

'Did you hear any of that row downstairs?' she asked, nonchalant.

'What row?' He decided to play dumb.

'My nanny's been – how shall I put it? – "having it off" with a friend of my husband's . . . and he's let them use this house to meet. According to the girl's grandmother, who cleans for us, he even screwed her in this bed. Can you believe that? Anyway, he's just given her her marching orders, so hopefully it's all over.'

'Is that right?' said Neil, trying to concentrate on copying accurately. To his relief, Caroline fell silent until he had finished his work. He turned to her. 'I think this carving used to be in the church. It matches up with the Jesse tree carvings we found in the grounds. And there was one missing. I think this is it.'

'Then why is it here?'

Neil tapped the side of his nose. 'That's all in the inscription.' He didn't know the answer to her question but he wasn't going to let her know that. Hoping he had been suitably mysterious, he left her. Once he was outside the house, he took his mobile phone from his pocket and dialled Wesley's number.

Chapter Sixteen

Have mercy upon me, oh God, after thy great goodness.
According to the multitude of thy mercies do away mine
offences.

I Simon de Stoke do confess my great wrong in that I did
cause an innocent woman to be hanged for a crime that she did
not commit. Let it be known to all people that I did cause the
death of Alice de Neston, cruelly hanged.

Let it be known also that I did cause this Tree of Jesse to be
raised in the church of St Peter as penance for my sin and
confession thereof.

Translated from the Latin text found on the carving in the
bedchamber at Stokeworthy Manor

'That's all Neil said. The nursemaid didn't do it.' Pam stirred the bolognaise sauce in the pan while rocking Michael's bouncing cradle gently with her foot. Not for the first time Wesley stood in admiration of the female sex's ability to do several jobs at once.

'What time did he ring?'

'About an hour ago. He asked if you were going for a drink tonight.' Pam made no comment but Wesley could sense her disapproval.

'Would you mind?'

'Suit yourself.' She turned away from him, frosty. He wanted to meet Neil in the Tradmouth Arms but he thought he'd better not push his luck. A bottle of wine and a video – a cosy evening in and an early night – might restore domestic harmony.

'Is anything the matter?' He thought he'd better ask, for appearance's sake.

Pam looked at him, her eyes glistening, close to tears. 'It's Michael.'

'What's wrong?' the anxious father asked, cursing himself for being so unobservant . . . so insensitive.

'There's nothing wrong with him. It's just that . . .' She hesitated. 'I'm back at work in September and I thought that finding a childminder would be easy . . . it all sounds so simple before they're born. But then it's there, your baby, needing you, and you feel . . . Oh, Wes, I can't leave him with just anyone. I keep hearing all these stories and then I look at him and I think . . .' The tears came. She picked the baby up and held him to her, rocking him to and fro while Michael gurgled happily at all the attention.

Wesley touched his son's soft baby hair. He understood. 'If you could find someone you had confidence in . . . would that make a difference?'

'Of course. But the ones I've seen so far I wouldn't even consider. I don't know what I'm going to do. We need the money . . . I know I've got to go back. And I miss the kids and the school even though I don't miss the paperwork.' She smiled weakly. 'And I've got the school holidays but . . .' She didn't finish her sentence. She just looked down at the baby in her arms. Michael took priority now. If he wasn't happy, neither was she.

'Something'll turn up,' said Wesley with a confidence he didn't feel. 'We've got till September. Don't let's worry about it, eh?' A drink with Neil would have to wait for another night. He took a bottle of Beaujolais from the wine rack and opened it, his mind on one question. If the nursemaid hadn't done it . . . who had?

Wesley left Pam in bed asleep the next morning. Michael had been up three times during the night and she was exhausted.

He drove down the narrow streets to Tradmouth police station, where he found Gerry Heffernan in his office, head in hands.

'We've had to release him, Wes. His son got some fancy solicitor down from London last night who reckoned we had no grounds to hold him.' He looked up with a sudden mischievous grin. 'We got a search warrant and a couple of our lads went through his things last night. His shoes and jacket are in the tender hands of forensic as we speak. We'll get him, Wes.'

Little more was said as they drove up the steep hill out of

Tradmouth, past the imposing bulk of the Royal Naval College and the less imposing council estate exiled on the edge of the town. Soon they had turned off the main road onto the winding country lanes walled with high hedges and concealing slow-moving farm vehicles round every corner. As he negotiated the lanes, on automatic pilot, Wesley's mind was on Neil's message. The nursemaid didn't do it. He dropped Gerry Heffernan by the steps of Stokeworthy village hall, saying that he'd had an urgent message from Neil at the dig and he wouldn't be long. It was always best to tell the truth . . . or an approximation of it.

He found Neil in the hut, sorting through finds from the newly dug village trench. Neil rushed over to him, took him by the arm and thrust a piece of expensive-looking notepaper into his hand. 'I found it . . . the last sculpture. Read that.'

Wesley began to read and found his rusty Latin wanting. He screwed up his face in concentration, translating slowly. 'I, Simon de Stoke, do . . . confess . . . my great . . . wrong . . .'

'The English is on the back.'

Peeved that Neil hadn't pointed this out earlier, he turned the paper over and read. 'I, Simon de Stoke, do confess my great wrong in that I did cause an innocent woman to be hanged for a crime that she did not commit.' Wesley looked up. 'That's a turn-up for the books.'

'Looking through the account books, I reckon this Simon must have been about five when his baby brother died . . . maybe as old as eight. How could he have blamed himself for her hanging? He was just a kid.' Neil thought for a moment. 'You don't think he could have killed his baby brother, do you? By accident or . . .'

Wesley shrugged. 'Children feel things very intensely. I can remember hating my sister at that age – really hating her, thinking she was getting all the attention. I can see a child of that age, jealous of the fuss over a new baby, lashing out, not knowing his own strength . . . or even picking him up and dropping him, then being too frightened to tell the truth when someone else gets the blame. What was this carving like?'

'There were figures . . . one man hitting another, with the names Cain and Abel underneath. Then this inscription.'

'Can I see it?'

'It's in my lady's bedchamber . . . above the fireplace. Probably taken from the church during the Reformation and put there. My

209

guess is that this Simon was so screwed up about this nursemaid being hanged that when the Jesse tree was broken up he had the statues buried with her ... making up for the fact that she was buried in an unhallowed grave by giving her all those saints or whatever to share it with, I suppose. Then he had that bit put in his bedroom so he'd see it every day ... so he'd never forget. Weird.'

'So how did you get to see it?'

'Don't ask, Wes ... just don't ask.'

Wesley raised his eyebrows. No doubt, over a pint in the Tradmouth Arms, he'd discover the truth one day.

'I'm off to the church to have a look at the Jesse tree frame. I want to check if it's in good enough condition to support the statues.'

'So they're going home ... to the church?'

'That's not my decision. But I must admit I'd like to see them restored *in situ*. I don't know if Caroline would donate her carving. I never got round to asking.' He winked.

'Maybe I'll ask when I pay her husband a visit. Is he in, do you know?'

'I think he is. As far as I know he's not been sighted by our friends up in the trees. I don't know what kind of mood he'll be in. Caroline's just discovered the nanny's been having it off with a friend of theirs – that Timothy Wills, the wannabe MP – using their house as his personal knocking shop. There was an almighty row when I was there. Are you coming to the church with me or have you got some poor prisoner to beat up?'

Wesley, used to Neil's jibes, ignored the last remark. 'I'll come to the church with you. But I'll have to make a phone call first.' He took out his mobile and dialled the number of the incident room.

Wesley stood behind Neil, his eyes on the great frame that had supported the Jesse tree figures but his mind elsewhere, racing with possibilities.

Neil interrupted his thoughts. 'I think it'll take the figures ... no problem. It'll be quite a sight. Must have been magnificent when it was all new and painted.'

'I didn't think you approved of religion,' said Wesley, absent-mindedly.

'I approve of art ... and this is bloody good art.'

'He certainly knew his stuff, this Thomas de Monte. I'm surprised he wasn't snapped up by some cathedral or . . .'

'He was. He worked on Exeter . . . I've checked. Another thing I found out from the manorial court records was that he and Alice de Neston were to be married.' Neil looked at Wesley, watching his face while the fact sank in.

'So that explains the crucifix that was buried with her. He made it. And it also explains why Simon asked him to carve the Jesse tree – it was a real act of penance, asking the girl's fiancé to carve the thing – and put that confession at the bottom. He must have been a brave man, Simon de Stoke.'

'Why brave?'

'To admit to what he'd done like that in front of the whole village when nobody would have asked any questions: he was lord of the manor. It must have taken courage.' Wesley had come across many sinners in his time in the police force . . . very few of them repentant.

'Good morning, Sergeant.' Wesley swung round to see the Rev. Brian Twotrees bearing down on him, a beatific smile on his face. 'Nice to see you again. And you too, Neil. How's the conservation going?'

'Fine . . . I think we've solved the riddle of the empty space underneath Jesse.'

'Really?' Brian Twotrees had been more intrigued by this mystery than he had cared to admit. 'Do tell all.'

'It involved entering a lady's bedroom,' said Neil, trying to keep his expression serious. 'Is Simon de Stoke buried here in the church?'

The vicar was surprised by this sudden change of subject. 'No. According to the church guidebook written in the time of my predecessor, he died while on pilgrimage to the Holy Land. But there's a family chapel over there with some impressive tombs,' he added pointing to the north aisle. 'There's someone in there at the moment actually, tracing his ancestors. We get a lot of that round here,' he said to Wesley confidentially. 'Americans mostly. They have a lot of links with Devon . . . Pilgrim Fathers sailing from Plymouth and all that.'

The church door creaked open. They turned and saw Rachel stepping into the church, tentative, respectful. She walked quietly across to Wesley and spoke in hushed tones.

'The boss is looking for you, Wes. He wants a word with Mr Thewlis up at the Manor.'

'Now?'

'Half an hour, he said.'

'You've got time to look at these tombs, then,' said Neil with a grin.

'That your idea of fun, is it?' Rachel looked at Neil as though he were mad, but followed the men into the de Stoke chapel.

The man they discovered there, bent over a worn effigy of a knight in armour, was no visiting American. Charles Stoke-Brown looked up nervously when he saw the group approaching.

'Don't let us disturb you, Mr Stoke-Brown. We've just come to have a look at the tombs. I hear they're very fine.' Charles looked at Wesley with disbelief. This was hardly the speech of a policeman.

'Relatives of mine,' Charles said. He leaned towards Wesley: his breath smelled of whisky. 'My glorious forebears,' he added with some bitterness.

Neil felt he had to put the man straight. 'Medieval life wasn't very glorious, even for the de Stokes of this world. Most of the time it was smelly, filthy, nasty and downright dangerous.'

Charles Stoke-Brown laughed. 'Oh, leave me with some illusions, please.' He looked at Wesley. 'Well? Have you checked my alibi?'

'Yes. As a matter of fact the landlady of the Wheatsheaf remembers you quite well . . . and the man you were with.'

'Man? She must have made a mistake.' Charles looked positively alarmed.

'Sarge.' Rachel touched Wesley's arm gently. 'Can I have a word?' She drew him aside, but before she could speak the vicar made a loud exclamation.

'It's back . . . the picture that was missing. It's back.'

Wesley left Rachel's side to see what the fuss was about.

'It's the picture I reported missing the other day. Someone's brought it back.'

They all looked at the tiny picture hanging on the stone wall: a tree, its branches bearing strange and intricate fruit. A preliminary sketch for the Jesse tree.

'Well, if it's police work, I'll leave you good people to it.'

Charles Stoke-Brown began to walk softly away down the aisle, as if afraid to wake anybody slumbering in the oak pews.

'Just a minute,' Rachel called after him. 'I saw that picture in your studio the other day.' Stoke-Brown stopped dead and turned to face Rachel, a smile of resignation on his lips.

'Can you prove it?'

Rachel looked at the picture. 'I remember it well. It was on your desk when I first visited you.' She looked the artist in the eye, challenging.

Stoke-Brown shrugged and put his arms out towards Rachel, as if anticipating handcuffs. 'A man's got to eat, Constable, er ... Tracey, isn't it?'

He was mustering all his resources of charm, but Rachel wasn't falling for it. She saw that Wesley was watching with interest. The missing church artifacts had been his case, she remembered, but it seemed that he was letting her get on with it. She recited the caution.

'I only borrowed the things,' Charles protested. 'I borrowed them, copied them, then passed the copies over to my contact. I put the originals back. I never actually stole anything.'

'Who was your contact?' It was time for Wesley to get involved.

'The man I met in the Wheatsheaf. He travels around, looks in churches for anything that looks saleable, I copy them, then he sells the copies as originals to collectors abroad who don't ask too many questions. It was a lucrative little business' – he sighed – 'while it lasted. My contact assured me that as the things were returned to their rightful owner, I wasn't breaking the law. What will you charge me with?' he asked self-righteously.

'I'm sure we'll think of something if we put our minds to it,' replied Wesley. 'Is that why you lied about your whereabouts on the night Pauline died?'

'Of course. If you'd gone looking for my contact in the Wheatsheaf ... I don't know his name, by the way. He just calls himself John.'

Wesley nodded at Rachel, who took Charles Stoke-Brown's arm and led him away. Wesley knew she could handle things on her own.

'Neat,' said Neil, who had been watching the proceedings with interest. He turned to Brian Twotrees, who appeared to be lost for words. 'At least you've got your picture back.'

'Sergeant,' Charles Stoke-Brown called from the church door, 'I had that thing out of its frame to copy it. There's some writing inside but I couldn't understand a word. You're the detective ... you have a look.' With that, the last of the de Stokes disappeared from view.

Wesley looked at his watch. 'Must go, Neil. I've got to meet the boss.'

Neil watched him walk away down the aisle before taking the picture down from the wall.

For the first time in their brief acquaintance, Wesley saw Philip Thewlis as Napoleon after Waterloo rather than Napoleon the conqueror of Europe. 'I don't think I'll ever forget that day,' he began quietly.

'Was there anything you didn't tell the police at the time?' asked Wesley.

Thewlis hesitated. 'I don't suppose it can do any harm now ... not after all this time. Pauline Quillon was quite right when she said I could clear her name ... not that I realised it at the time, of course. I was young and had other things on my mind. I never put two and two together.' He smiled wistfully.

'Go on,' prompted Wesley.

'I'd bought a pair of binoculars and I'd left them at the house. I think I mentioned it last time you were here.' Wesley nodded. 'I was getting bored playing with Tim – he was a lot younger than me – so I went to fetch them. On the way back I was using them and I saw Pauline going into the rose garden with Tim's father. I suppose she could have been with him when the baby died. I can't be sure, of course, but ...' He hesitated. 'I've been thinking about it since your last visit and I must admit that at first I thought the mother probably killed that poor baby ... but now ...' His voice was flat, unenthusiastic, as though he didn't want to believe what he suspected.

'What about Tim? If he was alone ...'

Thewlis nodded slowly as if he knew Timothy Wills could have killed his baby brother on that summer day thirty years before. In the back of his mind he had probably known it for years and had buried the thought deep in his subconscious. Now it emerged into the daylight, discomforting and bleak. 'Tim was certainly in a strange mood that day. He said his mother was sending him away. He was being a bit of a nuisance ... I think that's why I went off for the binoculars. I suppose he could have ... no, I can't believe it, but ...' He paused as if making a decision, then took a deep breath before he spoke again. 'I saw him. When I was coming back from the rose garden, I saw him running away from the trees where the baby was found. When I met up with him he was acting strangely. He wasn't being much fun so I went off home. I never asked him what was wrong: kids are pretty heartless about the feelings of others. Now that I think about that day ... yes, it is possible, it's just not something I've wanted to consider before ... but it all fits.'

'Did you tell Pauline this?'

'I must admit I did hint at it.'

'Did you tell Timothy Wills that Pauline had come to you to ask you to tell the truth?'

'She was dead before I saw him again. But I suppose she might have met him and told him what she knew,' he added thoughtfully.

'And the Saturday night – when Lee Telford died – did you see him then?'

Thewlis shook his head. 'You'd better ask Gemma, our nanny.' He paused. Confession was difficult for a man used to being in control. 'Gemma and Tim were having an affair. He was an old friend so I let them meet here; I turned a blind eye. Caroline found out, of course, and she didn't like it one bit. She thought Tim was abusing our friendship, using our house for ... you know. I didn't see Tim on Saturday night ... but Gemma might have. Shall I call her for you?'

'Yes please, sir, if you wouldn't mind. What about Friday? Did you see him on Friday night at all?'

'No. I believe he was at some sort of dinner over in Bloxham. Has my coat been examined yet?' he added casually.

'Yes, sir. As you said, the stain was rust.'

Thewlis smiled and walked over to the fireplace, where he pushed a button. Five minutes later Gemma Matherley glided into the room, her expression wary. When she saw the two policemen the colour drained from her face.

'Did you see Timothy Wills last Saturday night?' Gerry Heffernan came straight to the point.

The girl nodded. 'He was walking up the drive with someone,' she said quietly.

Wesley knew he wasn't mistaken. The nanny looked frightened.

Rachel was feeling pleased with herself. Charles Stoke-Brown was in custody at Tradmouth, her boyfriend, Dave, was taking her out for a meal that evening, and all was right with the world. She hardly noticed Steve Carstairs as he walked up the village hall steps in front of her.

'Hi, Steve,' a female voice called from over by the village shop. Rachel turned to see Leanne Matherley perched on the wall, hitching up her short denim skirt.

Steve hesitated, only to be rewarded by a sharp jab in the back. 'Ignore her, Steve,' Rachel advised. 'I suppose you know she's only fifteen?'

'Bloody hell. She told me she was seventeen.'

'She would. Take my advice, Steve: leave well alone.'

Steve, thinking of his narrow escape and the trouble he might have been in had things gone differently, walked on, subdued, and planted himself at his desk, head down, studying witness statements.

Rachel was surprised by WPC Trish Walton, who rushed up to her and whispered anxiously. 'There's a lady to see you. I've put her in the boss's office. She wants to make a statement.'

Rachel thanked her and marched purposefully towards Heffernan's lair. The woman who sat there looked up anxiously and pushed her long auburn hair back from her face. 'I believe you want to make a statement, Mrs Wills,' said Rachel as she sat down in the inspector's executive-style chair, trying it out for size.

Chapter Seventeen

15 April 1494
*The jury was told that John Fleccer, son of the late blacksmith
and ordered from the village many years since, did return and
my lord did order him close confined.*

*On this day John Fleccer, having returned to Stokeworthy
after these many years, is brought before the jury to answer for
his wrongdoing in the time of my lord's late father.*
From the Court Rolls of Stokeworthy Manor

Wesley and Heffernan found Robert Wills at home in Worthy
Court. His wife was out walking, he said. His daughter-in-law had
gone out, destination unspecified; and his son was canvassing in
Bloxham. He, Robert, had been left in charge of the children, a
grandfather's privilege.

Wesley drove steadily. Bloxham wasn't far; even allowing for
the car ferry at Tradmouth, they would be there in twenty
minutes.

'His alibi's watertight,' said Wesley, puzzled 'Over a hundred
people including the mayor and mayoress of Bloxham will swear
he was there on Friday night.'

'Yes, but I did a bit of checking myself. Nobody was with him
for the whole night. The do was held in the Queens Hotel. I've
been there for various things – divisional dinners, weddings. The
place is a suite of rooms, like a rabbit-warren. It'd be easy to
disappear for an hour or so ... everyone would think you were
mingling with the people in another room. He could have slipped
out and come back and no one would be any the wiser.'

'So we're making an arrest?'

'I've always wanted to arrest a politician,' Heffernan said, thoughtfully. 'It's a career best for me, this.'

They drew up by the harbour. Standing on a raised platform in front of a small crowd was a tall, fair-haired man with a large rosette in the buttonhole of his expensively tailored suit. He spoke passionately, his hand gestures emphasising each point. The crowd veered between jeering and applause. The two policemen got out of the car and stood at the back, watching and waiting.

They could tell when Timothy Wills had spotted them. He began to stammer, losing his train of thought. Eventually he wound up his speech, trying to retrieve the situation with a hearty ending. The rosetted men with him, presumably local party officials, muttered among themselves as Timothy pushed through the crowd, attempting to smile and shake the occasional hand as he went. He was soon at Heffernan's side.

'What the hell are you doing here?'

'I could say it's a public meeting and I'm a member of the public but that wouldn't be strictly true, sir.' The inspector put his hand on Wills's shoulder. 'Timothy Wills, I'm arresting you for the murder of Pauline Quillon. You don't have to say anything but . . .'

Wills looked at Heffernan in horror as he finished the caution, shaking his head. 'You're making a mistake. You've got the wrong man,' was all he could say as he climbed into the back of the car.

After they had been questioning Timothy Wills for an hour at Tradmouth police station, they felt in need of a break. They returned to the CID office and Wesley poured them coffee from the percolator in the corner of the room.

'He's stubborn, Wes. He'll be a hard one to break. And what were all those questions you were asking about his baby brother?'

'I think Timothy Wills killed his baby brother. He was upset that day, he'd just been told he was being sent away to school. I think he regarded that as rejection . . . and his mother didn't help by telling him she'd wished he and his brother had never been born. Philip Thewlis went off to fetch his shiny new pair of binoculars; the nanny was doing a bit of nature study with Robert Wills in the rose garden. She'd left the baby supposedly asleep and was lured off for a bit of hanky-panky. I think young Tim was angry at everything that had happened, maybe blaming the new baby for his troubles, especially if the mother had suffered from postnatal depression since the birth. Everything had changed since the baby came into the house ... and there he was, alone and vulnerable. I think Timothy took his anger out on the baby. And Thewlis saw him running away from the trees.'

Heffernan was silent for a while. Then he spoke softly. 'The old sibling rivalry, eh?' He scratched his head. 'But Wills still keeps denying it. He says he had nothing to do with his brother's death and nothing to do with our two murders.'

'Pauline Quillon was desperate to clear her name. She had her mind set on marrying Charles Stoke-Brown whether he liked it or not, and she'd have had to produce a birth certificate before the wedding, which means she'd reveal her true identity. She would have thought Charles would ditch her when he found out. I think she guessed what had really happened that day in 1969 and she pleaded with Timothy Wills to tell the truth so the case could be reopened and her name cleared. He was below the age of criminal responsibility: there wasn't much chance of him being locked up for it now. There have been so many cases of miscarriage of justice recently, why shouldn't she prove her innocence as well? You can see her point.'

'But if it all came out it'd probably scupper his parliamentary career. Imagine the headlines – MP kills baby brother. The tabloids'd love it.'

The phone on Wesley's desk rang. He answered it.

'That was Rachel, sir,' he said as he put the phone down. 'Jane Wills has been to see her at the incident room and she's made a full statement. She read it to me over the phone. I think we've got him.'

'Well, don't keep us in suspense,' said the inspector, finishing his coffee.

Back in the interview room Wesley switched on the tape machine as the solicitor looked on disapprovingly. 'We've had a statement from your wife, Mr Wills. It seems there are a few things you haven't told us.'

Gemma Matherley heard a soft tapping on her door. She lay on her bed, quite still. She had told the police the right thing ... used the right words. And besides, Tim had let her down; he was staying with that bitch of a wife, just when Gemma's hopes had been raised. He had said it was all over ... just because he wanted to be elected to Parliament. Why shouldn't he be arrested? He deserved all he got.

There was another knock on the door, louder this time. 'Come in,' she shouted. It was probably Mrs Thewlis wanting her to take charge of those brats of hers again. The door opened slowly and Gemma looked up. Philip Thewlis stood in the doorway watching her, as a cat watches a particularly juicy mouse.

'You did well, Gemma.'

'I don't owe him nothing.' She looked up. Thewlis stepped into the room, shutting the door behind him. 'It's a long time since I had a pay rise, you know ... and a friend of mine who's a nanny over in Morbay, she gets a car.' She looked at her employer expectantly. 'After all ... *sir* ... I've proved I'm good at my job. I'm more like one of the family, really. I know all the family secrets, don't I?'

Thewlis watched her for a while. The silence between them was making Gemma nervous. She began to fiddle with her hair. 'I'll have to discuss it with my wife. She's out at the moment.'

'Oh, I don't think your wife needs to know.' Gemma tilted her head coquettishly. 'Do you?'

'No, you're quite right.' He smiled, a warm friendly smile, putting her at her ease. 'As the children are out, why don't we go for a little sail? It's a lovely day ... blow the cobwebs out. We can discuss this, er ... pay rise, and we can be back in time for Caroline and the children. Come on.' He held out his hand, his smile avuncular and encouraging.

Gemma Matherley returned his smile and nodded.

'Your wife tells us that Pauline Quillon called on her early on Friday evening while you were out. She wanted to talk to you urgently. Your wife said she passed on the message and you said you'd talk to Pauline.' Heffernan sat back, awaiting a reply.

Timothy Wills thought for a few seconds. 'When my father told me he'd seen Pauline working at the doctor's surgery, I must say it was a shock. Not that the family ever talked about it ... I think the subject was too painful.' He paused. 'I was seven when it happened ... too young for it to mean very much. I think the prospect of being sent away to school upset me more that day than my baby brother's death.' He sat back in his plastic seat and glanced at the institutional clock on the wall of the interview room. His solicitor sat silently by his side, listening as intently as Wesley and Heffernan on the other side of the table.

'Did you kill your younger brother?' Wesley asked the question gently.

'No, Sergeant. I didn't. I always assumed it was Pauline: she'd been found guilty. I loved her, you know. She was gentle, kind . . . not neurotic like my mother. I asked my father about five years ago what had happened that day and he said he honestly didn't know. But he let it slip that Pauline had been with him. I was old enough by then to realise what that meant . . . I could tell from the way he said it. You don't think of your parents as sexual beings, do you? . . . or your nanny.' He took a deep breath. 'He never actually said it but I think he suspected that my mother had killed Peter. She hadn't been well at the time . . . mentally, I mean. For all those years I never thought of what happened to Pauline . . . maybe I didn't want to think about it.'

'So now who do you think killed Peter?'

'I didn't think about it again until a few years ago . . . not long after I'd discussed it with my father. I was at Philip and Caroline's when one of their children was a baby. We were in the garden of his London house and Caroline threw the baby up into the air and caught it. Just a game . . . the baby was laughing, enjoying it. Philip shouted at her to stop. He went quite . . . well, the colour drained out of his face. I thought about it for a few days after . . . it had been so unlike him to react like that. Then I remembered how he used to play that game with Peter; throwing him up in the air. I remember our housekeeper telling him off about it. I got hold of the transcripts of Pauline's trial and . . . I noticed there were inconsistencies. The statements implied that Philip went home to get his binoculars but I know for a fact he had them at our house.'

'Go on,' Wesley encouraged.

'I had an uneasy feeling – I wouldn't even describe it as a suspicion – but I told myself I must be wrong. And I had no proof . . . no proof whatsoever. Of course, I never mentioned it to Philip. We were close friends and he'd been very good to me . . . extremely good. He'd helped my career, got me the right contacts. I owed him a lot . . . and I was probably wrong. I tried to put it out of my mind . . . until now.'

'Did he ever mention Pauline to you?'

'No . . . never.'

'A witness saw you walking through the grounds of the Manor with Lee Telford last Saturday night.'

'Then they're lying. I didn't even know Lee Telford . . . I'd never even heard of him and I certainly wouldn't have recognised him. I was with my family all Saturday night. That's the truth. Whoever told you otherwise is lying.'

Heffernan changed the line of questioning. 'Did you call on Pauline on the night she died?'

'Yes. I saw her just before I went over to Bloxham. I felt I should talk to her. She'd called on my wife as you said. When I saw her she was very calm . . . very civilised. But as we talked she became more and more agitated and I realised that she thought I'd killed Peter. She'd had a lot of time to think about it in prison, she said, and she knew I'd been upset that day. She said she blamed herself for leaving me alone . . . and not looking after Peter while she . . .' He hesitated. 'She'd heard I was standing for Parliament and she threatened to make the whole thing public if I didn't help her clear her name. She said there were journalists who'd be only too happy to take up her case. I swore I'd had nothing to do with Peter's death.' He hesitated. 'I hadn't intended to tell her about Philip . . . but when she started talking about journalists it just, er . . . came out.'

'So what exactly did you tell her, Mr Wills?' Wesley had the feeling that he knew what the answer would be.

Philip Thewlis allowed Gemma to go first down the path which led to Knot Creek. He had never allowed anybody to stand in his way. Even as a child he had known how to manipulate, how to avoid trouble . . . how to engineer the truth.

Tim could be a liability . . . Philip had always wondered how much he knew about that day when his baby brother died. The day when Philip had left him alone to fetch his new binoculars from the Wills's house . . . always careful to call it 'the house' in any statements so that he couldn't be accused of lying but so it would be assumed that he meant his own house near by. He had run to the house, found his binoculars and, on the way back to join Tim, he had passed the rose garden. He had paused when he heard the sounds. The twelve-year-old boy had watched for a few seconds, fascinated as Tim's father writhed on top of the young nanny, emitting groans of what sounded like pain but which he now knew to be pleasure. Then, fearful of being discovered, he had run into the trees near the house, where he had found the baby awake and gurgling unguarded.

He knew little Peter's favourite game . . . being thrown high up in the air until he laughed with pleasure. It had started well; the child giggled with delight as Philip threw him higher and higher. Then came the awful, heart-stopping moment when he failed to catch him. The baby hit his head on the tree and went limp and pale. Philip had kept calm. He had run back through the trees, his heart pounding, almost on the point of vomiting when he thought about what he had done. But if he was careful, if he gave nothing away, nobody need ever know.

When Pauline Quillon had called on him so unexpectedly that Friday night all those years later, he knew Tim had said too much. But Tim was no real danger: nobody who wants to make it in the political world can risk being associated in the public mind with a scandal involving the death of a child. Besides, now that Pauline was dead, there was nobody who could prove anything against him. If he said that it was Tim who ran off towards the house that day thirty years ago, it would be Tim's word against his. And Tim owed him so much . . . he had always made sure of that.

He caught up with Gemma and they strolled along, side by side, to the creek. It would be best if it looked like an accident.

Neil Watson sat at the desk in the site hut in front of a flickering computer. The time had come to backfill the pit where the Jesse tree carvings had been found. He had left his colleagues to it and had taken refuge in the hut to finish recording the finds.

But his mind kept straying back to Alice de Neston, whose poor bleached skeleton now lay in Tradmouth mortuary, and the anguished confession of Simon de Stoke. The writing on the reverse of the sketch in the church had been no help: just a name, written over and over again. John Fleccer. As if the writer had been doodling – playing with the sound of the name. Neil had recognised it from the court records: the blacksmith's son who had become, in modern-day parlance, a young offender – a nasty bit of work in his own or any other century.

Two large volumes lay on the shelf above the desk. He had

brought the accounts book back to the site, intending to return it to the muniment room: the court roll translation he would hang on to a little longer as he had only reached the trial and execution of Alice de Neston.

Intrigued to know what had become of the village delinquent, Neil lifted the court records from the shelf, put his feet up and made himself comfortable. The recording of the finds could wait half an hour.

He flicked through the leather-bound volume, seeking references to John Fleccer – but he found nothing. Fleccer had either died, left the village for good or gone straight.

Neil turned the pages, year after year of petty wrongdoings and neighbourly squabbles passed through his fingers in seconds. When he reached 1494 – two years after the Jesse Tree had been carved – he saw it. 'John Fleccer is returned to the village and my lord orders the constable to keep him close confined.'

So the village bad boy had returned from his travels only to be banged up on the orders of the new lord of the manor, Simon de Stoke. Neil read on.

'John Fleccer, having returned to Stokeworthy, is brought before my lord and the jury to answer for his wrongdoings many years past in the time of my lord's late father. My lord states that as a child he did see John Fleccer enter the chamber of my lady, his mother, and feloniously take a jewel belonging to my lady, his mother. He did also slay my lady's babe by stopping the infant's cries with most grievous force and did make terrible threats to my lord, then a young and innocent child, that if he did betray him he would return and kill him. My lord, in fear, stayed silent and the nursemaid, Alice de Neston, was hanged for the crime. The jury state that John Fleccer is to stand trial for this dreadful offence at the assizes in Exeter and should stay close imprisoned until that time.'

So that was it. John Fleccer had killed the child: Simon had kept his mouth shut at the time, probably through fear, and Fleccer had disappeared from the scene – probably up to no good somewhere else. But years later Simon found himself in a position of power and could ensure that justice was finally done when Fleccer returned to his home village. But he hadn't lived easily with the knowledge that Alice had died because of his silence. He had been haunted by guilt for the rest of his days, had blamed himself; had commissioned the Jesse tree and had ended his days in pilgrimage.

Betting wasn't one of Neil's vices, but if it had been, he would have laid money that the repeated writing of Fleccer's name on the reverse of the Jesse tree sketch had been done by Simon, obsessed by his guilt, doodling the name at the forefront of his mind. Neil picked up the phone and dialled the number of Wesley's mobile.

Wesley answered almost immediately and announced that he was on his way to the Manor and couldn't talk long. Neil quickly gave him the outline of his discovery about John Fleccer. Wesley said nothing but Neil could sense the workings of his brain.

'Thanks,' Wesley said at last. 'Is Thewlis in, do you know?'

'I've not seen him leave.' Before Neil could continue he heard a commotion some way off. The noise seemed to come from the trees, then it surrounded the site – rhythmical, swaying, growing louder as more of the protesters joined in. 'Sorry, Wes, I'm finding it hard to hear you. Our eco-warriors here seem to be up to something.' He put a dirty finger in his ear. The noise was growing as Squirrel and his colleagues chanted and drummed. 'I'll ring you later. Okay?'

Neil pushed the court rolls to one side and rushed out of the hut. 'What the hell's going on?' he asked Matt, who shook his head and leaned on his spade.

Jane came running up. She had been at the medieval-village end of the dig and knew more. 'They've decided it's time to take the protest to Thewlis,' she announced, breathless. 'They're staging a peaceful vigil round the Manor.'

'Come on, then,' said Neil. 'I reckon we can leave the students to it for half an hour . . . see the fun.'

Wesley and Heffernan found Caroline Thewlis comforting a pair of whinging children, looking more than a little annoyed. 'I don't know where she's got to . . . and Philip said he'd be working here all day . . .'

'You mean Gemma's not here?'

She shook her head, tight-lipped with annoyance.

'You can't get the staff these days,' said Gerry Heffernan, tongue in cheek. 'Where's your husband?'

For the first time Caroline Thewlis looked apprehensive. 'I don't know. Why?'

The two policemen didn't answer.

'I think we should head for the creek,' said Wesley, quietly, when they were out of earshot.

'Is that your considered opinion, Sergeant?' Wesley nodded. 'What's that awful noise?'

'Sounds like ... drums. And voices. It seems to be getting nearer.'

It would be easy. Gemma was off guard, relaxed. Philip Thewlis was good at charm, putting people at their ease. Pauline Quillon had been relaxed before he had strangled her, convinced by his stories of Tim Wills's guilt. He had walked with her down the drive, done her the courtesy of seeing her off the premises. He had offered to go with her as far as the churchyard and she had been pathetically grateful. Then he had struck.

He had had to act quickly before she had a chance to think his arguments through. It would only be a matter of time before she realised the truth, spoke with Tim again and pronounced his secret to the world; a world so ready to bring down the successful like jackals attacking a weakened lion. He had fought and clawed his way to the top of the tree; exchanged a Dorset village council house for Stokeworthy Manor; had become not just another avaricious businessman but a public figure ... one of the country's great and good. He wouldn't be brought down by one mistake; a moment of carelessness so many years ago.

He had remembered the court records in the library which he had read with considerable interest when he had moved into the Manor, become Lord of Stokeworthy ... quite an achievement for the son of the Wills's odd-jobman; the child condescendingly allowed to play with the family's son, Tim ... as long as he knew his place and kept to it.

He had found the rope and a ladder in the churchyard and it had seemed like an amusing touch ... the hanging. He had assumed the local police would take it for suicide. But, it seemed, he had underestimated them.

He hadn't realised that he had been seen until he had noticed that stupid youth urinating behind a gravestone near by. He had been vacant, unaware ... drugged up, most likely, but one couldn't take risks. He had followed him, and when his friend had gone into the Ring o' Bells he had persuaded him to take a walk, to talk ... to have a drink at the Manor. He had led him to the creek and pointed out his boat, the *Pride of de Stoke*. When the boy was off his guard he picked up an oar and knocked him off balance, then held him beneath the water. It had been high tide ... easy to dispose of Lee Telford's scrawny body.

Now Gemma was there, strolling in front of him, so trusting. But she knew that it wasn't Tim Wills who'd been walking through the grounds with Lee Telford that Saturday night. She had been watching from the window, watching for Tim, and had recognised her employer. It was only self-interest and fury at Tim's rejection that had made her lie to the police. One day she might choose to tell the truth ... and Philip Thewlis was not prepared to risk everything he had – the wealth, the reputation, the power, the respect – on the whim of some silly girl, employed to look after his children.

It was high tide. He knew. He wasn't a man who left things to chance. They reached the end of the path. Where there had been an expanse of muddy sand at low tide, there was now water, lapping up to the sandy, tree-lined bank. Philip took Gemma firmly by the shoulders and pulled her down until she knelt by the water. When the shock wore off she began to struggle, to scream. Philip clapped his hand over her mouth and pushed her head down towards the water. But her arms and legs were free, kicking, fighting him. He took his hand from her mouth and grabbed her hands, forcing her downwards. Lee had been drunk; Gemma was putting up more of a fight.

Her head hit the water while she continued to struggle. Philip held it there, avoiding her flailing limbs. Then he heard the drumming, distant at first but coming nearer, and for a moment his hold relaxed and Gemma's face shot out of the water.

It had been Earth's idea to come down to the creek and hang a banner from Thewlis's boat, the *Pride of de Stoke*, before starting their vigil at the Manor. The noise of the protesters grew nearer ... and there was another sound, like police car sirens. The drumming, rhythmic and primitive – the drumming of

227

hunters after their prey – made Philip grab Gemma and renew his efforts.

Squirrel was in high spirits, running along the path. He didn't see Gemma at first, just a man leaning over the water. He grabbed the man's shoulders and pulled him back, thinking he was drowning. Then he saw Gemma, unconscious, her head in the water. It was while he was trying to save her that Philip Thewlis escaped.

'Someone get him. He's trying to swim for it.' Gerry Heffernan, puffing behind his fitter sergeant, shouted as police officers mingled with eco-warriors, all in pursuit of a common goal.

Wesley got to Gemma first. 'She'll be okay, pig,' said Squirrel casually. 'I've given her the kiss of life.'

Wesley looked down at Gemma. Her eyes were opening and she was coughing healthily. He ensured she was in the recovery position, and as he radioed for an ambulance, he felt a hand on his shoulder, pushing him away from the girl's prone body. It was Leanne.

'Gemma . . . what's happened?' She looked Wesley in the eye. 'Do something.'

Steve and Rachel appeared, running out of the trees, and Leanne, determined, spotted Steve. She called out to him, but he pointedly ignored her and darted off to where a group of uniformed colleagues were gathering by the shore. Rachel hurried over to Leanne and placed her jacket round the girl's bare shoulders.

Gerry Heffernan took charge. 'Your sister'll be all right, love,' he assured Leanne. 'Anyone seen Thewlis?'

There were too many answers to that question. The waterfront was crowded – eco-warriors, Neil and his colleagues from the dig, policemen, and Leanne and Jo, who had been hanging round the village as usual waiting for something to happen when they had heard the drumming and followed the sound. Thewlis, it seemed, had last been seen swimming fully clothed towards his boat. Knowing the currents in Knot Creek at high tide, Gerry Heffernan didn't fancy his chances.

Neil, now face to face with Wesley in the lounge bar of the Tradmouth Arms, repeated his story.

'So Alice didn't kill the baby. Simon could have told the truth but he kept quiet. He was probably terrified of this Fleccer character but, from the carving he had made, it was clear he blamed himself. It haunted him all his life.'

'Poor man,' said Wesley. There were some secrets that shouldn't be kept. The truth would have saved Pauline Quillon from fifteen years in prison ... and would have saved her life.

'It was good of your baby-sitter to have Michael too,' said Pam to Anne as she sat down beside Neil. She raised her glass of white wine. 'Here's to Mrs Miller.'

'Who's Mrs Miller?' asked Neil.

Anne grinned. 'I brought Pam some good news today. Mrs Miller's my childminder. One of the women she minds for is moving out of the area in August so she'll have a vacancy for Michael when term starts in September. Pam's been round to see her today and it's all settled.'

Neil gave a weak smile and looked away: people's domestic arrangements didn't really interest him.

'Since my husband died,' Anne continued, 'she's been such a help. More like a member of the family than a childminder.'

This captured Neil's attention. 'You're a widow, then? You're on your own?'

Anne nodded and Neil edged closer to her, a secret smile playing on his lips which only Wesley, as a detective, noticed. Neil asked her if she'd like another drink.

'Mrs Miller was so lovely with Michael, Wes,' said Pam with enthusiasm as Neil rose to go to the bar. 'You should have seen her ... just like a granny.' She took her husband's arm and gave it a squeeze.

'I'll drink to that,' said Wesley with some relief. 'Here's to Mrs Miller.'

'Who's Mrs Miller?' A familiar voice, reminiscent of the River Mersey, boomed behind Wesley. Gerry Heffernan stood at the bar of the Tradmouth Arms looking smarter than usual. Behind him, to Wesley's amazement, stood Susan Green.

Wesley moved up to make a space. 'Won't you join us?'

'No, ta, Wes. We're off out for a meal. Something exotic.'

'Where are you going ... Chinese? Indian? Thai?'

Heffernan looked at Wesley and winked. 'Susan here

recommended it. There's a place near Neston that runs these banquets. We're just off for a medieval.'

Wesley, who had had enough of medieval intrigue and deception for one day, put his arm round his wife and took a sip from his twentieth-century glass of best bitter.

Epilogue

Three weeks later

The body of Philip Thewlis was found in the River Trad by fishermen four days after he was last seen alive. The national newspapers carried glowing obituaries of the man who had risen to great heights from humble beginnings, whose incandescent life had been so cruelly cut short by a boating accident. Even the more inquisitive tabloids didn't guess the truth. His was a quiet funeral. The Rev. Brian Twotrees, rather overwhelmed by the importance of the man he was seeing to his last resting place, said very little about the lord of the manor of Stokeworthy, who had rarely, if ever, set foot in his parish church.

The police case was closed. A sparse press statement issued at the time said that a man had been found dead and the police weren't looking for anyone else in connection with the deaths of Pauline Brent and Lee Telford. Gemma Matherley had returned to the bosom of her family on the Stokeworthy council estate, acknowledging that her brief encounter with the political world was over as Timothy Wills, now Bloxham's Member of Parliament, resolutely spent more time with his family. Robert Wills was often seen walking arm in arm with his wife down by the creek. The shadows of suspicion lifted, they seemed to have found a quiet, sad contentment. The village had returned to some sort of peace.

On a warm day in July, Neil invited Wesley to witness the return of the Jesse tree figures to the church. Wesley had expected to find a select band of experts and bigwigs from the County Museum there. But to his surprise, the sunlit church was packed with villagers and the students who had helped to unearth the treasures.

Squirrel stood awkwardly near the door with a couple of his colleagues. Now that Thewlis was dead and his widow had announced that she was selling the Manor and moving up to Gloucestershire to be near her parents, the plans for the holiday development had been shelved. Squirrel was moving on. There was a proposed airport expansion up north that required his attention.

The Jesse tree, now bearing its richly carved fruit, dominated the south wall of the church. The figure of Christ at the top sat in splendour with a hand raised to bless the congregation. Brian Twotrees, having overcome his puritanical sentiments, looked at the thing in wonder and proudly posed for photographers from the local papers.

Twotrees cleared his throat. As vicar, he felt obliged to say something on such an occasion. 'I'd just like to thank you all for coming today to witness the return to our church of this magnificent Jesse tree. I'd like to thank Neil Watson of the County Archaeological Unit and his team for their efforts in bringing the tree back to life, and I'd also like to thank Detective Sergeant Wesley Peterson of Tradmouth CID for explaining one or two things to me about its history.'

Wesley looked round, slightly embarrassed, only to see that Gerry Heffernan had crept quietly into the church and was standing behind him grinning. The inspector poked him in the ribs good-naturedly as the vicar proceeded to recite the story of Alice de Neston's trial and death.

'A woman,' continued the vicar, 'Alice de Neston, was hanged for a crime she did not commit and, as some of you will know, there were echoes of this sad case in the events that occurred in our village a few short weeks ago. I would, therefore, like to dedicate this plaque.' He produced a brass rectangle from behind a pew like a conjurer revealing a rabbit. 'To the memory of two women who lived five centuries apart but who were hanged unjustly, innocent of any crime.' He read from the plaque. 'This Jesse tree was restored in memory of Alice de Neston and Pauline Quillon. The Lord knows all truth.'

Gerry Heffernan began the applause which spread throughout the congregation and rippled out on the summer breeze into the churchyard, where the freshly dug graves of two women lay side by side, covered with offerings of summer flowers, beneath the hanging tree.

232

The Armada Boy
Kate Ellis

A West Country murder mystery

Archaeologist Neil Watson did not expect to find the body of American veteran Norman Openheim in the ruins of the old chantry chapel...

He turns to his old student friend, Detective Sergeant Wesley Peterson, for help. Ironically, both men are looking at an invading force – Wes the WWII Yanks and Neil a group of Spaniards killed by outraged locals as they limped from the wreckage of the Armada.

Four hundred years apart two strangers in a strange land have died violently – could the same motives of hatred, jealousy and revenge be at work? Wes is running out of time to find out...

"traditional detective fiction with a historical twist – fans will love it"
                                                    Scotland on Sunday